CHASING MONSTERS

A Bailey Flynn FBI Mystery Thriller, Book Three

Melinda Woodhall

Melinda Woodhall
Visit my website at www.melindawoodhall.com
Printed in the United States of America
First Printing: June 2024
Creative Magnolia

CHAPTER ONE

It wasn't quite dawn when the guard came for Gayle Kershaw. She caught a glimpse of the uniformed man's dour face, still puffy and creased with sleep, before he turned to escort her down the drab hall of Rock Ridge Detention Center's psychiatric ward. Swiping his security badge through a reader on the concrete wall, the guard waited for the metal door to swing open, then led her through a maze of corridors to the Inmate Processing Center.

Thirty minutes later, she stepped out into the bitter chill of a North Virginia winter. Long strands of ash blonde hair whipped around her face as she stopped beside the waiting taxi to look up at the exterior of the prison.

Scanning the imposing stone building, Gayle fixed dark, wary eyes on the window to Dr. Jude Varney's office, half-expecting to see the psychiatrist's cap of short, dark hair and round, bespectacled face appear behind the smudged glass.

But the window remained dark and empty as Gayle climbed into the back seat of the yellow cab and gave the driver the address to her mother's house an hour away in Crimson Falls.

By the time she mounted the porch steps of her childhood home and gave her waiting mother an impatient hug, the sun had started to rise behind a shroud of thick gray clouds.

"I'm only stopping long enough to change clothes and pack a bag," she said as she checked her watch. "I need to get going if I'm going to make it down to Belle Harbor in time for dinner."

Ignoring her mother's startled protests, she hurried up to her room to exchange her cheap prison outfit for slim-fitting black jeans, a soft cashmere sweater, and knee-high boots with three-inch heels.

Once she'd thrown the necessary travel essentials into an overnight bag and pulled on a heavy winter coat, Gayle went out to the garage and slid behind the wheel of the big Cadillac her dad had driven up until his sudden death three years earlier.

"Honey, I don't think you're supposed to leave Crimson Falls," her mother called through the closed driver's side window. "And you've got an appointment with Dr. Varney tomorrow. If you don't show up they'll come looking for you. What will I tell them?"

Dismissing the question with a distracted wave of her hand, Gayle adjusted the seat, started the engine, and unfolded the letter she'd tucked into her pocket upon leaving her cell that morning.

She doublechecked the address before entering her destination into the satnav. With her mother's anguished face receding in her rearview mirror, Gayle pulled out of the driveway and headed south toward the interstate.

Twisting a knob on the dashboard, she smiled as the first few haunting notes of Patsy Cline's *Crazy* filled the car, pleased to note that the radio was still tuned to the Classic Country station her dad had always enjoyed.

As Gayle hummed along to the familiar music, her mind turned to the man who waited for her down in South Florida.

Mason Knox, the man she'd been convicted of stalking two years earlier, had finally come to his senses. And now that the trials and tribulations of the last two years were behind her, they could be together just as fate had always intended.

Setting the car's cruise control to eighty miles per hour, Gayle noted the diminishing snow and ice outside her window with satisfaction as she crossed the state lines of North Carolina, South Carolina, and Georgia.

By the time she spotted the *Cheap Gas & Good Grub* sign halfway down the Florida coast, she had traded in her heavy winter coat for a lightweight, waterproof jacket that offered protection against the soft rain pattering against the Cadillac's windshield.

Pulling up to the nearest pump, she swiped her mother's credit card and inserted the nozzle. As she waited for the big tank to fill, she once again pulled the letter from her pocket even though she'd already read it from beginning to end a dozen times.

Of course, she'd known all along that somehow she and Mason would be together again but the arrival of the letter had still come as something of a surprise. A very welcome surprise.

It surely meant that he'd forgiven her for getting a little carried away with their relationship. He'd come to realize that she'd never meant to hurt him, despite the whole gun incident and her attempt to shoot him.

Unable to resist, Gayle read the letter again, silently mouthing the treasured words she'd already memorized by heart.

Dearest Gayle,

I've thought of you often over the last year with both longing and regret. Although we're forbidden from contacting each other, I'm writing to you with the hope that we can give our relationship another chance.

According to my sources up in Crimson Falls, you've got a parole hearing coming up. With any luck, you'll be walking out of Rock Ridge next week.

If you want to try again, meet me for dinner at my new home in Belle Harbor after you're released. I'll be eagerly awaiting your arrival.

Mason

A street address in Belle Harbor and a contact phone number had been written in blue ink at the bottom of the letter.

Gayle traced the words with a gentle finger, lingering over each letter, imagining she was touching the man who'd written them.

She shivered with pleasure at the thought of seeing Mason again.

Who cared about the no-contact agreement she had signed prior to the parole board granting her early release? And why should she listen to Dr. Varney's advice to stay far away from Mason?

She's just jealous and miserable and doesn't want me to be happy.

Sticking the letter back into her pocket, Gayle returned the nozzle to the pump and screwed on the gas cap.

As she climbed back into the car, she thought about the parole hearing she'd attended the week before, recalling Dr. Varney's adamant objections to her release.

"Ms. Kershaw still suffers from the same obsessive thoughts and delusions that led to her crime in the first place."

When a parole board member asked for an official diagnosis, the psychiatrist had instantly responded.

"At this point, Ms. Kershaw is unable to take into account other people's feelings or to respect their boundaries. She exhibits clear signs of narcissistic personality disorder, which makes her highly reactive to rejection, as well as borderline personality disorder, which causes extreme mood swings and impulsive acts of anger. She shows no sign of repentance or improvement."

Gayle had been offended by Dr. Varney's brutal assessment.

Okay, so I tried to kill Mason. But I'd been in the midst of a stressful break-up. I wasn't exactly thinking straight. And I was also still grieving the death of my father. It's no wonder I momentarily lost my temper.

But now she was better.

Especially after receiving Mason's letter.

She was ready to restart their relationship, this time without the drama. Ready to put the disappointments of the past behind her.

Of course, there was no way she could have told Dr. Varney what she had planned. The malicious woman would never have let Gayle leave the psych ward if she'd known where she was headed.

Just for spite, I should invite vindictive Varney to the wedding when Mason and I get married. Although, I'm not sure where we'll hold the ceremony. One thing's for sure, it won't be in Belle Harbor.

Gayle shuddered at the thought of the small, coastal town.

She couldn't imagine what Mason had been thinking to accept a position in South Florida.

Isn't it hot and humid nine or ten months out of the year? Not to mention chock full of alligators, insects, and tackily dressed tourists.

But she suspected she knew his reasoning.

Based on the research Gayle had done in the prison's small library, Belle Harbor and the surrounding Summerset County appeared to be a hotspot for murder and the discovery of unidentified dead bodies.

Her mind flashed back to the various newspapers she'd scoured in recent months, hoping for news about Mason.

The city didn't exactly sound like a safe place to live or a prime location to have a wedding.

However that many dead bodies could mean job security for a medical examiner like Mason.

The *Crimson Falls Tribune* had run a series of front-page stories about the capture of Dr. Carter Delaney, a prolific serial killer the press had started referring to as the Bone Cutter after he'd hidden dozens of dismembered bodies in the old Belle Harbor Burial Ground.

Delaney, who had worked as a professor in the anthropology department at Lyndhurst College, had been identified as the biological brother of Chadwick Hearst, a man who'd been accused of his own string of murders before he'd fallen to his death from the deck of the Belle Harbor Lighthouse earlier in the year.

One newspaper article had accompanied a photo of Carter Delaney being escorted into the courthouse. The serial killer had been dressed in an orange jumpsuit, his dark hair disheveled above a pale, thin face as he aimed cold eyes and a thin, calculating smile at the camera.

A smaller photo further down the page had shown an attractive woman with shiny auburn hair standing behind a lectern.

The caption had identified the woman as Cate Flynn, an assistant state attorney tasked with prosecuting the Bone Cutter.

The man she was questioning on the witness stand was none other than Mason Knox.

Swallowing back a pang of jealousy, Gayle recalled the photo, picturing the affectionate expression on Mason's handsome face as he'd looked at the attractive prosecutor.

If I didn't know better, I'd say there was a definite spark between them.

Anger surged through her at the unwelcome thought and she gripped the steering wheel tight enough to make her hands hurt.

Imagining the *I-told-you-so* expression Dr. Varney would surely assume if she could see her now, Gayle forced herself to loosen her grip and exhale.

"Remember what it says in Proverbs," she murmured to herself. "A peaceful mind gives life to the body, but jealousy rots the bones."

The image was unpleasant, and Gayle certainly didn't want her bones to rot, but the seeds of jealousy had taken root, and the familiar ache in her stomach hinted at the bitter harvest to come.

I'll just have to make sure Mason has no cause to see that woman again. I'll see to it we move back to civilized society as soon as possible.

As she merged the Cadillac onto the Belle Harbor exit, butterflies began to flutter in Gayle's stomach. She'd been waiting to be reunited with Mason for so long that she could hardly believe she was only minutes away.

Pressing her boot down hard on the gas pedal, she sped through the streets, eager to arrive by the agreed-upon hour.

It wouldn't do for her to be late.

No, tonight of all nights, everything has to be perfect.

But the giddy thought curdled as she reached Belgrave Avenue to find an old silver sedan sitting in the driveway of Mason's lovely new house.

As she parked the Cadillac behind it, Gayle frowned.

Surely that isn't Mason's car?

He'd been driving a late-model Audi when he lived up in Virginia, and she'd been looking forward to taking long, leisurely road trips together.

But I certainly won't be going anywhere in that old thing.

Pulling out her cell phone, which she hadn't used in

almost two years, Gayle tapped in the number Mason had written on the bottom of the letter.

She held the phone to her ear with nervous anticipation. Listening to the phone ring again and again without answer, her excitement soon turned to frustration.

With an annoyed sigh, she climbed out of the car and stomped past the sedan toward the front door. As she reached the porch steps, she inhaled a rich, delicious aroma.

Her irritation faded as she realized the wonderful smell was drifting out of the front door, which had been left slightly ajar.

Knocking softly, Gayle called out for Mason, then pushed open the door and stepped inside.

"Hello?" she called again in a playful voice. "Is anyone home?"

Her eyes dropped to the foyer's hardwood floor and she gasped in pleasure to see a trail of rose petals leading down the hall.

The fragrant trail led to the dining room, which was lit only by candlelight, and she stopped in the doorway and blinked in surprise as she saw the elaborate feast laid out on the table.

Moving into the room, she smiled when she saw that a chair had already been pulled out and that a glass of red wine was waiting.

No matter that I only drink white. I'll have Mason trained soon enough.

Music began to play as Gayle crossed to the chair.

She cocked her head and closed her eyes, listening to the

haunting notes of the piano coming from the sound system.

Recognizing Chopin's Piano Sonata No. 2 in B-flat minor, she frowned, wondering why Mason would choose to pair a morbid funeral march with a romantic dinner.

He does have a lot to learn. But he'll be worth the effort in the end.

Smiling at the thought, she looked down at her dinner plate.

A quarter-sized pendant had been carefully placed in the middle of the white porcelain dish. Straining to see in the dim light, Gayle leaned forward to get a better look.

The sterling silver had been engraved with the anguished face of a young woman. Was the woman holding a cross?

Or is that a sword?

"Go ahead and take a seat. Mason should be here soon."

Gayle jumped and spun around to see a dark shadow in the kitchen doorway.

"Who are you?" she asked.

She looked back at the table, her eyes narrowing.

"And what *is* all this?"

"It's a very old custom. When someone you love dies, you hold a funeral feast."

Taking an instinctive step back, Gayle frowned in confusion.

"Someone died?" she asked

She strained to see through the shadows, making out two shining eyes in a pale face.

"Is that why Mason's late?"

The figure nodded and moved closer.

"If you want to be the wife of a medical examiner, you'll have to get used to death intruding at the most inopportune moments."

The comment sent an unwelcome shiver up Gayle's spine.

"Why is *that* on my plate?" she asked, looking down at the pendant with distaste. "Is it a gift from Mason? I don't like silver jewelry. I prefer gold or platinum."

"That's Saint Olga, the patron saint of revenge."

The shadowy figure in the doorway moved forward to stand beside her, balancing a wide, silver tray in one hand.

Gayle looked down, struggling to make sense of the items on the tray. Before she could move, the sharp blade of a scalpel slid under her ribs, releasing a warm gush of blood as it entered her liver.

Staring down in disbelief, she grabbed for the knife just as the second scalpel sliced neatly across her throat.

She collapsed onto the table, blood mixing with the wine as she sent the tray clattering to the floor.

A hand reached forward and grabbed a fistful of blonde hair, jerking Gayle down into the waiting chair.

"I said to take a seat, didn't I? Mason will be here soon."

CHAPTER TWO

Special Agent Bailey Flynn quietly opened the door to the Belle Harbor Police Department conference room and followed Ludwig inside. The German shepherd crossed to his usual spot by the window as Bailey sank into an empty seat next to Detective Jimmy Fraser.

Murmuring an apology for being late, she turned her attention to the front of the room where Dr. Eloise Spellman stood beside a smartboard.

"Thanks for coming, Agent Flynn. I hope you don't mind, but I asked the team if we could use our time today to run through the DNA results from the unidentified remains in the crypt."

The forensic anthropologist flashed Bailey a rueful grin.

"I'm sorry if we're covering old ground, but I'd like to understand where we're at as far as identifying the victims."

"That sounds like a good idea to me," Bailey said. "I'm sure we could all use a refresher on what we've found so far."

Sitting back in her chair, Bailey followed along as Eloise pulled up a diagram of the Belle Harbor Burial Ground and methodically ran through the location of all the human remains found so far.

The abandoned graveyard had been an active excavation site for months, although Eloise hadn't joined the task force until after it had been discovered that serial killer Carter Delaney, also known as the Bone Cutter, had been using the site to hide his many victims.

So far, they'd found the remains of dozens of victims, some of whom had been dissected, sliced, or cut up into manageable pieces and then stacked inside the burial ground crypt.

Other victims had been buried in unmarked, shallow graves, or dumped on top of bodies that had been buried in the graveyard over a century earlier.

Once she'd finished reviewing the diagram with the team, Eloise looked around the room with pale blue eyes.

"Okay, now that we all know *where* our victims are, I'm interested in finding out *who* they are."

She aimed a smile at Madeline Mercer.

"How about we let our fearless CSI team leader lead this part?"

Jumping to her feet, Madeline hurried to stand beside Eloise.

At five-foot-eight, she was a good six-inches taller than the forensic anthropologist, and her ink-black bob was a sharp contrast to Eloise's wispy, wheat-colored hair.

Standing together, they looked vaguely mismatched.

"Let's start with our teenage Jane Doe in the crypt," Madeline said. "I think we're getting close to figuring out who she is."

She turned to the smartboard and tapped on the

touchscreen, opening a folder and then selecting an image file.

Bailey stared at the photo that appeared on the screen. A delicate-looking skeleton had been laid out on a metal dissecting table. The bones had been pieced back together with meticulous care, like a macabre jigsaw puzzle.

"Based on the condition of the bones, and the hair attached to the skull, we believe the remains of teenage Jane Doe have been in the crypt between two and three years," Madeline said. "We were able to use her hair to obtain a DNA profile and got a hit in CODIS."

Bailey nodded at the words.

"That's right, the victim's DNA was found to be a partial match to an incarcerated criminal," she said. "A man who's serving life in the Summerset County Detention Center for a double murder. His name is Desmond Bolt."

Her voice hardened on the name.

"According to the DNA, our teenage Jane Doe is Bolt's daughter," she continued. "Only, when the warden out at the prison told Bolt about the discovery of his daughter's remains, the man refused to speak. He refused to acknowledge even having a daughter."

"And so far we can't find any record of Desmond Bolt having a child," Special Agent Aisha Sharma said. "We can't find a record that he has any living family at all."

A frown settled between her honey-brown eyes as she began digging through a stack of folders. Locating the one she was looking for, she opened it and flipped through the documents inside.

"Two pieces of jewelry were found with the victim's remains," Sharma said as she pulled out several photos. "A silver necklace pendant and a charm bracelet."

She slid a photo toward Bailey.

"One charm was in the shape of the letter B."

Bailey stared down at the delicate gold chain and the attached charm that had been entangled with the dead girl's wrist bones.

"Well, the B could stand for Bolt," Fraser said.

Eloise nodded.

"That's a possibility, of course," she conceded. "But it's hardly conclusive evidence of the girl's identity. Which is why the lab conducted isotope ratio analysis on almost thirty centimeters of the hair attached to the skull."

"What's isotope ratio analysis?" Fraser asked.

The forensic anthropologist smiled at him indulgently, giving Bailey the impression she'd hoped someone would ask the question.

"It's a process used to measure a person's exposure to naturally occurring isotopes in the environment," Eloise said, speaking slowly as if she was explaining the concept to a very small child. "The ratio of these isotopes are different in different geographic regions of the world, so measurements can identify where a person has lived or traveled."

"In this case, the length of the girl's hair made it possible," Eloise said. "She'd grown it out over years, which allowed us to measure isotope ratios and pull together a rough timeline of where she lived and traveled during that time."

All eyes around the table looked at her expectantly.

"In this case, the tests indicated our teenage Jane Doe had been living in north Florida in the years leading up to her death, somewhere around Jacksonville. She had traveled to south Florida only a few weeks before she died."

"I think I saw something about Jacksonville in Desmond Bolt's file," Sharma said as she dug through the folders in front of her.

She grabbed one and flipped through the contents, then gave a satisfied nod, causing a strand of dark, silky hair to fall over one slim shoulder.

"I knew I'd seen something about Jacksonville," she announced. "According to his birth certificate, Desmond Bolt was born in Verbena Beach, a small town north of Jacksonville."

Passing the document to Bailey, she sighed.

"Unfortunately, from what I can tell, that's about all we know about Bolt," she admitted. "Other than he's a convicted murderer."

"It's as if someone out there wiped the slate clean when it came to his prior history," Bailey fumed. "And from the police reports and court transcripts, it appears he kept his mouth shut."

She handed the document back to Sharma.

"Okay, so we know the girl lived in Verbena Beach," she said. "And then she came down to South Florida a few weeks before she died. Could she have come down here for her father's trial?"

Sharma checked the dates in Desmond's file.

"It's possible," the agent confirmed. "Bolt was convicted three years ago. And as Eloise just stated, they've estimated the girl's remains have been in the crypt for at least two years."

As Sharma flipped through the rest of the file's contents, Fraser's phone vibrated on the conference room table.

The detective glanced down at the display, then sat up straight in his chair and grabbed the phone off the table.

Turning to Bailey, he stared at her with wide eyes.

"A homicide's been reported on Belgrave Avenue," he said. "At the residence of Dr. Mason Knox."

Bailey shook her head, thinking he must be joking, or maybe mistaken. But the shock on his face told her he was deadly serious.

"I've got to go," Fraser said, looking up at Eloise and Madeline as he jumped to his feet. "There's been a homicide and–"

"And I have to go with him," Bailey added, already moving toward Ludwig with his leash. "You all go on without us."

She followed Fraser out of the room, her mind spinning with questions. Had Mason Knox been killed in his own home?

What will Cate do when she finds out?

"I'll drive," Bailey said as they hurried outside to the parking lot. "My Expedition's just over there."

Ten minutes later they were pulling into a quiet neighborhood made up of large, well-maintained houses with long driveways and wide lawns of lush, green grass.

Turning onto Belgrave Avenue, Bailey saw several police

cruisers with flashing lights outside an elegant two-story Mediterranean-style house with white stucco walls and terracotta tiles on the roof.

Detective Killian Rourke's charcoal gray Interceptor was parked along the curb but there was no sign of Fraser's new partner as they climbed out and hurried toward the house.

As they passed a big Cadillac in the driveway, Bailey noticed that the vehicle had Virginia plates. Her eyes momentarily rested on the state's slogan that *Virginia is For Lovers* before moving to the porch.

Mason Knox stood in the arched doorway, his handsome face pale beneath his dark, tousled hair, his chiseled jaw clenched.

Stepping back as they approached, the Summerset County medical examiner allowed Fraser and Bailey to step into the warm foyer, which was dimly lit by the glow of candlelight.

Bailey looked down to see rose petals scattered on the floor.

"In the dining room," Mason said in a dazed voice that hinted at mounting shock. "It's Gayle Kershaw. My stalker. She's dead."

CHAPTER THREE

Mason's legs were heavy as he led Bailey Flynn and Detective Fraser down the hall. His head felt strangely fuzzy and his hands were shaking as he forced himself to walk back to the nightmarish scene in the dining room. Wondering if he was going into shock, he looked up to meet Killian Rourke's accusing glare.

The newly promoted Belle Harbor PD detective was standing in the doorway tugging on the lapel of his ill-fitting suit. When he saw Fraser and Bailey behind Mason, Rourke's freckled face flushed red, matching the shade of his gelled-back hair.

"What's the FBI doing here? This is BHPD jurisdiction."

Fraser ignored Rourke's belligerent question as he brushed past Mason and followed Bailey into the dining room. He jerked to a stop as he caught sight of Gayle Kershaw's lifeless body.

Propped up in a chair, she was slumped forward, her long blonde hair crimson at the tips where it rested on the blood-stained table.

Although it wasn't visible from where he stood, Mason knew that her neck had been neatly sliced open from ear to ear. He'd discovered the wound when he'd attempted to check her pulse.

"You said that you know this woman?" Fraser asked, taking a cautious step into the room as if trying not to disturb any trace evidence.

Mason tried to speak but found that his mouth was too dry to make a coherent sound, so he simply nodded.

Gayle Kershaw had terrorized him for months before she'd been locked away in the psychiatric ward at Rock Ridge Detention Center in Crimson Falls, Virginia for aggravated stalking.

Her obsession, and his fear of what she might do upon her inevitable release, had ultimately driven him from his home town, prompting him to accept a position at the medical examiner's office in Summerset County, Florida.

But now, looking over at her lifeless body, despite everything she'd done, Mason felt a wave of sadness wash over him at the senselessness of her death.

Having no doubt that Gayle had been mentally unbalanced when she'd attacked him and that she'd suffered some sort of break from reality, he didn't hold her actions against her.

After all, she hadn't been in her right mind.

And now she'll never get a chance to recover.

"He claims the dead woman's been stalking him," Rourke said, directing suspicious eyes in Mason's direction. "Although, that doesn't really gel with the fact that somehow *she's* the one who ended up dead at his dining room table."

Again, Fraser ignored Rourke's outburst.

Turning to Mason, he met and held his eyes.

"I'm sure you've already told my partner, Detective Rourke, what happened. But I need you to go over it again with me."

He put a hand on Mason's arm and guided him back toward the living room, leaving Rourke grumbling behind them.

Mason looked up to see Bailey's green eyes on him as he passed her in the hall but she remained silent as he took a seat on the sofa beside Fraser.

"I need some water," he managed to rasp. "My throat-"

"I'll get it," Bailey said, hurrying out of the room.

When she returned with a brimming glass, Mason drank it down in two long gulps, then set the glass on the coffee table.

"Ok, now, tell me what happened here," Fraser said.

"I really don't know," Mason replied truthfully. "I got home from work about an hour ago and saw a car in the driveway that I didn't recognize."

He shook his head.

"The front door was open and there were rose petals and candle light and...well, I walked into the dining room and I saw Gayle."

His voice faltered at the memory.

"She was just sitting there at the table," he said. "It was as if she had been lying in wait for me. Only...she was already dead."

Clearing her throat, Bailey spoke for the first time.

"Could Gayle have done this to herself?" she asked. "I mean, could her wounds have been self-inflicted?"

Rourke scoffed from the doorway, having come down the

hall to listen in but Mason ignored him.

"That's what I thought at first," he admitted. "I thought that maybe she wanted me to...to find her like this. But, based on what I could see of the wounds, I don't think that's possible."

He looked up at Bailey, then turned his gaze to Fraser.

"I checked her pulse even though...well, I've worked with enough dead bodies. I could tell right away she was dead. But I had to be sure and so I put my fingers to her neck and..."

Lifting his hand as if to reenact the moment, Mason saw that his fingers were covered in Gayle's blood.

"I knew she was dead," he repeated, dropping his hand into his lap. "Of course, I knew it was too late, but I called 911 anyway. I wasn't sure what else to do."

Fraser nodded as if he understood, then cocked his head.

"Let's back up a little bit," he said. "You say she was already in the house sitting at your dining room table when you got home from work?"

Mason nodded.

"That's right."

"Okay, then. Do you have any idea how she could have gotten into the house? Did you leave the door unlocked?"

This time Mason shook his head.

"No, I never leave my door unlocked," he said firmly. "And I have no idea how she made it past my security system."

His head was clearing and his voice was stronger now.

"After what happened up in Virginia, when Gayle tried to shoot me...well, I became very security conscious. I put in a security system as soon as I moved here."

A spark of hope lit in his chest as he pulled out his phone.

"In fact, I didn't even think. I can check the cameras," he said, tapping quickly on the icon for the security system. "Maybe the cameras will show what happened. Maybe they-"

He stared in dismay at the red *SYSTEM DEACTIVATED* message displayed across the top of the security system app.

"Put your phone down!"

Suddenly, Detective Rourke was looming over him, his voice deafening in the quiet room as he pointed at Mason's phone.

"That phone may contain crucial evidence," Rourke barked at him. "We can't have you tampering with it."

He plucked it from Mason's hand before he could react.

"I'll hold on to this until the CSI team arrives," he said. "They should be on the way."

Fraser glared up at his partner but made no move to retrieve the phone. Instead, he waited until Rourke had retreated into the hall, then turned back to Mason.

"Does anyone else have access to your house?" he asked. "Have you given anyone else your security code or a spare key?"

Thinking of Cate Flynn, Mason shook his head.

He'd been considering offering the woman he'd been dating his spare key to the place but hadn't gotten up the courage.

His budding relationship with the assistant state attorney was still relatively new and he hadn't wanted her to think he was putting pressure on her or moving too fast.

God only knows what she's going to think now.

He winced at the thought of Cate's reaction to the discovery of a woman's dead body in his house.

I'm guessing she won't be requesting that spare key any time soon.

The thought was interrupted by footsteps on the porch. The crime scene team had arrived.

Mason looked up to see Madeline Mercer enter the hall wearing white protective coveralls and protective booties.

The CSI team leader gave him a weak smile before she pulled up her mask and headed toward the dining room.

"Stay here and try to think of anyone that may have done this," Fraser said as he got up from the sofa. "I'll be back shortly."

Motioning for Bailey to follow him, Fraser stepped into the hall.

As soon as they had disappeared into the dining room, the front door swung open again.

Finola Lawson stepped inside.

The assistant medical examiner was carrying the big bag she always took with her to death scenes.

Her eyes widened as she looked over to see Mason sitting on the sofa. He quickly got to his feet.

"I didn't know they had called you already," he said, feeling awkward as she stared over at him. "I guess you're going to have to handle this scene on your own."

She nodded and bit her lip.

"You okay?"

Her normally flippant tone was gone, replaced by concern.

"Yes, I'll be fine," he said. "I was pretty shaken up at first, but since I'm not the one who needs the attention of a medical examiner, I guess I'm the lucky one."

Pointing down the hall toward the dining room, he sighed.

"The scene is that way. Sorry I can't help."

Finola nodded solemnly, then turned and made her way down the hall. As she went, Mason followed after her, stopping outside the dining room to watch the team working the scene.

He stepped back as Madeline appeared in the doorway, carrying a small silver pendant in her gloved hand.

"Is this yours?" she asked, holding it up for him to see.

Leaning forward, Mason studied the unfamiliar pendant, noting the image of a woman holding a sword, then shook his head.

"I've never seen that before," he said. "It must be Gayle's."

The CSI team leader turned and called to Bailey Flynn, who was standing beside Fraser.

As the FBI agent approached, Madeline held up the pendant.

"Is this what I think it is?" she asked.

Bailey's eyes widened.

"It sure looks similar to the pendant found with our teenage Jane Doe in the crypt," she said. "Although, I can't be sure it's the exact same design. Where did you find it?"

"This was on the dinnerplate in front of the body in there," Madeline said. "I'll bag it and we can see if it matches once I get back to the lab."

Before Mason could ask what they were talking about,

Detective Rourke appeared in the hall, accompanied by two officers in Belle Harbor PD uniforms.

"Mason Knox, we need you to go down to the station for an official interview regarding the homicide of Gayle Kershaw," the detective said with obvious satisfaction. "These officers will escort you in their cruiser."

"But, I've told you everything I know," Mason protested, shaking his head. "I don't know what happened. I have no idea how Gayle got in here or who did this to her. You don't really think that I could have done this…that I'm a suspect, do you?"

Rourke stepped closer, making no attempt to hide the sneer of contempt on his face as he pointed toward the front door.

"You can walk out to the cruiser on your own or–"

"That's enough, Detective Rourke."

Both men spun around to see Jimmy Fraser standing in the doorway, his face hard and disapproving.

"I'm sure Dr. Knox has no problem giving an official statement at the police station if we explain that it's standard procedure."

He turned to Mason.

"Would you mind going with these officers and filling out a statement, Dr. Knox? It will help us with the investigation," Fraser said quietly. "I'm sure you are as eager as we are to find out who did this to Gayle and make sure they can't do it to anyone else."

Knowing he had no choice but to agree, Mason slowly nodded his head. With a sigh, he followed the officers to the front door.

As he was led down the porch steps, Mason saw Cate Flynn's white Lexus pull into the driveway. He watched as she climbed out and hurried toward him.

"Mason? What's happened?"

Before he could answer her, one of the officers opened the back door to the cruiser and motioned for Mason to get inside.

He turned to meet Cate's frantic green eyes.

"Where are they taking you?" she called out as he slid into the backseat. "Are you being arrested?"

"I didn't do this. I didn't kill her!"

But his words were drowned out as the door was slammed shut.

Looking through the back window as the cruiser pulled away, he kept his eyes on Cate, assuring himself that everything would be okay. But he had a bad feeling.

Somehow, I don't think this is going to end well.

CHAPTER FOUR

Jimmy Fraser lunged forward to grab Cate Flynn's arm, pulling her back and out of the way just as the black and white police cruiser pulled away with Mason Knox inside. Wrenching her arm from his grip, the assistant state attorney spun around to glare at him with bright green eyes full of outrage.

"What's going on?" she demanded as she stared after the cruiser. "You aren't arresting him, are you?"

"No one is being arrested," Fraser said. "At least not yet. But Mason Knox reported a homicide at his house, so of course, he'll be considered a person of interest for the time being."

Suddenly, he stopped and frowned at her.

"Why are you here, anyway?" he asked. "Surely the state attorney's office hasn't been called in to advise on the case this quickly."

He raised an eyebrow.

"And why are you jumping in to defend Mason Knox? Last time I checked you were a prosecutor, not a defense attorney."

"Don't you know?" Rourke asked as he came up behind

Fraser. "The assistant state attorney here is dating our suspect."

"Is that true?" Fraser asked, unwilling to take anything Rourke said as fact without verification.

Sucking in a deep breath, Cate nodded.

"Yes, if you must know, I've been seeing Mason Knox for a few months now," she admitted. "But it's not anything serious. And it certainly won't affect my judgment when it comes to my job."

Rourke snorted and shook his head.

As his partner turned and walked away, still laughing, Fraser studied Cate's face, noting the flush of anxiety painting her cheeks.

Her obvious distress suggested she was more serious about the medical examiner than she wanted to admit, perhaps even to herself.

There was no way she could be allowed to get involved with the investigation into Mason or his potential prosecution.

Stepping closer, he lowered his voice.

"Come on, Cate. We both know that anyone who is romantically involved with a witness or a suspect can't be considered objective in a case like this. And they certainly can't be involved with the investigation."

He cleared his throat.

"I assure you that we won't act rashly or arrest anyone without conducting a full investigation. Now, why don't you go home and–"

"I want to know what happened," she said, starting

toward the house. "You said it's a homicide but who's the victim?"

Fraser moved quickly to block her path.

"You can't go in there," he said. "The CSI team and the assistant medical examiner are working the scene. As for the identity of the body, that information will be released to the public in due course."

Looking back at the house, he saw Bailey step out onto the porch.

Cate caught sight of her sister at the same time he did.

She darted around Fraser, managing to make it to the front steps before Bailey intercepted her.

"Just tell me what's going on," Cate insisted. "I don't understand what's happened. Why has Mason been taken in?"

"I'm sure the Belle Harbor PD just want him to make a statement," Bailey said, shooting Fraser a quick *at-least-I-hope-that's-the-case* look. "He came home to find a dead body in his house. The official investigation needs to take its course. And you can't interfere. Now go home. I'll see you there later."

Backing away from the porch, Cate exhaled in frustration.

"I wish everyone would stop telling me to go home," she said. "I have no intention of going home. Not until I find out what exactly is going on here."

As she walked back to her Lexus, she stared over at the Cadillac with narrow eyes. Spotting the Virginia license plate, she took out her phone and snapped a photo.

Knowing it would only take a matter of minutes for Cate to

find out that Gayle Kershaw's father owned the Caddy, Fraser shrugged.

The whole damn town is going to know soon enough.

The thought made him picture Sabrina West and the other reporters who would soon be swarming the scene.

Spotting Madeline Mercer retrieving a stack of coveralls and masks from the CSI van, he jogged over to her.

"Can you get your team to cordon off the driveway?" he asked. "I think we'd better treat that Caddy as part of the crime scene. Maybe we should even cover up the plates. That'll help us keep the victim's identity under wraps until we can notify next of kin."

Madeline gave him a thumbs up.

"You got it," she said. "And I need you to do something for me."

She tossed him a coverall, booties, and a mask.

"Put those on before you go back into my scene."

As she hurried back into the house, Fraser followed orders and pulled the coveralls on over his clothes, slid his shoes into the booties, and positioned the mask over his face.

Heading back into the house, he passed Rourke on the porch.

His partner was talking animatedly on the phone and didn't seem to notice Fraser as he slipped by in his protective gear, catching a snippet of the conversation.

"...lying through his teeth and thinks we're all stupid enough to buy his innocent routine. I'd say we should-"

As the front door shut behind Fraser, he rolled his eyes.

He'd heard enough of the conversation to figure out that

Rourke was talking to Millicent Pruett, Belle Harbor's new chief of police.

The man's efforts to suck up to the woman were nauseating.

As soon as the new Chief of Police had been introduced to the team, Rourke began a campaign to win over his new boss.

The worst part was that Chief Pruett seemed to enjoy Rourke's obsequious attitude. She was buying his act hook, line, and sinker.

Knowing there was little he could do about his new partner for the time being, Fraser swallowed back his frustration and strode down the hall to the dining room.

Bailey was standing beside Finola as the assistant medical examiner took photos of Gayle Kershaw in situ, getting shots from every conceivable angle.

She turned as Fraser approached.

"There you are," Bailey said. "I wanted you to get a look at this pendant before the CSI team bags it."

She pointed to the table.

A silver pendant was lying on a dinner plate. Fraser bent down to study the woman's image engraved on the surface.

"That looks familiar," he said.

"Yeah, we saw one like it earlier," Bailey reminded him. "Remember, the teenage Jane Doe in the crypt?"

Before he could reply, Finola spoke behind them.

"I think I've found something."

The assistant medical examiner held out a worn piece of paper that had been loosely folded.

"Looks like it's a letter," she said. "It was in her pocket."

Fraser took the paper in his gloved hand and spread it open on the table. His pulse quickened as he read it.

Finola was right, it was a letter.

And it had been written by Mason.

"This was in her pocket, too," Finola said, holding up a phone.

Quickly refolding the letter, he called over Madeline and asked her to bag it, then picked up the phone.

Fraser frowned down at the little device and tapped on the display, surprised to find that it wasn't passcode protected.

Instinctively, he pressed redial and held the phone to his ear.

It rang again and again without answer.

"Hold on, what's that sound?" Bailey asked

They all grew quiet and listened to a soft buzzing from somewhere nearby. Fraser stood and followed the sound down the hall to the front door.

He paused beside the coat rack, reached into the pocket of a jacket hanging on the rack, and pulled out a small flip phone.

"What's that?"

Rourke was standing in the doorway, staring at the phone.

"Is that one of those burner phones that criminals use?" he asked, frowning at the jacket. "Was that in Mason Knox's jacket?"

Deciding there was no point in withholding the information from Rourke, Fraser nodded.

"This was the last number Gayle called before she died."

* * *

Millicent Pruett parked her white Interceptor along the curb outside the scene. Climbing out of the official vehicle, she stood still, looking up toward the house with brooding eyes as if she was a model posing for a photoshoot.

Lifting a hand to make sure her sleek blond pageboy bob was still perfectly in place, she adjusted her navy blue skirt and white blouse which were still fresh and crisp after a long day in the office, and headed up the driveway to where Fraser and Rourke were waiting on the porch.

For the last thirty minutes, Rourke had been arguing that Mason Knox should be arrested and booked right away, while Fraser was adamant that they complete the investigation, first.

"Why would Mason Knox have a burner phone?" Rourke asked as Chief Pruett mounted the steps. "And why would he send the woman who had tried to kill him a letter asking her to come to his house? It's obvious to me."

Wishing he hadn't had to show Rourke the letter or the phone until he'd had a chance to interview Mason, Fraser shook his head, sensing he was going to lose the argument.

"We don't know if Mason sent that letter," he insisted. "And it's not a crime to own a flip phone."

Throwing his hands in the air, Rourke turned to Pruett.

"I recommend we charge Mason Knox with murder," Rourke said as he defiantly crossed his arms over his chest. "But for some reason, Detective Fraser prefers to give him special treatment just because he works for the county and has been dating assistant state attorney Cate Flynn."

Before Fraser could protest, Chief Pruett cleared her throat.

"I'm glad you're passionate about your work, Detective Rourke, but you do need to remember that only the state attorney's office can charge a suspect with murder," she said smoothly. "Which is why I've put in a call to my contact there. I expect to get a call back shortly."

Relieved that someone was finally talking sense, Fraser exhaled and let his shoulders relax. He realized he'd let down his guard too soon when Chief Pruett turned to him with a frown.

"I have to say I'm disappointed to hear that you're not taking this case more seriously," she scolded. "I don't appreciate having to come out here to remind you how to do your job."

Putting up a warning finger to stop the protest she saw brewing on his face, she continued.

"I advise you to treat this case and the suspect as you would any other case, regardless of your personal feelings. No preferential treatment will be tolerated."

She lowered her voice.

"I'm sure I don't have to remind you that you're skating on thin ice as it is. Two of your partners have died during investigations over the last six months, and there's pending litigation over the last one. I would be very careful if I were you."

Fraser exhaled deeply, trying to conceal his irritation, wanting to dispute Raya Valera's allegations, but knowing it would do no good.

It wasn't the time or place to discuss Rita Valera's daughter and the wrongful death lawsuit she'd filed against the department.

His late partner had been attacked, drugged, and dumped in the Bellamy River. Although she'd been pulled from the water by Dalton West and Bailey Flynn, who had been conducting a search in the area at the time, Detective Valera had died later that night in the hospital after a ventilator had mysteriously failed.

The cause of the equipment failure had never been explained, and a week after her death, Valera's estranged daughter had arrived in Belle Harbor to collect her mother's body.

After speaking to a lawyer, Raya Valera had vowed not to leave town until someone paid for her mother's murder. And she meant that literally.

The woman's lawyer had already filed a wrongful death lawsuit against the Belle Harbor PD asking for a million dollars in damages.

Needless to say, Chief Pruett and Mayor Sutherland weren't very happy. They were looking for a scapegoat, and Jimmy Fraser knew that as Valera's ex-partner, he fit the bill.

"I'd also advise you to take good care of Detective Rourke," Pruett said as she brushed an invisible crumb from her pristine blouse. "If something happens to him, it'll be three strikes against you. And you know what that means."

Fraser was saved from responding to the infuriating advice by a buzz from the pocket of Pruett's well-tailored skirt.

Pulling out her phone, she smiled.

"That's the state attorney calling back," she said, moving down the steps and onto the lawn to answer the call.

Minutes later, the call was over and Chief Pruett was back.

"Good news, the state attorney has assigned a prosecutor to work with us on this case," she said. "Assistant state attorney Henrietta Trilby will determine if we have enough evidence to arrest and charge Mason Knox with Gayle Kershaw's murder. We'll set up a meeting first thing tomorrow."

As she turned to go, Pruett spotted Bailey Flynn standing just inside the door, talking to Madeline Mercer.

Her eyes flicked to Rourke, who shot her an *I-told-you-so* scowl.

"One more thing, Detective Fraser."

Pruett's voice was ice cold.

"We don't need or want FBI assistance here. Make sure I don't have to tell you twice."

Once the chief was gone, Bailey slipped out of the house and stood next to Fraser on the porch.

"Don't worry, I heard what she said."

Bailey looked out at the street, avoiding his eyes.

"I've got to get going anyway. I need to check on Cate. She was pretty upset. Maybe I'll talk to you tomorrow."

She started to walk away, then hesitated.

"I've been thinking I'll go talk to Desmond Bolt over at the Summerset County Detention Center tomorrow," she said. "I want to see what I can find out about our teenage Jane Doe and that pendant. I guess you'll be too busy with this scene to come along."

Fraser nodded.

"Yeah, it looks like it," he agreed. "But you go talk to Bolt. And be sure to tell me what you find out."

Bailey walked out to her Expedition and climbed in, giving him a tired wave as she drove away.

Watching the Expedition until it reached the end of the street, Fraser sighed and took out his phone. He'd have to call Linette and tell her to put the girls to bed without him.

Before he could tap on his wife's number, the front door opened to reveal Finola Lawson, who was trying to push out the gurney with the body on it by herself.

Hurrying over to help her, he grabbed one side of the gurney, then jumped back as the sheet caught against the doorjamb, revealing Gayle Kershaw's pale hand.

It looked to Fraser as if the dead woman was pointing at him.

As if she was warning him that he could be the next to die.

CHAPTER FIVE

Bailey woke early the next morning to find Cate pacing the living room floor and watching the local news, having already downed her second cup of coffee. Her sister hadn't come home until after midnight, and based on her red, puffy eyes, Bailey could tell she hadn't gotten much sleep.

"Someone in the Belle Harbor PD must have leaked the story to Channel 3 News," Cate said. "Gayle's murder is the top story. They're saying the police are interviewing a person of interest, although they haven't named Mason yet."

She stifled a wide yawn.

"And they've assigned Henrietta Trilby to the case. She's new to the area and doesn't even know Mason."

"That's the way it's supposed to work," Bailey said. "You're not supposed to prosecute people you know."

Cate shot her sister an angry glare and stormed out of the room, not bothering to turn off the television as she went.

Reaching for the remote, Bailey was about to press the *POWER* button when she realized what she was seeing on Channel 3 News.

Although she had expected to see footage of Mason Knox

being driven away in a police cruiser, instead she saw a woman being interviewed in front of the Belle Harbor Police Department.

She frowned as she heard a familiar name.

Looking more closely at the screen, she recognized Raya Valera.

"Detective Jimmy Fraser and the Belle Harbor PD are hiding something," the woman claimed. "My mother's dead, and I want answers. I want to know what really happened to her."

Bailey sighed and turned off the television, wondering if they would ever find out what had really happened to Rita Valera.

Had someone deliberately turned off her ventilator or had it just been a tragic, unexplained accident?

She suspected Fraser would never be truly at peace until he found out the truth and cleared his name.

Leading Ludwig out to the Expedition, she settled him into the back seat, then drove out to the Summerset County Detention Center where Desmond Bolt was being held.

When she got to the visitor's entrance and explained that she had arranged to visit Desmond Bolt, the guard at the desk frowned.

"Dessie hasn't had any visitors in a while."

He checked the log and lifted an eyebrow

"I guess you must be someone special," he said, making the comment sound like an insult. "The warden signed for you personally."

His eyes flicked down to Ludwig.

"No dogs allowed in the private interview rooms," he said, his voice gruff. "You'll have to leave him in your vehicle."

"But he's a search and rescue dog," Bailey said. "He's trained to behave in any environment and-"

The guard shook his head.

"I said no dogs," he repeated. "If you want to go in, he's got to go out. It's up to you."

"I'll watch him for you."

Spinning around, Bailey saw a second guard standing by the bank of lockers where visitors were required to leave their phones and valuables before going in for visitation.

The guard, whose name tag read *Officer Boswell*, was a short Black man with a small paunch and a round, friendly face.

"I like dogs and they tend to like me, too," he said, looking down at the German shepherd. "What's his name?"

"His name's Ludwig," Bailey said.

Boswell smiled.

"Like the composer?"

"Yep," Bailey said. "Just like the composer. And he's got a friend named Amadeus, as well."

The guard laughed and waved to an empty corner by the lockers.

"He can hang out over there," he said. "He'll be fine."

Ignoring the dirty look the other guard was sending his way, Boswell helped Bailey lock up her phone and handed her a little key.

She followed the surly guard into the back, walking down a stark, brightly lit corridor to one of the little, windowless rooms where the inmates and their lawyers could meet in private.

Desmond Bolt was already in the room waiting but he didn't look pleased to see her.

"I'm Special Agent Bailey Flynn with the FBI's Miami field office," she said. "I appreciate you meeting with me, Mr. Bolt."

"My name's Dessie. And I didn't have a choice," he said. "Once you get locked up in here all your choices are made for you."

The man didn't sound bitter, only resigned.

His dark hair had started to sprout gray at the temples and his face was worn and creased with lines that made him look older than his thirty-six years. His shoulders were broad and strong but they were lowered in the slumped style of a defeated man.

"Well, Dessie, it's good to meet you," she said in a quiet voice. "I'm here to ask about your daughter. I'm very sorry for your loss."

She watched for his reaction, noting that his back had stiffened at her words, but he didn't respond.

"I'm part of a task force that's investigating multiple homicides down in Belle Harbor. I'm sure you've heard something about the case. About Carter Delaney? He's in here, too."

Dessie stared down at the floor, his jaw clenched.

"Your daughter was found in the crypt at the Belle Harbor Burial Ground. We're trying to understand what happened to her. We want to give her a proper burial but we don't know her real name."

A flush of color was creeping up the man's neck as if it was a strain on him to maintain his silence.

"We believe she was living in Verbena Beach up until a few weeks before her death. But we can't figure out why she came down to Belle Harbor."

She cocked her head and frowned.

"Was she down here in South Florida with you? Was she at your trial? Or was your daughter a runaway? Was she into drugs or-"

"Birdie wasn't a runaway and she sure as hell wasn't doing drugs," Dessie snapped. "She wouldn't have just disappeared like that willingly. Someone must have taken her."

"Birdie? Is that your daughter's name?"

Dessie's face hardened.

"Just leave me alone," he muttered. "What does it matter anyway? Nothing I tell you will bring my baby girl back."

Shaking his head, he lifted a hand and began fidgeting with a pendant that was hanging around his neck on a chain.

Bailey's eyes widened.

"What's that?" she asked leaning forward. "Is that pendant the same kind that your daughter was wearing? What does it mean?"

The question seemed to cross whatever boundary Dessie had set. He banged his fist down onto the table between them and yelled toward the door.

"Guard! We're done here."

He stood and turned his back on Bailey, refusing to look at

her again as the guard appeared and led her back out to the visitor's center where Ludwig was waiting with Officer Boswell.

"He's been a good boy," Boswell said as Bailey retrieved her phone from the locker.

As she snapped on Ludwig's leash, the guard spoke to her in a low voice, making sure no one else could overhear.

"You should be careful around Dessie Bolt," he said. "Rumor has it he's connected to the Tumba Cartel. They're bad news."

Looking up, she saw concern in the man's eyes.

"Thanks for the heads up," she said quietly. "And for watching Ludwig. I really appreciate it."

After leaving the jail, Bailey settled Ludwig into the back seat of the Expedition before tapping in a text message to a number stored in her phone as Andi Parker.

Can we meet? I have a question.

A few minutes passed and then she got a response.

"Okay, meet me at Summerset Park at noon."

Staring down at the text, Bailey felt her heartbeat quicken.

Summerset Park, and the events that had taken place there several years earlier, still loomed large in her nightmares.

She hadn't been back since she'd been a detective with the Belle Harbor PD responding to the reported abduction of twelve-year-old Dolores Santos.

That had been the day she'd ended up shooting and killing Ronin Godfrey. The day she'd arrived too late to save the life of the girl he'd abducted. Too late to stop the bullet that cost Sid Morley his leg.

Bailey's throat tightened as she thought of Morley, the career FBI agent who had trained most of the search and rescue dogs in Summerset County.

After losing his leg to Godfrey's bullet, he had been forced to retire from the Bureau but he'd still managed to train Bailey how to handle a search and rescue dog and had supported her request to become Ludwig's handler.

Glancing in the rearview mirror, she smiled at the German shepherd, grateful for the dog and the help he'd provided in several recent cases. Grateful that at least one good thing had come out of that dreadful day.

But the thought of going back to the park now caused her hands to grow clammy as they gripped the steering wheel.

"The only way to overcome your fear is to face it head on," she said in Ludwig's direction, repeating the advice her sister liked to dole out after she'd heard it during one of her therapy sessions with Dr. Chung.

The dog stared at her in silent agreement.

Before Bailey could change her mind, she tapped in a response to the text from Andi Parker.

Okay, see you there.

* * *

Bailey stopped the black Expedition just outside the open gate, suddenly hesitant to cross the barrier into the past.

Of course, she'd driven past Summerset Park plenty of times over the last few years but she'd never had the guts to pass through the gate and walk down the path she'd followed that fateful day.

Sucking in a deep breath, she pressed her foot on the accelerator and made a sharp right turn into the park.

As she nosed the Expedition into an empty space in the shady parking lot, her thoughts turned to the woman she was about to meet.

Although the contact record in her phone listed the woman as Andi Parker, Bailey had a hard time thinking of the FBI special agent by any name other than Charlie Day.

She'd met Charlie at the Washington D.C. field office the previous spring during a serial homicide investigation in Virginia.

The experienced agent had taken a leave of absence soon after the case had been successfully solved, only to turn up in South Florida six months later with a new name, identity, and appearance.

Her shoulder-length, golden hair, and somber, tailored suits had been replaced by a sleek, dark bob and colorful leisure wear that fit in well with the jet-setting, resort-hopping scene in Miami.

They had met up at various locations over the last few months. Ever since Carter Delaney had been captured and outed as a hitman for the Tumba Cartel.

Only a few people knew that Charlie was operating undercover in Miami and Latin America under the name Andi Parker in order to infiltrate the dangerous trafficking gang.

Their mutual boss up in the D.C. field office, SAC Roger Calloway, had decided the two agents could provide mutual assistance, especially now that Carter Delaney, a serial killer, and self-confessed hitman, was behind bars, and Charlie was getting closer to uncovering the identity of the cartel's top guy, known only as Mr. Tumba.

Sucking in a deep, calming breath, Bailey climbed out of the SUV and opened the door for Ludwig. She snapped on his leash and allowed him to lead the way past the basketball court and soccer fields toward the five-mile nature trail that circled the park.

They were approaching the entrance to the trail when Bailey saw Charlie sitting on a bench, her dark hair tucked under a newsboy cap and her gray eyes hidden behind dark sunglasses.

"What's the question?" she asked as Bailey sat down beside her on the bench. "Is it about the homicide in Belle Harbor last night? Cause I have no clue what's going on there."

Bailey smiled.

"That makes two of us," she admitted. "But that's not what I wanted to ask. I just met with Dessie Bolt at the Summerset Detention Center, and I heard that he might have connections to the cartel. I was wondering what you know about him."

Taking off her glasses, Charlie turned her eyes to Bailey.

"Why were you meeting with Dessie Bolt?" she asked.

Her gray eyes showed rare surprise.

"Dessie's daughter was one of the victims we found in the Belle Harbor Burial Ground. He called her Birdie, but I don't know her real name. We're trying to figure out what happened to her."

Charlie nodded slowly.

"I have heard about Dessie Bolt," she admitted. "He was a loyal associate in the cartel before his arrest and conviction."

"Word in the cartel is that Dessie had someone working with him the night he was making a delivery and got ambushed by two men. Both men ended up dead and the cops arrived to find Dessie there on his own. He refused to name anyone else, so he ended up doing all the time."

She shrugged.

"But, I never heard about a daughter. Especially a dead one."

The idea seemed to intrigue her.

"Let me see what I can find out," she said. "In the meantime, you should definitely find out what you can from Carter Delaney. He's responsible for most of the bodies in that crypt, right? So, wouldn't you think he killed Bolt's daughter, too?"

"It's possible," Bailey admitted. "And I definitely plan on asking Delaney about it if I get the chance, although I doubt I'll get a straight answer. It's unlikely he'll help us find her real name or tell us how she ended up in that crypt."

An image of the silver pendant lying among the girl's bones flashed behind Bailey's eyes.

"There was something else," Bailey said, pulling out her phone. "We found a pendant in the crypt with Birdie's bones. A similar pendant was found at the scene of a homicide last night, and I just saw Dessie wearing one as well."

Scrolling to the photo she'd taken of the pendant the night before at Mason Knox's house, Bailey showed it to Charlie.

"Have you ever seen one of these before?"

Charlie studied it, then shook her head.

"No, I don't think so. But send me the photo. I'll ask around."

She stood up from the bench, then bent to scratch Ludwig behind the ears.

"And don't forget to talk to Delaney as soon as possible," she said. "He knows a great deal more than he's told us. We've got to keep working on him."

Bailey nodded.

"Maybe I can make another trip over to the Summerset Detention Center tomorrow," she said. "I think they're starting to like me there."

"Okay, just be careful," Charlie said. "Carter Delaney and Dessie Bolt are both in for murder. And they both have connections to the cartel. They're both dangerous men with nothing to lose."

The words sent an unpleasant shiver down Bailey's spine as Charlie headed toward the parking lot beside the nature trail.

She watched as the undercover agent climbed into a black Navigator with dark-tinted windows. She caught a glimpse of a dark-haired man in a white Polo shirt and mirrored sunglasses in the driver's seat before the door slammed shut.

Turning to leave, Bailey's eyes drifted to the path that led down to the pond where Ronin Godfrey had hidden Dolores Santos' body.

As her heart began to thud rapidly in her chest, Ludwig pulled on the leash, urging her back toward the Expedition.

Perhaps he remembers that path, too. After all, he was there with Morley that day. He was-

She jumped as her phone buzzed.

Looking down, she saw Fraser was calling.

"The assistant state attorney has decided not to charge Mason," he said as soon as she answered. "At least, not yet."

Bailey breathed a sigh of relief.

"But he's been suspended from his position with pay, and he's been asked not to leave the area while we continue the investigation. At this point, he's our only person of interest."

Bailey thanked him for sharing the news, then ended the call with a heavy heart. As she walked back to the parking lot, she gave one last wary look toward the nature trail.

CHAPTER SIX

Cate parked her white Lexus in the tiny parking lot outside Dr. Mandy Chung's office and looked in the rearview mirror. Inhaling deeply, she smoothed back her auburn hair and wiped a speck of mascara from under one puffy eye. Glancing at the clock on the dashboard, she saw that she was a few minutes early for her eleven o'clock appointment but opened the door and climbed out anyway.

As she entered the quiet office, she gave a listless wave to Cecilia. The gray-haired receptionist was just returning to her desk holding a steaming cup in one hand and a file folder in the other.

Motioning for Cate to have a seat in the waiting area, she pulled her heavy knit sweater around her and took a sip from her cup.

"You want some herbal tea while you're waiting?"

Cate shook her head.

"I'm not a big fan of tea, but coffee would be nice."

"Sorry, but Dr. Chung doesn't like patients to be caffeinated during a session," the receptionist said in a hushed voice as she looked toward the closed door. "I'd sneak you a cup but she always seems to know. She's got an unusually keen sense of smell."

Looking around at the expensively furnished office, Cate's natural skepticism kicked in. She surreptitiously scanned the room for tell-tale signs of a hidden camera.

"I guess I'll have tea, then," she said, trying to sound more enthusiastic than she felt.

She watched as the older woman set her own cup on the desk, along with the file folder, and turned back toward the kitchen.

Cate's eyes fixed on the name on the folder.

Mason Knox.

She knew she shouldn't be surprised.

She'd been the one who had recently recommended that Mason see her therapist after he'd finally broken down and told her about Gayle Kershaw.

Cate had figured having a woman stalk you for months before trying to shoot you qualified as trauma.

As Cecilia disappeared into the kitchen, Cate looked around again for a hidden camera. Seeing nothing suspicious, she stood and strode across the room, flipping open the folder before she could change her mind.

She skimmed the first page, then used a finger to flip to the next.

Her eyes widened as she saw the final comment jotted down at the end of the session notes.

...anger and frustration appears to be reaching a breaking point. Lack of sleep has contributed to memory loss and blackouts.

Cate jumped as the door to the session room swung open to reveal Mandy Chung's trim, athletic figure.

The psychiatrist had her head turned to the young woman behind her, giving Cate a chance to step away from the desk just as Cecilia bustled back into the room.

Accepting the offered tea, Cate took a long sip of the hot liquid before stepping toward the window. She gazed out at the parking lot as the therapist led the departing patient to the door.

Once the woman was gone, Dr. Chung turned to Cate.

"I hope I didn't keep you waiting," she said, checking the delicate gold watch on her wrist as Cate moved toward the open door.

Instead of following Cate into the room, Dr. Chung turned back.

"Cecilia, did you find that folder?" she asked. "I told Mr. Knox I'd try to squeeze him in after my next appointment."

Cate strained to listen as she stepped into the room.

She'd been seeing the therapist now for several months.

Mandy Chung was considered to be an expert in treating post-traumatic stress disorder and was well-regarded in the community for her outreach programs.

She'd helped Cate deal with the fallout of being drugged and kidnapped by Chad Hearst, the Summerset Stalker. While Bailey had arrived in time to save her from being thrown off the deck of the Belle Harbor Lighthouse, the experience had been traumatic and Cate was still having nightmares and panic attacks.

Dr. Chung had been helping her come to terms with her trauma.

Taking another sip of the tea, Cate winced as the hot liquid burned her throat, still brooding over the words in the folder.

What was Mason so angry about? And was he really having blackouts?

Cate had tried to call him that morning but he hadn't answered. Was he still at the police station or was he avoiding her call?

She turned to see Dr. Chung standing in the doorway, smiling at her with a curious expression.

"You seem jumpy. Is everything okay?"

Cate nodded.

"Yes, everything is fine," she lied.

"Okay, then let's get started."

* * *

Cate was sitting at her desk trying to keep her eyes open when Bailey popped her head into the office.

"I thought I'd come by and check on you," her sister said as she led Ludwig into the room. "I also spoke to Fraser and thought you might want an update."

Suddenly, Cate was wide awake.

"What happened? What did Fraser tell you?" she demanded. "Has Mason been arrested?"

Sinking into a chair across from her, Bailey sighed.

"He said the assistant state attorney has decided not to file charges yet, but that Mason is still their one and only suspect in Gayle Kershaw's murder. Apparently, Mason's also been suspended from his job with pay pending the outcome of the investigation."

Not sure if she should be relieved or worried, Cate slumped back into her chair, glad now that she hadn't given into the temptation to stomp down to Henrietta Trilby's office and demand an update.

"I also was going to mention that I saw an *old friend* of yours today," Bailey said. "Or maybe *old enemy* would be more like it."

Cate raised an eyebrow.

"I went to the Summerset County Detention Center and spoke to Desmond Bolt," she admitted. "You do remember him, right?"

"Of course, I do," Cate agreed. "That was a big case. I wasn't sure the jury would convict but they recommended a life sentence."

She frowned.

"Why did you go to see him?" she asked.

"His DNA was in CODIS and it flagged as a partial match to a homicide victim," Bailey said. "A teenage Jane Doe in the crypt. Turns out the victim was his biological daughter."

Forgetting her worry about Mason for the first time all day, Cate leaned forward with interest.

"The lab had performed an isotopic analysis of her hair to help determine where she lived leading up to her death. Turns out she lived in North Florida up until a few weeks before she died."

"Right, and Dessie was born up in Verbena Beach," Cate said. "I remember that. Although the man refused to speak. He wouldn't tell us anything about himself."

Thinking back to the trial, she pictured Dessie's closed

face.

"Well, he let his mask slip and called his daughter Birdie," Bailey said. "He also insisted she wasn't on drugs or a runaway. It was very clear to me that he had a relationship with her and is devastated by her death."

Cate considered the information.

She had to admit she was surprised that Bailey had gotten Dessie to open up. The convicted murderer had kept his mouth tightly shut even at his sentencing hearing.

Instead of pleading for mercy or presenting evidence to mitigate his sentence, he had maintained a stony silence that had earned him a life sentence.

"You sent him down about three years ago, right?" Bailey said.

She didn't wait for Cate's confirmation.

"And it was around that same time that his daughter ended up in the crypt. This means before the task force performed the DNA analysis and informed him that she was dead, he had gone years without being sure what happened to her."

"Unless he's the one who killed her," Cate said, recalling Dessie Bolt's inscrutable eyes. "After all, we don't know enough about him to be sure what he's capable of doing."

Bailey shook her head.

"I don't think so. He seemed torn up when he finally broke down and talked about his daughter," she said. "That wasn't the reaction of a murderer. He was in pain."

But Cate wasn't convinced.

"You still don't know who his daughter is...or was," she

reminded Bailey. "And with Roderick Payne as his lawyer pushing for a new appeal, you can bet he's not going to talk now."

She grimaced as she thought about the prosecutor-turned-judge who'd recently had to resign from the bench after being photographed exchanging money for drugs on a local street corner.

"You do know that Payne is back at work defending his sleazy list of criminal clients, don't you?" Cate asked. "And top of the list is likely Dessie Bolt.

"Well, talking of sleazy criminals...I'm planning to visit Carter Delaney as soon as I can make the arrangements," Bailey said. "Maybe as soon as tomorrow. You want to go with me?"

Before Cate could reply, there was a soft rap on the door. It swung open to reveal Henrietta Trilby.

The prosecutor's profusion of fluffy black and gray curls framed a broad face and wide, alert eyes behind oversized glasses.

She was wearing a form-fitting sweater dress that emphasized her generous curves and stylish, low-heeled riding boots.

"Henrietta, I've been meaning to come see you," Cate said as Bailey quickly stood and headed for the door. "Come in."

She waved goodbye to her sister, who ushered Ludwig into the hall with a reassuring smile and shut the door behind her.

"Yes, I heard you had some concerns about a person of interest in Gayle Kershaw's homicide," Henrietta said. "Mason Knox is a *friend* of yours?"

Her arch tone sent a ripple of irritation down Cate's back. The woman had clearly heard that she and Mason were dating.

"I realize that my personal friendship with Mr. Knox precludes me from becoming involved in the investigation or potential charges against him," Cate acknowledged. "But I do want to make you aware that he is an upstanding member of the community who has been a victim of stalking and harassment himself."

Raising a perfectly plucked eyebrow, Henrietta put both hands on her substantial hips.

"But you do understand the woman who stalked him is dead?"

Her blunt statement made Cate wince.

"Of course, and whoever killed Gayle Kershaw needs to be found and prosecuted," Cate said. "The fact that she stalked Mason doesn't mean she should have been killed. All, I'm saying is..."

She faltered and sighed. Not sure what she was trying to say.

"Listen, I get it. You're worried for your friend. But I assure you, as long as I'm involved, Mr. Knox, and any other suspect in the case, will be given fair treatment under the law."

Knowing there was little more that could be said, Cate watched with miserable eyes as Henrietta left the room.

After a long beat, she picked up her phone and tried Mason's number again. He still didn't answer.

But her heart jumped seconds later when a text came in.

Sorry, can't talk now. Just on the phone with my lawyer.

She instantly texted back.

Who did you retain?

She crossed her fingers, hoping it wasn't going to be Payne.

The answer came back only slightly better.

Tony Brunner.

The news wasn't terrible. After all, Brunner was one of the best defense attorneys in the area.

She'd gone up against the man many times and was now glad to remember she'd recently lost a case to him.

Looking out the window, she saw the clouds had dissolved into rain, which beat against her office window like angry tears.

CHAPTER SEVEN

Light rain drizzled down from a gray sky as Dalton West opened the door to find his sister Sabrina huddled under an umbrella. While she was dressed for her job as a reporter in slim black pants, a white blouse, a ruby red jacket, and a full face a make-up, her short blonde hair was disheveled and her hands were covered in what appeared to be motor oil.

"The van won't start," she fumed, pushing past him into his apartment. "There's a breaking story and I need a ride...now!"

"Have you ever heard of Uber?"

"Why should I pay someone to drive me around when I have a perfectly reliable big brother living right next door?"

Dalton checked his watch.

He had just taken on a new missing person case and had a list of things to do before his next meeting with his client.

But then, the whole reason he was living in the less-than-ideal Arbor Apartments was to keep an eye on his younger sister.

His father had made a deathbed request for him to rebuild his relationship with Sabrina. Giving her a ride when her car broke down seemed like the easier part of the deal.

"Fine," Dalton said. "But you'll need to get another ride back."

Holding the umbrella for her as they walked out to his black Dodge pickup, Dalton paid little attention to what Sabrina was saying until he heard Mason Knox's name.

"...woman was killed at his house," she said. "No one's been arrested yet as far as my sources know, but it sounds as if an arrest is imminent."

Dalton opened his mouth to tell his sister that he already knew about the murder, then decided not to open himself up for the inquisition that was sure to follow.

He'd seen Bailey the night before after managing to talk her into meeting him for a quick bite to eat, and she'd been preoccupied and worried about Cate.

He couldn't say he blamed her.

Running through all the details she'd shared, everything pointed to Mason Knox as the prime suspect in the murder.

And Bailey's sister is devastated. She's head over heels for the guy.

The thought was followed by an unsettling question.

Would Bailey be devastated if I'd been the one accused of murder?

Dalton wasn't sure he wanted an answer. His relationship with Bailey wasn't something he was ready to analyze. At least, not this early in the morning.

As soon as the Dodge pulled up to the curb outside Mason's house, Sabrina climbed out, hitting the ground running as she saw the crime scene swarming with activity up ahead.

Dalton stepped out after her and stood on the street with the group of reporters and curious neighbors that had gathered past the yellow crime scene tape.

He saw a small woman with glasses and a dark cap of hair approach a man he recognized as Detective Killian Rourke.

"Oh my goodness, what's happened?" the woman asked, grasping at the detective's arm.

"Ma'am, you'll need to step back," Rourke barked, wrenching his arm away. "This is a crime scene. There was a homicide last night and-"

The woman's high-pitched cry of dismay turned the heads of everyone in the crowd.

"I'm too late!"

She stared at the house with an anguished expression.

"I thought...well, I *hoped* that I'd get here in time to stop this from happening."

Rourke frowned down at her.

"You knew a murder was about to take place?" he asked. "Who are you?"

"I'm Dr. Jude Varney," she said. "I work at the Rock Ridge Detention Center in Crimson Falls, Virginia. In the psychiatric ward. One of my patients is...*was* a woman named Gayle Kershaw."

The woman seemed flustered as she spoke.

"Two days ago, the board decided to grant Gayle early release over my objections. The officer cleaning out her cell found this in the trash can."

Dr. Varney held up a wrinkled piece of paper.

"It's a letter addressed to Dr. Mason Knox, the man Gayle

had been convicted of stalking almost two years ago. Considering the contents, I figured she'd break her no-contact order and head down here."

"And you thought you'd chase after her by yourself?" Rourke asked. "Why not call us and–"

"I had no legal right to stop her myself," Dr. Varney protested. "But I had a moral obligation to try to warn her victim."

She looked toward the house.

"But I'm too late," she said, shaking her head in despair. "Even after everything she told me, I can't believe she really killed him."

"*She* didn't kill *him*," Rourke snapped back. "*He* killed–"

"That's enough, Detective Rourke," a deep voice interrupted as Detective Jimmy Fraser appeared. "The identity of the woman who has been killed hasn't been officially released yet pending notification of next of kin."

He flashed Rourke a warning look.

"You mean Mason Knox isn't dead?" Dr. Varney asked, confused.

"No, Dr. Knox is not dead," Fraser said. "But, as I said, the identity of the victim hasn't been released to the public yet."

He looked over at Dalton, and then his eyes moved past him to where Sabrina stood with an umbrella in one hand and a microphone in the other.

"I'm going to need you to come down to the station with me," Fraser said, putting a guiding hand on Dr. Varney's arm. "We can–"

"But, who died?" she cut in.

Eyes widening, the doctor once again gasped.

"Is it Gayle? Is Gayle Kershaw dead?"

Suddenly, Sabrina was beside her.

"You said Gayle Kershaw was a stalker?" she called out.

The doctor gave a stunned nod.

"I can't believe she's dead," Dr. Varney murmured. "I'm not surprised someone died. I just thought it would be Mason."

"We haven't confirmed the identity of-"

Fraser's protest was drowned out by Sabrina's next question.

"Could Gayle have come here on a murder-suicide mission?"

"No more comments," Fraser snapped as he ushered the doctor toward an Interceptor parked further down the road.

Once the vehicle had pulled away, Dalton turned back to see Sabrina tapping wildly on her phone.

"What are you doing?" he asked, coming up beside her.

"I'm pulling up Gayle Kershaw's arrest records," she said, her eyes already gleaming. "And looking for her socials."

"Just make sure you have all the facts before you start spreading false information," he warned her. "You can't believe everything you find online, you know."

But she only waived him away.

"You can go," she said. "The station manager will send someone to pick me up when I'm done here."

Dalton sighed and checked his watch.

He was already late for his appointment with his new client.

As he got back into the Dodge, he wondered why he hadn't mentioned the new case to Bailey the night before.

Something had held him back.

Perhaps the feeling that if she knew what he was doing and who he was working for, she wouldn't approve.

* * *

Dalton sat across from Neil Ashworth at the Summerset Espresso Café, listening as the man told him everything he could remember about his father, Chuck Ashworth, who had disappeared when he was still a teenager.

After recently celebrating his own fortieth birthday, Neil had retained Dalton's services to find out what had happened to his father. He wanted to know why the man had simply disappeared from his life for the last twenty-five years.

He'd explained to Dalton that he had already submitted a sample of his DNA to all publicly available ancestry and genealogy databases but had found no matches or clues to his father's current whereabouts. He figured a private investigator was his only option.

"Okay, I think for now I have enough to get started," Dalton said. "I'll contact you later in the week with an update."

As he started to get to his feet, Neil reached out to stop him.

"Remember what I said. This is between me and you. I don't want my mother to know anything about this."

The request wasn't unusual. Many people hired a private

investigator because they were looking into things they didn't want other people to know about.

And Dalton was familiar with Neil's mother, Nigella Ashworth.

On the surface, the woman appeared to be a popular member of the city council and a successful local business owner.

But she'd also been accused of bribery and he'd heard tales of her sharp tongue and fiery temper.

"My mother has always been angry that my father left," Neil said. "She would never permit anyone to speak of him in her presence, even me."

Lifting a hand, he absently tucked a long strand of hair under the blue bandana he had tied around his head

"And lately, she's been extra...sensitive," he added, carefully selecting his words. "Even though the bribery case against her was dropped by the judge, she's been extremely paranoid and suspicious lately. It's like she thinks everyone is out to get her. Anyone who's connected to the prosecutor, Cate Flynn, is on her list of enemies."

Dalton hesitated, wondering if he should mention Bailey.

Does dating someone's sister mean you're connected to them?

After a moment's thought, he decided it didn't. His love life and who he chose to date weren't relevant to the case.

Besides, his relationship with Bailey was fated to end.

Although he wasn't sure when, she had made it quite clear she would be rejoining the FBI special crimes unit in the D.C. field office once her current case was closed.

After leaving Neil sitting at the table sipping his second

cup of green tea, Dalton hurried off to do his errands, not wanting to be late for the Tuesday night tacos and tequila get-together that Sid Morley had arranged.

When he finally pulled up to the retired FBI agent's house, the rare winter rain had already stopped and Morley and his black German shepherd Amadeus were sitting beside the back fence.

As Dalton approached, he could see that one of the more adventurous gopher tortoises who'd been rescued from the Sun Creek preserve had decided to make an appearance and was sitting calmly on the other side of the chain link fence.

"That's Shelley," Morley told Dalton as he took a seat in an empty chair. "She came for the party."

"How can you be sure she's a Shelly and not a Sheldon?" Dalton asked, raising a doubtful eyebrow.

Morley shrugged.

"I'm as sure as I can be. I got a look at her plastron when she got herself stuck under that fence a few weeks ago. It was flat, which means she's a female."

Opening his mouth to ask what a plastron was, he was interrupted by the sound of tires on gravel.

He looked over to see Bailey's Expedition pull up to the house.

Moments later Ludwig was bounding toward them.

Bailey followed the German shepherd looking decidedly less exuberant than the dog.

"You look tired," Morley called out, waving her toward a lawn chair. "Have you been over at the crime scene at the medical examiner's house? Have they charged him?"

The question earned a grim shake of her head.

"I'm not working the case, so I don't have all the details," she admitted. "Millicent Pruett, the new Belle Harbor chief of police doesn't want the FBI involved."

She sank into an empty chair and gratefully accepted the frosty margarita Morley handed her.

"All I really know so far is that the victim was a former girlfriend of Mason Knox. She spent the last few years in prison for stalking and attacking him."

Morley whistled.

"So, it was self-defense?"

Bailey hesitated, not sure how much more she should say.

Remembering that she wasn't officially working the case, she decided she had no real obligation to hold back her opinion.

"Actually, it doesn't look that way," she said. "The woman drove there willingly and went into the house. Dinner was laid out on the table and there was no real sign of a struggle. She was just sitting at the table with her throat cut."

She took out her phone.

"There is something that has me wondering though," she said, scrolling through her photos. "There was a pendant on the plate in front of the victim."

Handing the phone to Morley, she sighed.

"I noticed it because we found a similar pendant on one of the victims in the crypt. A teenage girl whose father is a convicted murderer and suspected associate of the Tumba Cartel."

Dalton leaned over to look at the phone, frowning down at

the silver pendant, which wasn't much bigger than a quarter.

"The man was wearing a pendant just like this when I saw him this morning at the Summerset Detention Center."

As Morley zoomed in on the pendant to study the engraved design, Dalton glanced up at Bailey.

"Are you thinking it's a coincidence that this same type of pendant was found with both bodies or could the cases be linked?"

Before she could answer, Morley spoke up, his eyes still glued to the photo on the phone.

"That's a Saint Olga medal," he told them. "I recognize it because I was raised in the Orthodox church."

He cocked his head.

"If I remember my lessons well, St. Olga is the patron saint of revenge."

CHAPTER EIGHT

Traffic was heavy as Bailey fought the morning rush through downtown Belle Harbor, heading west toward the highway. She had invited Cate to go with her to interview Carter Delaney at the Summerset Detention Center but had decided to make a short detour first.

"Sid Morley sent me the contact details for the priest at a local Orthodox church," Bailey said, glancing over at Cate, who was staring morosely out the window. "He thought the reverend may be able to tell me something about the Saint Olga pendant we found the other night at Mason's house."

"If it could help Mason, it's fine with me," Cate said. "Just as long as no one tries to save my soul. I'm not in the mood."

Deciding silence may be the wisest response, Bailey followed Morley's directions to the All Saints Orthodox Church of Summerset County, which was set on a wide tract of land just west of the slow-moving Bellamy River.

Pulling up to the big domed church, Bailey admired the high, narrow windows and graceful arch of the front door.

As they walked into the quiet, dimly lit building, a balding man in flowing black robes hurried down the aisle to greet them.

"I'm Reverend Schroeder," he said, inclining his head with a welcoming smile. "Please, come into my office where we can talk."

Bailey and Cate followed the big man past an elaborate altar and into the back administrative area.

As they settled into plastic folding chairs around a small table, Reverend Schroeder gestured to a selection of tea and cookies he had laid out in anticipation of their visit.

"I'm sorry to put you to so much trouble," Bailey said as she took a cookie off the tray and nibbled at it. "We really can't stay long, but I was hoping you could tell me something about this."

She scrolled to the photo of the pendant and set the phone down in front of the priest.

He squinted at the screen, then nodded.

"Yes, that's Saint Olga, just as Mr. Morley had determined," he said. "It's impressive that he remembered."

Looking up at Bailey, he produced a wry smile.

"There are over two hundred million members of the Eastern Orthodox church worldwide. Over half a million parishioners live in the US alone," he said. "Sometimes it feels as if we have just as many saints. There are thousands and each one has a feast day."

He glanced back at the phone.

"It's hard to remember them all, even for me."

"With so many saints, how does a person decide which saint to honor?" Bailey asked. "For example, why would a member of the church wear one of these Saint Olga pendants?"

Reverend Schroeder clasped his hands and leaned forward.

"Those in our faith are given a Christian name which matches the name of their patron saint."

Bailey nodded.

"And how is a patron saint selected?"

"There is no set rule," Reverend Schroeder admitted. "But the child's day of birth or baptism usually falls on the patron saint's feast day."

Trying not to get too excited, Bailey kept her voice calm.

"So, a woman who wears this pendant could be named Olga?" she asked. "And could have been born on Saint Olga's feast day?"

The reverend frowned.

"Possibly, but not necessarily," he admitted. "People often wear pendants honoring a relative or loved one's saint, or they may choose several saints to honor based on divine inspiration."

Bailey's hope dimmed as she and Cate stood and followed the priest back out to the sanctuary.

As they neared the front door, she stopped in front of a poster showing a group of laughing teenagers. It was an announcement for an upcoming fundraising event for the church's youth shelter.

She turned back to the priest.

"Is there a way to find out if a teenage girl named Birdie ever came to your shelter?" she asked. "The girl would have been wearing one of these Saint Olga pendants. It would have been two or three years ago."

The reverend frowned as she continued.

"She was originally from Verbena Beach and would have been new to Summerset County. Most likely on her own."

"A runaway?" the reverend asked with a concerned frown. "Our food bank and youth shelter are very active. I will ask our volunteers and let you know."

"Thank you, Reverend Schroeder. I'll be in touch."

* * *

Once they left the church parking lot, it was only another twenty-minute drive until Bailey was pulling up once again outside the Summerset County Detention Center.

She was pleased to see that Officer Boswell was on duty in front of the lockers.

He didn't seem surprised to see her again so soon, and he quickly offered to let Ludwig hang out with him while she and Cate went in to meet with Carter Delaney.

"You keep some dangerous company," Boswell said under his breath as she placed her phone in the locker.

He looked as if there was something else he wanted to say, but the other guard was waiting by the door with a grim, put-upon expression, so Bailey had no choice but to turn and hurry after him.

She and Cate were led to the same small room she'd been in the day before when she'd met with Dessie Bolt, and they sat silently at the little table for the next ten minutes, waiting for the serial killer to be brought down from his cell.

Jumping as the door banged open, Bailey watched the guard push Carter Delaney into the room and cuff his leg to the table, which was bolted to the floor.

Since the same precaution hadn't been taken the day before with Dessie, Bailey suspected that Delaney must be classified as a high-risk inmate.

Based on the dozens of victims he'd left behind, she couldn't say she disagreed, although she doubted the leg cuff would do much to stop Delaney if he decided to jump across the table at her.

"What do you want, Agent Flynn?" Delaney asked once the guard had stepped out into the hall. "You know, I could file a harassment suit against you and the FBI if you keep coming here trying to pressure me."

"I just have a few questions," Bailey said. "If you tell me what I want to know, I'll leave you in peace."

Running a restless hand through his short, dark hair, Delaney scoffed loudly at the comment

"There's no peace in this place," he said. "Only boredom."

"Well, maybe instead of peace I can offer you something to think about then," Bailey countered. "We've uncovered information about another one of the victims in the crypt and I wanted your input."

When Delaney didn't object, she continued.

"What do you know about a man named Desmond Bolt?"

"What makes you think I know anything?" he asked.

"I heard he works for the Tumba Cartel and he's in prison for murder," Bailey said. "So, it seems you two have a lot in common."

Delaney shrugged and quickly looked away. Too quickly.

"What about Birdie?" she asked. "You know, Desmond

Bolt's teenage daughter."

A tightening in Delaney's jaw let Bailey know she'd hit a nerve.

"I'm surprised you managed to get any information out of Dessie," Delaney said. "But if he's been bragging about his association with the cartel...

He let out an exaggerated sigh.

"I'm guessing his indiscretion explains the recent, tragic event."

"What do you mean? What tragic event?"

"Oh, you'll find out soon enough."

Bailey wanted to push him for information, then decided it would only give Delaney pleasure. The serial killer obviously enjoyed toying with them.

She considered asking him about the pendant Dessie had been wearing, then decided it wouldn't be a good idea. She'd already given him enough information without getting anything in return.

There was no point in giving him anything else he might be able to use to his advantage.

Delaney seemed to sense her change in mood.

Leaning back in his chair, he turned his head and began to study Cate as if she were a specimen in a jar.

"You must be good at your job," he finally said. "Considering you managed to lock Dessie up for life. It's not easy around here to get a conviction against an associate in the cartel. Although, I can't say you managed to take all responsible parties off the street."

It was clear he wanted them to think he knew what had

happened the night Dessie had been arrested.

He wanted them to think he had inside information.

As far as Bailey knew, he probably did.

"That's old news," Bailey said. "We want to know about Birdie. What happened to her?"

"Birdie?" he asked, almost playfully. "You want to know what happened to poor little Birdie? Well, let me tell you."

Bailey's mouth went dry as she saw something in Delaney's dark eyes that told her he wasn't lying. Maybe he really did know what had happened to the girl.

But will he tell me the truth?'

Holding her breath, she waited, knowing that further prodding would only incur his wrath.

He'd enjoy nothing more than to bring her to the edge of anticipation before refusing to speak, leaving her once again unsatisfied.

The petty manipulation of her emotions was the only power he had left. That, and the information he kept to wield over anyone who tried to question him.

Growing bored with her silence, Delaney sat forward in his chair and propped his elbows on the table.

"I didn't kill Birdie. But I know what happened to her."

He grinned.

"Let's just say she flew too close to the sun."

"What's that supposed to mean?" Cate asked.

Delaney tutted as if disappointed.

"Don't you know what a metaphor is?"

When neither Bailey nor Cate answered, he exhaled.

"Fine, I'll spell it out. Birdie got too close to the top. She made someone mad and they wanted her eliminated."

"The cartel put out a hit on a teenage girl?" Bailey asked, not sure she believed what he was saying. "But you weren't the one who carried it out?"

He shook his head.

"It wasn't me."

His dark eyes met hers, giving nothing away as she tried to decide if he was lying.

But, if he did kill Birdie, why deny it?

"So, you know who ordered the hit?"

"Few people actually know Mr. Tumba's true identity. Those who find out don't seem to live very long."

Considering his words, Bailey made a mental note that Delaney hadn't actually denied knowing who the leader of the cartel was.

"Tumba is the Spanish word for *tomb*, isn't it?" she asked.

"So I've heard," Delaney agreed. "Which is why they say that working for the Tumba Cartel is like entering a tomb. Once you enter, you never leave alive."

She heard the truth behind his words. And the fear.

"You're scared," she said. "Even in here, you think if you say too much you could be killed by the cartel."

Delaney didn't deny it.

"Life in here isn't exactly exciting but it's better than spending the rest of eternity in *la tumba*."

His mocking tone was back.

"There won't be any grand tomb for you," Bailey said. "They bury lifers out back in the prison cemetery. And they normally use a cardboard box."

"Then they're probably constructing another box right now."

Delaney's eyes lit up as he called for the guard.

Replaying his words as she and Cate followed the guard back to the visitor's area, Bailey found Boswell and Ludwig waiting.

As she used her key to open her locker, Boswell leaned in.

"Dessie Bolt was found hanging in his cell last night," the guard said in a low voice. "He's dead.

CHAPTER NINE

Olga ran full out on the treadmill, her leanly muscled arms and legs pumping with focused determination as the high-quality surround sound system blasted a dance remix of Blondie's *One Way or the Other* into the mirror-paneled home gym.

The frenzied words to the song had been playing on a loop in her head ever since she'd left Gayle Kershaw's dead body propped up at Mason Knox's dinner table.

What better song is there to commemorate the death of a stalker?

Smiling grimly at the thought, Olga jabbed a sweaty thumb at a button on the treadmill's control panel, increasing the already steep incline of the machine as she ran in time to the track's quick tempo, which closely matched her heart rate of 160 BPM.

If she had her way, Olga would set every scene of her life to music, even if the music was only playing in her head.

Luckily, the luxurious house she was currently squatting in included a stellar sound system throughout both levels, similar to the one Mason Knox had installed in his house, which had allowed Chopin's *Funeral March* to accompany

Gayle Kershaw's last supper.

While Gayle had only been a pawn in the bigger game that Olga had now set in motion, she had played her unwitting role perfectly.

And there was no need for Olga to feel guilty. The stalker who had terrorized Cate Flynn's lover had gotten what she deserved.

Olga had set the Blondie song on repeat and as it started over, she decided the song might make a satisfying soundtrack for her future encounter with Cate Flynn as well.

"Oh yes, I'm coming for you, Cate," she muttered as she ran. "And I'm definitely going to get you."

Just then, she felt the buzz of her smart watch on her wrist.

Slowing, Olga looked down to see an incoming call alert on the tiny display and grimaced, making no attempt to stop the sweat on her forehead from dripping onto the sleek black device.

She ignored the call for now, but she'd have to get going soon or people would start asking questions.

For someone secretly working for the Tumba Cartel as a fixer, it wasn't a good idea to make people too curious about her whereabouts.

Her ability to fit in within normal society enabled her to operate as a killer under the radar.

No need to stir up trouble now just when she was so close to carrying out her plan of revenge.

That plan was the only thing keeping her going.

No matter how long it took, she would make Cate Flynn

pay for what she'd done.

Climbing off the treadmill, still panting, she tried to catch her breath, mopping at her face with a towel as she started toward the kitchen, her hand instinctively reaching for the Saint Olga pendant hanging from the silver chain around her neck, before remembering that she'd taken it off and left it on the dinner plate at Mason Knox's house.

She'd have to remember to get a replacement soon.

But it was probably best to wait.

At least for now.

It wouldn't do for anyone to see her wearing it.

She was halfway across the living room when she saw the special bulletin on Channel 3 News.

Reporter Sabrina West spoke into the camera.

"Convicted murderer Desmond Bolt is dead. The warden of the Summerset County Detention Center said Bolt, who was serving life in prison for a double murder, was found dead in his prison cell."

Olga stared at the television in shock. Pain knifed through her as Dessie's photo appeared on the screen.

Sinking to her knees, she let out a high-pitched keening sound that competed with the blaring music.

She killed him. That bitch killed Dessie.

The thought crashed through her head like a tidal wave.

First, she locked him up forever. And now she's gone and killed him. Or as good as. It's all her fault. Dessie would still be alive if it wasn't for Cate Flynn.

Shaking her head in rage and anguish, Olga got to her feet just as Sabrina West spoke again.

"And in other news, the Belle Harbor Police announced that the person questioned in relation to last night's homicide on Belgrave Avenue has since been released."

Choking back her rage, Olga headed upstairs, muttering a verse from Leviticus as she went.

"Facture for fracture, eye for eye, tooth for tooth..."

Her plan would need to be updated. Now that Dessie was dead, Mason Knox would have to die, too.

CHAPTER TEN

Finola Lawson normally enjoyed the quiet solitude of the autopsy suite when she was preparing a body for a post-mortem. But today she was on edge and jumpy as she worked in the quiet medical examiner's office, carefully photographing the deep wounds on Gayle Kershaw's neck and torso, and recording the body's current weight, height, and body temperature.

Looking down at the mutilated woman, she wondered if Mason really could have inflicted the fatal wounds she had documented.

She checked the clock on the wall, wishing she could have gone home an hour ago like everyone else.

Once the body was prepped, she would store it in the cooler in advance of the autopsy she would most likely have to perform on her own the next day.

But she could handle it. She was an assistant medical examiner, after all. Not a lowly forensic technician as most people assumed.

She had performed many autopsies on her own. However, in a small office, the junior examiner often got left with the grunt work.

If Mason is charged with murder, I might even be promoted.

The thought was quickly replaced by a depressing alternative.

"Or someone much more difficult than Mason to work with could be hired in as the new chief medical examiner. And that M.E. might want to bring their own staff with them."

Her heart dropped.

Mason's loss of a job could lead to the loss of her own.

And, even worse, a good man could be wrongly convicted.

Because, from everything she'd seen during her work at the medical examiner's office, he was a good man.

He was kind but reserved, not trusting people easily.

Not even people he worked with on a daily basis.

He'd rarely let her get past his professional veneer.

But on occasion, Finola had seen a flash of vulnerability and emotion in his eyes that made her think he'd quit his prestigious job up in Virginia because he was running away from someone or something. And she hadn't blamed him.

It was tempting to just walk away from all the problems of life that sometimes seemed too hard to face.

She'd been tempted to pull up stakes and leave Summerset County herself a few times. Her mother, who suffered from bouts of depression exacerbated by a drinking problem, and her father, who dealt with her mother's drinking and mood swings by working late most evenings, would be unlikely to miss her.

Only her on-again, off-again boyfriend Terrance would likely be upset by her sudden departure. Although she had a feeling he wouldn't wallow in a single state very long.

Terry would be out at the bar before I got to the county line.

The thought sent a sharp pang of jealousy through her.

As she bent over the dead body on the metal dissecting table, she wondered if jealousy had been the cause of Gayle's death.

She'd heard the detectives discussing the allegations against the woman. They'd said she'd been convicted of stalking Mason. Of even trying to kill him.

But then she'd found that letter in Gayle's pocket.

Could Mason have been trying to lure the woman down to Florida so that he could kill her? Had he been seeking revenge?

The thought was chilling.

Had he stabbed her in the heart and slit her throat in a calculated move to make sure she could never threaten him again?

Her morbid thoughts were interrupted by quiet footsteps in the hall. She jumped as the door swung open.

Turning around, she saw Mason standing in the doorway.

"What are you doing?" she asked, her voice faltering at the words. "You aren't supposed to be here."

She stared at her boss, surprised by the dark circles under his eyes and dark stubble on his jaw.

"I came by to pick up some of my stuff," he said. "I've been suspended as I'm sure you've heard. But it'll be fine. It'll all work out and I'll be okay."

"Well, you look terrible," she said, feeling a pang of pity for him.

But then Mason's eyes fell to the table where Gayle's body lay.

He stared at the dead woman and took a step forward.

As they both looked down at his ex-girlfriend, Finola's pity suddenly turned to fear.

After all, they were alone. And if he'd already killed one woman, what would stop him from killing another?

Positioning the dissecting table between herself and her boss, she picked up a scalpel and held it out in front of her.

"You need to leave," she said, trying to sound firm. "If you don't, I'll call the police."

Mason lifted his eyes, which looked dazed and unfocused.

"You've got to know I didn't do this," he said. "I would never have hurt Gayle. And I would never hurt you."

He shook his head in confusion.

"Her killer is still out there, you know. Whoever did this is still out there and we're all still in danger. You need to-"

"All I need is for you to go back through that door and leave me here to do my job. Otherwise..."

She let the implied threat linger, not sure what she would do if he made a sudden move.

Mason sighed, then nodded.

"Okay, I just need to get a few things from my office and I'll go."

His shoulders slumped as he turned and walked back through the door. Seconds later, she heard his office door close behind him.

Feeling suddenly foolish for doubting him, she turned back to Gayle and continued her work. As she bent over the body, she heard the soft swoosh of the door opening again.

Finola turned, expecting Mason, prepared to say her

goodbyes.

Instead, a woman was standing in the doorway.

She was dressed all in black. Her hair was tucked under a black knit cap, her eyes covered by a pair of dark glasses.

"How did you get inside?" Finola asked. "Who are you?"

The woman stepped forward, walking toward the gurney with slow deliberate steps.

"I'm the one responsible for *her*."

She gestured toward Gayle's lifeless body on the table.

Shaking her head, Finola took a step back.

"You're not her next of kin," she said.

There was no doubt about that. She had spoken to Gayle's mother earlier in the day. The poor woman had been devastated and had asked for more time to figure out how to get her daughter's body back to Virginia.

"No, that's not what I meant," the woman said. "When I said I'm responsible, I meant responsible for her death."

Before Finola could react, the woman reached toward the autopsy tray and grabbed up a scalpel.

With a vicious lunge forward, she swiped the blade in the air, narrowly missing Finola's throat as the assistant medical examiner jerked backward to evade the blow.

Instantly, the woman was circling the table, moving fast as Finola tried to run for the door.

She was halfway across the room when a hand reached out and grabbed her ponytail, yanking her back, and sending her crashing into a metal tray, which crashed down around her.

Stainless steel tools clattered to the floor as Finola scrambled back to her feet. She staggered as the woman landed a solid blow to her chin, knocking her back to the floor, where the back of her head banged painfully against the concrete.

Standing over her, her attacker lifted the scalpel above her head.

Finola closed her eyes and braced herself for a fatal blow. But it didn't fall. The woman had stopped and was listening to footsteps that were coming down the hall.

As Finola opened her eyes, she saw her attacker turn and step into the shadows behind the door.

She sat up and tried to call out as Mason appeared in the doorway but her throat was tight with panic and pain.

"What's going on in here?" he asked.

His eyes widened as he saw Finola struggling to get to her feet, her face lined with blood and fear.

"Wait..." she managed to rasp out, but it was too late.

As Mason crossed the room, the attacker stepped forward, holding the big metal tray.

Lifting it up, she brought it down with full force over his head, causing him to stumble back and fall to the floor.

Suddenly, Finola was back on her feet, taking off through the door and running down the hall, heading toward the loading bay.

She was out through the loading bay door before she risked looking back over her shoulder. She screamed again.

Her attacker was running after her.

CHAPTER ELEVEN

Bailey pulled up to the curb outside the Sanctuary Apartments and brought the Expedition to a stop. She waited impatiently as Cate opened the door and climbed out of the passenger seat. Her sister had insisted on being dropped off at home before six o'clock, claiming she needed to complete the work she'd missed that afternoon by going on their little field trip, although Bailey suspected she just wanted to be alone to call Mason Knox.

And maybe she'll call Henrietta Trilby, too. She's got to be dying to find out if the prosecutor is planning to file charges against Mason.

Once Cate was safely inside, Bailey pulled back onto Sanctuary Street and headed toward downtown. Turning onto Grand Harbor Boulevard, she drove toward the medical examiner's office, hoping that Finola Lawson would be working late.

After all, the woman's boss was suspected of murder. It seemed likely that she would want to determine what had really happened before she went home for the evening.

And Bailey was eager to find out if the assistant medical examiner had collected any biological evidence off Gayle

Kershaw's body that might be linked to the perpetrator.

Perhaps there had been blood or tissue under the dead woman's fingernails. The evidence could clear Mason, putting Cate out of her misery. Perhaps the answer would set her own mind at ease as well.

Bailey hadn't been able to stop thinking about the Saint Olga pendant that had been left on the dinner plate in Mason Knox's house. She couldn't explain away the fact that Dessie Bolt and his daughter Birdie had both worn identical pendants.

Was it really just a coincidence that a third pendant had been found in the house of a man who had helped excavate Birdie's skull and bones?

The odd connection seemed too strange to just discount or ignore. It was the type of connection FBI profiler Argus Murphy would identify using one of his algorithms.

A seemingly circumstantial connection that might ultimately point to a link between Gayle Kershaw's death and Birdie's remains.

And what about Dessie's sudden demise?

Could he have been killed because he knew too much? Or had he taken his own life after the impact of his daughter's death and his own incarcerated future sunk in?

As she pulled up outside the medical examiner's office, Bailey saw that two cars were still parked in the lot.

She recognized one of them as Mason Knox's black Audi.

"What's he doing here?" she murmured to Ludwig as she opened the door and waited for him to jump down.

Hurrying up the sidewalk, she found the door to the office

unlocked and stepped inside, wincing at the pervasive smell of death and chemicals.

The office was eerily quiet as she walked past the reception desk and made her way into the back.

"Mason?" she called out. "Finola?"

When no one answered, she hesitated in the hall.

Suddenly, Ludwig barked, making Bailey jump.

The German shepherd looked up at her and barked again, then scurried down the hall, tugging her along after him.

Letting Ludwig lead, she followed him into the autopsy room, then came to a sudden stop.

Gayle Kershaw's dead body was lying on a metal dissecting table in the middle of the room. A metal tray had been knocked over and stainless steel tools were scattered all over the floor.

She gasped as she saw the pool of blood and the trail leading through the door and out toward the loading dock.

Moving quickly, Bailey slipped her Glock from her holster and followed after Ludwig, who was tracking the scent and the blood with excited barks.

She stopped him at the loading bay door and looked out at the back lot, which was lit by two harsh floodlights.

"Hold on, boy," she said softly, scanning the lot and the woods beyond. "I've got to make sure no one's out there."

The dog turned and barked as something moved in the woods.

A voice called out.

"We need help! Call an ambulance!"

Bailey recognized Mason's voice.

"Finola's been hurt!" he shouted again. "Hurry!"

Taking out her phone, Bailey tapped in 911, then held the phone to her ear and waited for the emergency operator to pick up.

Once she'd asked for an ambulance and police back up at the medical examiner's office, she allowed Ludwig to pull her out of the building and across the lot toward the woods.

She was holding her Glock in a ready position when she saw Mason kneeling over Finola's bloody, motionless body.

"She's still breathing," he called out. "But just barely. She's been stabbed and I think she may have hit her head."

As he turned his head to look over at her, Bailey was startled by the dark, glassy look in his eyes.

"Someone attacked us," he added as she drew nearer. "I didn't see who it was. I came into the autopsy suite and Finola was on the floor and then someone hit me over the head and...'

He lifted a hand to his head and winced.

When he pulled his hand back, his fingers were wet with blood.

Staring at him, still holding the Glock, Bailey tried to think. She needed to figure out what had really happened.

Did he attack Finola? Was he the one who stabbed her?

She found it hard to believe that the concerned man kneeling on the ground could be a killer. But you never knew what was inside someone. Even a seemingly nice guy like Mason could in reality be a monster masquerading as an ordinary man.

As if sensing her doubt and fear Mason called out again

"I didn't do this, Bailey. You've got to believe me."

Stepping forward, she stared down at Finola.

"Move away from her, Mason," she ordered. "Move back and wait for the ambulance to get here. It's on the way."

Before he could respond, something moved in the woods behind them, causing Ludwig to bark toward the dark shadows.

There was a rustling sound in the trees and then silence.

Is there an animal out there? Or maybe a person?

Bailey considered investigating the noise, then decided she couldn't leave Finola alone with Mason.

"If I leave her like this she could bleed out," Mason said. "Once the ambulance is here you can do whatever you want. I'll tell you everything I know. But first I need to help her."

When Bailey didn't lower the gun, Mason shrugged his big shoulders and sighed.

"Shoot me if you have to," he said, pulling off his jacket and holding the soft material against the wound in Finola's chest. "I can't just sit here and let her die."

His words were followed by sirens in the distance.

Hoping she wouldn't regret it, Bailey stuck her gun back in her holster and dropped to her knees to help him.

Together they wrapped the jacket around Finola and secured it tightly, trying to stem the flow of blood seeping into the ground.

"Stay!" Bailey ordered when Ludwig started toward the woods.

He stopped and followed orders but allowed himself a rebellious bark toward the shadows.

Suddenly, the paramedics were there, taking the coat from her hands, and attaching some sort of electrodes to Finola's chest.

As Bailey backed away, she could see the urgency and tension on the paramedics' faces as they lifted Finola onto a gurney and raced her toward the waiting ambulance.

"We're losing her," someone said as the door slammed shut.

Seconds later, the ambulance was speeding away.

Turning back toward Mason, she saw him staring after the flashing lights with glassy, disbelieving eyes.

CHAPTER TWELVE

Mason swayed on his feet as he stared down at the bloody patch of grass, trying to make sense of what had happened. Who had attacked Finola, and why? Was it the same person who had killed Gayle Kershaw? The only thing he knew of that connected the two women was him. Was this all somehow his fault? If so, what had he done and to whom?

Looking over at the fading lights of the ambulance, he saw Bailey watching him. Doubt filled her green eyes, which were so like her sister's. She opened her mouth as if to ask him a question, then closed it as hurried footsteps sounded behind her.

Suddenly, Detective Rourke appeared in the darkness, followed by several uniformed officers. He lifted his Glock and pointed it directly at Mason, who held up his hands and took a stumbling step backward as he tried to explain what had happened.

"I came to pick up some of my stuff from my office," he said in a hoarse voice. "Finola was in the autopsy suite and I spoke to her. She seemed a little jumpy but fine."

He lifted a hand to massage the back of his head as he

spoke but kept his eyes on Rourke's gun.

"I went to my office and started packing up a box. That's when I heard something. It sounded as if she'd knocked over a tray."

"When I came to check on her, I saw something was wrong. She was bleeding and...well, that's all I can remember. Someone hit me over the head. I fell and must have momentarily blacked out. When I regained consciousness, I saw that Finola was gone."

Rourke emitted a hollow laugh.

"That's pretty convenient. How'd you both end up outside?"

"I followed the blood trail out through the loading bay," Mason said. "I saw Finola on the ground. She'd been stabbed and I guess she collapsed. She wouldn't respond. Then Bailey arrived and-"

"And you didn't see who attacked Finola?" Rourke demanded.

He sounded incredulous.

"You didn't see the person who hit you over the head?"

"No, I didn't," Mason said, his voice a dull croak. "Whoever it was must have come up behind me."

Suddenly, Bailey Flynn was there, standing between Rourke and Mason, her green eyes bright with worry.

She turned to Rourke.

"Where's Detective Fraser?" she asked. "I'm sure he knows Mason well enough to know he's not acting normally. He's sustained a head injury and needs medical treatment."

"Jimmy Fraser's at home with his wife and kids," Rourke

said. "He's made it clear that the BHPD isn't his number one priority. If you've got a complaint about me, I suggest you talk to Chief Pruett. She's the one you need to convince to give Mason Knox a pass, not Fraser and not me."

The detective stepped closer, keeping his hostile eyes on Bailey.

"And didn't the chief tell you that the Belle Harbor PD takes care of their own cases? The FBI has no role here."

Bailey didn't bother protesting as Rourke turned to greet the crime scene team. She gave Mason a long look, then turned and strode away with Ludwig following close behind her.

* * *

Mason's head was pounding and his vision was blurry as he was led into the Belle Harbor police department and placed into an interrogation room.

Sinking into a chair, he rested his head on the table, allowing himself to drift off to sleep.

He woke with a start as Detective Rourke strode into the little room and slammed the door.

The detective lowered himself into the chair across from Mason. Leaning back, he folded his arms over his chest and frowned.

"I guess you thought that hot prosecutor girlfriend of yours would figure out a way to save your ass," he said. "Too bad she wasn't assigned to the case."

Mason didn't respond but his jaw clenched at the thought

of Cate, wondering what she must be thinking about him now.

Is she thinking I'm a killer?

Or was it possible that she would actually believe his story when no one else would? But even if she did believe him, could he really put her through the humiliation and stress of having to defend him to her colleagues?

No, that wouldn't be fair. I'll have to end things.

He should have done it sooner, but he'd been hoping for a reprieve. Hoping there would be a break in the case or an unexpected confession.

Determined not to rise to Rourke's bait, he exhaled slowly.

"I want my lawyer. I want to talk to Tony Brunner."

Before Rourke could respond, Chief Pruett opened the door and stepped into the room. She had her blonde hair pinned up and was wearing a black silk dress and an annoyed frowned.

It looked to Mason as if she'd been having dinner out when she'd been called back to the office. She didn't look happy about it.

The police chief was followed into the room by a curvy woman in a gray pantsuit. Her wild headful of black and gray curls seemed to contrast with the business-like attire.

"Hello, Mr. Knox, I'm assistant state attorney Henrietta Trilby," she said, making no move to offer Mason her hand.

Henrietta gestured for Rourke to move, and the detective got up from his seat with an ungracious huff.

"I want to speak to my lawyer, Tony Brunner," Mason repeated as the room began to sway around him.

"Yes, Mr. Brunner has been called," Henrietta said. "But, it is after hours. I can't be sure how long it will take for him to arrive."

Glancing up at Chief Pruett, she gave her a thin smile.

"You can leave," she said. "As can Detective Rourke. We won't be able to question Dr. Knox until Mr. Brunner arrives."

The police chief huffed and then nodded. As Pruett followed Rourke out the door, Henrietta turned to Mason.

"Perhaps, while we wait for your lawyer to get here, you and I can have a little chat. Off the record."

Mason stared at her, trying to focus on her face, but his eyes didn't want to cooperate.

"Anything you tell me now I'll consider to be inadmissible and off the record," the prosecutor said. "Now, if you didn't kill Gayle Kershaw, who did? Who would want to kill *your* stalker?"

Her question seemed sincere. It was the same question Mason had been asking himself. He'd been thinking of nothing else for the last forty-eight hours.

Who could hate him enough to set him up for Gayle's murder? Or Finola's for that matter? Who would be willing to kill two innocent women? Women who had nothing in common but their connection to him.

"I don't know who did this," he admitted as he banged his fist against the scarred wooden table in frustration. "But someone out there is holding a grudge. I don't know who and I don't know why. All I'm sure of is that someone is trying to frame me for murder."

Henrietta's big brown eyes looked almost sad

"Well, if your theory is right, they're doing a damn good job."

She opened a folder on the table.

"The forensics have come back on several items collected at the crime scene," she said. "Your prints were lifted off the letter sent to Gayle Kershaw. Tests on the scalpel used to slit her throat and the burner phone recovered from your coat pocket were inconclusive."

The prosecutor jotted down a note on her pad as she spoke, then checked her watch.

"Hopefully, Mr. Brunner will be here soon. In the meantime, I suggest you consider cooperating. If you got angry and snapped, it could be understandable. The fact that you were stalked..."

She hesitated.

"Well, we'd better wait for your lawyer to get here before going into all that. He can help you understand your options."

Mason wasn't sure anyone could help him now.

Certainly not this sad-eyed woman. Perhaps not even slick, fast-talking Tony Brunner would be able to help now.

He thought longingly of Cate, then quickly dismissed the idea.

He couldn't ask her to compromise her job by trying to help in his defense.

For now, he was on his own.

CHAPTER THIRTEEN

Cate paced the living room floor, leaving the work she had intended to complete untouched on the table as she brooded over the strange circumstances surrounding Desmond Bolt's sudden death. Inevitably, her thoughts soon turned to Mason's predicament. She couldn't stop herself from picturing him the way he'd looked the last time she'd seen him, his dark curls disheveled and his brown eyes full of anguish and regret.

Crossing to the table, she looked down at the folders of documents waiting for her. She knew she should be working on the case against Phil "Phoenix" Thayer and Kelvin "Kato" Miller, who had both been recently indicted for trafficking in illegal firearms.

The two men had supposedly worked as security guards for Jordan Stone's Sun Creek Nature Preserve before the cryptocurrency billionaire had jetted off to an unknown location.

Since Stone's sudden departure, the privately held preserve had been put up for sale and the illegal operations within had been disbanded, at least for the time being.

Unless she could get Phoenix and Kato to turn on their

fellow traffickers, Cate knew that a new operation would pop up somewhere else soon enough.

If she was lucky, she might even convince them to give evidence against Stone, who in her mind must have been the ringleader.

There was also the question of drug dealer Lando Gutierrez's dead body, which had been found floating in the Bellamy River just outside the preserve. Killed by blunt force trauma to the head, his murder still hadn't been solved. Could Kato or Phoenix have silenced the man?

Or was it Jordan Stone trying to protect his operation?

She strode to the television, wanting to see if there were any updates on Channel 3 News about Gayle Kershaw's murder, fearful that Mason had been officially named as a person of interest.

Before she could turn on the television, she heard keys in the door, and then Ludwig was bounding in, obviously eager for his evening meal.

Bailey followed the dog inside, looking somber.

"I'm surprised you're home this early," Cate said, trying to act normal as if her heart wasn't broken. "I thought you'd be with Dalton."

"I wanted to tell you what's happened before you heard it from someone else," Bailey said. "There's been another attack."

Taking Cate's arm, Bailey led her to the sofa. Sitting down beside her, she inhaled deeply, then exhaled slowly.

"Finola Lawson was attacked tonight at the medical examiner's office," Bailey said. "They don't think she's going to survive."

Cate shook her head in denial.

"That can't be...why would anyone..."

Her words died away as she registered the grim look on Bailey's face. There was more that needed to be said.

"I was the one who found her," Bailey continued. "I stopped by the medical examiner's office hoping she'd be there. I wanted to find out what the autopsy had revealed."

She held Cate's eyes.

"Ludwig and I went inside. We found blood and signs of an attack. There was a trail of blood leading outside. Finola was there on the ground and Mason was kneeling over her."

Pushing away Bailey's hand, Cate jumped up from the sofa.

"What are you saying?" she demanded. "Are you saying that Mason did this? That he attacked Finola?"

"No, I'm just telling you what I found," Bailey said. "Mason denied he'd hurt Gayle or Finola. He insisted he was attacked, too. That he was hit over the head and when he came to he tried to save Finola. To be honest, he looked as if he'd been hit."

Cate stared down at Bailey, allowing herself to voice the question she'd been thinking all evening.

"If Mason didn't kill Gayle, then who did?"

"I keep thinking her murder must somehow be linked to Birdie and Dessie Bolt," Bailey said. "The Saint Olga pendants might be a coincidence...but then, maybe not."

A spark of something like hope flickered in Cate's chest.

"So, you believe Carter Delaney?" she asked numbly. "You believe he didn't kill Birdie? That someone else did? Someone still on the outside? Someone who could have killed Gayle?"

Bailey nodded.

"I think it's a possibility. I don't like coincidences. And Delaney said the cartel sent another fixer after Birdie. He might actually be telling the truth for once."

Cate wondered if her sister could be right, or if they were both just grasping at any possibility to exonerate Mason.

"Tell me the truth," she said, looking down at Bailey, her voice ragged. "Do you think Mason could have done this? Do you think he could have killed Gayle and then attacked Finola when she found evidence during autopsy that implicated him?"

After a long beat, Bailey shook her head.

"My gut tells me no," she admitted. "I guess it's impossible for me to think like a prosecutor or someone who knows nothing about him. We both know Mason. We know he's a good person."

She took Cate's hand.

"We also know it's unlikely he would plan out a murder in his own home, and then follow it up with an attack at his own office."

Cate nodded, knowing Bailey was right.

Her heart lifted.

Even if Mason was a secret serial killer under his good-guy routine, he wasn't stupid. In fact, he was one of the smartest men she knew.

If he was going to commit murder, there was no way he would make such a mess of it.

She grabbed her jacket and purse.

"Where are you going?" Bailey asked.

"To Mason's house," she said. "I've got to talk to him."

"Mason's not at home," Bailey said. "He's at the Belle Harbor Police Station."

"Then that's where I'll go," Cate said. "I'm going to talk to Henrietta Trilby and Chief Pruett. I'm going to talk some sense into them if it's the last thing I do."

* * *

Cate made a sharp turn into the parking lot outside the Belle Harbor police station and parked her Lexus along the curb, not caring if she got a ticket.

As she hurried toward the entrance, she was surprised to see Mason being led out of the building, flanked by two uniformed officers, and followed by Killian Rourke and Henrietta Trilby.

They appeared to be leading him to a waiting police cruiser.

"What's happening?" she called to him. "Where are you going?"

"They've arrested me," Mason said. "For murder."

His words hit Cate like a punch.

"Actually, he's been charged with one count of murder and one count of attempted murder," Rourke corrected. "And he's being taken to the Summerset County Detention Center to await an arraignment hearing."

"Where's Detective Fraser?" Cate asked. "I want to talk to him."

"He's probably at home with his wife and kids," Rourke scoffed. "I bet he's tucking the kids in right about now."

The disdain in his voice was evident. Cate knew there was no point in talking to the man.

She turned to Henrietta.

"Rourke said *attempted* murder. Does that mean that Finola Lawson is still alive?"

"Barely," Henrietta acknowledged. "And don't get any big ideas. You're not assigned to the case and you have no right to go to the hospital and interfere. Let justice take its course."

But Cate wasn't listening. She was already heading to her car.

She would go see Finola for herself.

She'd make the woman admit Mason hadn't tried to kill her.

But when she neared the Lexus, she saw that Tony Brunner was leaning against the hood waiting for her.

Stopping to allow a silver sedan to pass, she heard Freddy Mercury's falsetto ringing out as the radio blasted *Killer Queen* through its open window.

Brunner spoke before she could ask him what he was doing to get Mason out of jail.

"My client asked me to give you this note," he said, holding up a piece of paper. "And I'll give you some free advice while I'm at it."

He flashed her a sardonic smile.

"We've gone up against each other enough times for me to determine that you're not stupid or careless. Don't make me change my opinion of you now. Listen to your boyfriend."

He handed her the note.

Cate read the words with a sinking sensation in her stomach.

> *Dear Cate,*
>
> *I didn't kill Gayle or anyone else. In your heart, I'm sure you know that. However, having a relationship with a suspected murderer will compromise your position and may complicate matters for us both, so it's best if we end things now. I wish you well.*
>
> *Mason*

Tears prickled the back of her eyes but she managed to blink them away as she looked up to see Brunner studying her.

"You seem to have a hard time hanging on to men," he said, lifting an eyebrow. "First you run Jordan Stone out of the country, and now Mason Knox doesn't want anything more to do with you."

He reached out and rested a finger under her chin, lifting her face so that their eyes met.

"I'm available if you need someone to console you," he said softly, allowing his eyes to assess the soft curves of her body. "I have no qualms about consorting with the enemy when the necessity arises."

Resisting the urge to give him a sharp knee to the groin, Cate jerked her face away, repulsed by the man's touch. Without another word, she climbed into the Lexus and sped away. She didn't notice the silver sedan pull out behind her.

CHAPTER FOURTEEN

Bailey was startled to see her mother sitting at the kitchen table across from a tearful Cate when she and Ludwig returned from their morning run. Jackie Flynn ran a disapproving eye over Bailey's red, sweaty face before silently handing her a dish towel and motioning for her to have a seat.

"Mason broke up with her," Jackie said, speaking in the same hushed, somber tone she had used when their grandfather had died.

Sniffling into a tissue, Cate turned angry eyes to Bailey.

"He didn't even have the guts to tell me face to face," she sniffled. "He just gave a note to Brunner."

Smoothing back a strand of silver hair, her mother shrugged her thin shoulders and sighed.

"He's obviously not thinking straight," Jackie said. "Why else would he let a catch like you get away? But if there's any possibility he really has attacked these women, I'd say you're better off without him, wouldn't you agree, Bailey?"

Wiping the sweat from her forehead, Bailey rolled her eyes.

"Yes, if Mason is a serial killer I agree Cate would be better off without him," she said dryly. "Only, he's not a serial killer. And he's obviously trying to do the honorable thing by releasing Cate from any sense of obligation she–"

"Can you two quit talking about me as if I'm not here?" Cate snapped. "Neither one of you knows how I feel. And you certainly aren't qualified to decide what Mason's motives were in breaking up with me. If he wants to dump me, I'll just have to live with it."

She gathered up her laptop bag.

"But you can bet I'm not going to let the real person who killed Gayle and attacked Finola get away with it," she added, before turning on her heel and striding out of the room.

Jackie tutted quietly as she picked up a glass off the table and carried it to the sink.

"You certainly put your foot in it that time," she said, shooting a disapproving look in Bailey's direction. "You know your sister doesn't like anyone sticking their nose in her business."

Before Bailey could reply, Jackie continued.

"Now, do you really think Finola Lawson will survive?"

She cocked her head as she started running water into the sink.

"I have half a mind to go down there and ask who attacked her. She can tell us who's right about Mason. Because I'm not so sure I believe him. Most men can't be trusted, you know."

Biting back the indignant reply that came to mind, Bailey decided it wasn't worth it.

"Finola's still unconscious," she said instead. "And I don't think she'll be accepting random visitors anytime soon."

Jackie didn't reply. She just finished washing and drying

the dishes, then gave Bailey a peck on the cheek and left, saying that she was heading to a meeting with Mayor Sutherland about the city's purchase of the Sun Creek Nature Preserve.

Once Bailey had showered and dressed, she and Ludwig drove over to Jimmy Fraser's house. She had agreed to drive him to the task force meeting at the Miami Field office.

As she parked in the driveway, Linette opened the front door.

Two small girls who looked like miniature versions of their mother hovered in the hallway behind her wearing backpacks.

Bailey climbed out and waved to the girls, who ran over with round, excited eyes, giggling and wanting to pet Ludwig.

"Jimmy's in the kitchen washing up the breakfast dishes," Linette said after she too took a turn scratching the German shepherd behind the ears. "I think he's been feeling down."

She motioned toward the house.

"The door is open. You can go on in."

Following Linette's advice, Bailey walked to the front door and pushed it open, then called down the hall.

"Fraser? You in there?"

When no one answered, she stepped inside and walked to the kitchen, stopping in the doorway. Fraser turned to see her standing there and jumped, almost dropping a cereal bowl in the process.

"You scared the life out of me," he said, shaking his head.

Bailey smiled, noting how his Jamaican accent always seemed to come on stronger when he was startled or scared.

As he finished rinsing out the bowl, Bailey updated him on the events at the medical examiner's office the night before.

"I didn't hear until this morning about the attack on Finola Lawson or Mason Knox's arrest," he admitted. "I think Chief Pruett and Rourke are trying to push me out. They think they know best. But they don't really know much."

Suspecting he was right, Bailey nodded and checked her watch.

"We better get going if we're going to make it to Miami on time for the task force meeting," she said. "Agent Sharma said there will be a special guest at the meeting, so I don't want to be late."

* * *

Bailey followed Fraser and Ludwig into the conference room, then stopped short, startled to see Special Agent Argus Murphy seated at the conference room table along with Aisha Sharma, Ford Ramsey, and Eloise Spellman.

The profiler and analyst with the FBI's Behavorial Analysis Unit in Quantico, Virginia usually joined the meetings remotely.

"I'm here for a few days helping out on another case," he said with a secretive smile. "February in Virginia is miserable. I jumped at the chance to get some Florida sunshine."

"Well, your timing is perfect, because we've been trying to figure out what happened to our teenage Jane Doe, who we now know is Dessie Bolt's daughter, Birdie."

Adjusting his glasses, Argus sat forward with interest.

"Yes, I just heard the news that Dessie is dead," Argus said. "And Sharma was filling me in on your theory that there's a connection between the murder of Gayle Kershaw and the death of Dessie and his daughter."

"You really think there's a connection?" Fraser asked. "Gayle Kershaw lived up in Virginia and Dessie Bolt lived in Verbena Beach. As far as we know, they never even met. They never moved in the same circles. They had nothing in common."

Bailey arched an eyebrow.

"What about the Saint Olga pendants?"

"Right, the pendants," Argus said, pulling up an image on the screen. "This same pendant was found on the dinner plate at the scene of Gayle's murder and in the crypt where they found Birdie's body, right?"

He seemed intrigued.

"Yes, and Desmond Bolt was wearing an identical pendant when I saw him two days ago," Bailey added. "Then yesterday, he was found dead in his cell. Foul play involving the Tumba Cartel is suspected."

"Of course, the pendants could be a coincidence," Bailey admitted. "Reverend Schroeder at the All Saints Church of Summerset County said there are over a half million Orthodox parishioners in the U.S., as well as hundreds of millions of people worldwide. So, I'm guessing these pendants aren't exactly rare."

Argus frowned.

"Well, I'm pretty sure that finding one on a dinner plate at the scene of a gruesome murder *is* rare," he said. "Have you considered that it was left as an intentional clue? That maybe the killer left the pendant on the plate so we'd connect Gayle's death to Birdie or Dessie? Maybe the killer wants us to know he's killed them all."

"Possibly," Aisha agreed. "Or maybe Gayle's killer just wants us to think that, to throw us off the scent."

As the team threw out other ideas, Fraser held up a hand.

"Hold on, let's think this through. Who knew that Birdie was wearing a pendant when she was found?" he asked.

Bailey's face fell.

"Mason Knox obviously did. Along with pretty much everyone on the task force, including the Belle Harbor PD detectives, the crime scene team, and the FBI agents assigned. Oh, and Eloise's students."

Bailey glanced at the consulting forensic anthropologist who'd replaced Wendy Wharton as the forensic expert on the excavation site at the burial ground. It hadn't been easy to find someone brave enough to take on the role after two students working on the dig had been killed and their professor abducted.

Thus far, Dr. Eloise Spellman had proven to be a valuable replacement, managing to instill a sense of order and calm to the excavation site as she took on the difficult task of finding and identifying human remains along with the rest of the team.

"None of my students have a reason to kill anyone," Eloise said indignantly. "They're good kids."

"Okay, then what about the press?" Bailey said, quickly moving on. "The information about Birdie's pendant wasn't released to the media, was it?"

Everyone around the table shook their head.

"Well, Dessie Bolt must have known his daughter wore that pendant," Aisha said. "So, maybe he told someone. And he had one around his neck, too. Maybe whoever killed Gayle was a cellmate or associate of Dessie."

"How much do we know about Dessie Bolt?" Argus asked.

Tapping on his keyboard, he opened the task force database.

"Okay, so he was born in Verbena Beach, had a daughter he called Birdie, and was a rumored associate of the Tumba Cartel?"

He frowned.

"If he worked for the cartel, could he have been working with Delaney?" he asked. "I mean, Delaney admitted to working as a hitman for the cartel and he's been killing people and dumping them in the burial ground for years. Are we sure Delaney didn't kill Birdie?"

"When I saw him yesterday, Delaney insisted he didn't kill her," Bailey said. "I have to admit I believe him. Why would he lie now?"

"To protect himself from Dessie?" Fraser suggested. "If Dessie was an associate of his, Delaney wouldn't want him to know he killed his daughter."

Bailey considered the idea, then shrugged. It was as good a theory as any other. Then she remembered something else.

Something Delaney had told her soon after he'd been

arrested.

"Delaney said the Tumba Cartel has someone else working in the area as a fixer. I took that to mean he wasn't their only hitman."

"And you think this other *fixer* may have killed Birdie?" Fraser asked. "But why? If Dessie was a loyal associate of the cartel, why would the cartel order a hit on his daughter?"

"Maybe it wasn't a sanctioned hit," Bailey said, warming to the idea. "Maybe this other killer went rogue."

CHAPTER FIFTEEN

Fernando Borja looked in the full-length mirror, admiring the handsome, chiseled features and piercing amber eyes that gazed back at him as he straightened his red bowtie and rolled up the sleeves of his white cotton dress shirt to reveal tanned, leanly muscled forearms.

Checking the titanium Rolex on his wrist, he picked up a tray of drinks and made his way back onto the main deck of the luxury yacht, stopping to offer a drink to a sultry woman whose silky sarong was the same delicate shade of pink as the diamond in her wedding ring.

He stopped beside a tipsy couple dressed in the kind of haute couture fashion that looked vaguely ridiculous off the runway.

As they took their time selecting a drink from the tray, Borja decided his cover as a waiter at the exclusive private party had been a bad idea. He was attracting too much attention.

Most of the women and several of the men in attendance had already made their interest known with inviting smiles, sideways glances, lingering strokes of his arm, and phone numbers hastily scribbled onto napkins and tucked into the back pocket of his snug, black pants.

Any other night, he might have taken the woman in the pink sarong up on her unspoken but quite obvious invitation. He'd have enjoyed making her regret her indiscretion.

Fortunately for the woman, he didn't have time to act on his baser instincts. Right now, he was only interested in one thing.

He needed to eliminate his latest target while the yacht was still in international waters. Once he'd completed his task, he had an escape dinghy already waiting for him in the water, ready to go.

With any luck, his target would be dead and he'd be back in Miami by dawn. The tight timeline prevented him from indulging in the activities that had earned him the nickname *El Monstruo* within the cartel's inner circle.

The Spanish word for monster seemed a strange nickname for a man who looked more like an angel.

But it hadn't been Borja's looks that had earned him the title, it had been his monstrous actions.

He'd earned the name after bragging about the torture he inflicted on his victims as he carried out his paid hits. His boastful words had been backed up by the grisly mess he often left behind.

Carrying the tray of drinks past the galley, he hurried down the passageway, stopping in front of his target's cabin.

After looking around to make sure he was alone, he tapped on the door and waited. Seconds later the door swung open to reveal a pot-bellied old man in a silk robe.

"I'm sorry to disturb you, Mr. Murdock, but I have a

message for you from the captain. May I come in and set down my tray?"

The man hesitated, then shrugged, and stepped back.

That's the trouble with most people, they don't listen to their instincts.

Stepping inside, Borja used his right foot to kick the door shut behind him, then set the tray down on the table.

As he turned toward the old man, he reached into his pocket and pulled out a folded piece of paper. He handed it to the man with a small bow, then waited as if expecting a tip.

Murdock unfolded the note, glanced down at it, then opened his mouth to scream. But Borja was too fast for that.

The straight-edge razor sliced through the old man's jugular with ridiculous ease, sending a hot spray of blood across the room.

Thirty minutes later, Borja was motoring through the waves. As he passed Bellamy Beach and the Belle Harbor Inlet, he thought about the fun he'd had in the quiet little town.

The first time he'd been there he'd killed Dessie Bolt's daughter.

The girl called Birdie had been a tall, gangly teenager with an attitude. She hadn't gone peacefully or quietly.

And he hadn't been able to tell anyone about his deadly deed, or the fun he'd had with rebellious Birdie before he'd taken her life.

The only ones who'd known he'd killed the girl had been the big boss, Mr. Tumba, and the fixer who'd swooped in to clean up after him.

Perhaps I had a little too much fun that time.

Unfortunately, his second trip to Belle Harbor hadn't offered up as much entertainment. He'd been sent to take out Lando Gutierrez, a local, low-level drug dealer who'd been caught beating up the young women he'd recruited as drug couriers.

Gutierrez's antics had caused the sort of trouble and attention that Mr. Tumba tried to avoid, so Borja had been dispatched.

A clandestine meeting at the river's edge had given him the opportunity to bash the weaker man's skull against a large Cypress tree. He'd almost been disappointed to find he'd managed to kill Gutierrez on the first try.

Never one to clean up after himself, Borja had left the drug dealer floating in the river. And now it looked as if Mr. Tumba might have another very special job for him to perform in Belle Harbor. Something he'd never done before. He had never been asked to take out one of the cartel's other secret assassins.

But it appeared that the woman known to him only as the Saint had gone rogue and the big boss needed Borja to do something about it. Something he knew he would enjoy very much.

CHAPTER SIXTEEN

Olga lifted the Sig Sauer pistol and aimed it at the steel target, picturing Cate Flynn's face on the bull's eye as she pulled the trigger. The bullet clanged off the center of the bright red circle with satisfying force. The prosecutor was the one responsible for all her pain, and eventually, she would die for her actions. But first, she would have to suffer, as was just and fair.

The stupid woman had prosecuted Dessie, an innocent man.

Persecuted is more like it.

The prosecutor had started a chain of events that had destroyed her family, taking her husband and her child from her.

Her joy in life had died along with them, leaving her body a stone-cold tomb in which to store her frozen heart.

The only thing that lived inside the tomb now was hate. And the only thing that now mattered was revenge.

She would follow in the footsteps of Princess Olga of Kiev, who had earned her sainthood after waging a bloody, brutal campaign of revenge against the enemies who had killed her husband.

The shared anguish of lost love and the thirst for revenge bonded the two women despite the millennia that separated them.

Firing another round, Olga thought through her plan.

Her first objective in coming to Belle Harbor had been to set up Mason Knox, ensuring that he was arrested and convicted of a murder he hadn't committed.

That was the only way Cate Flynn would know what it was like to watch the man she loved being dragged away to prison in handcuffs, just as Olga had been forced to watch Dessie being dragged away and locked up forever.

But now that Dessie was dead, the objective would have to change.

The punishment must fit the crime.

"Fracture for fracture, eye for eye, tooth for tooth."

Olga muttered the verse from Leviticus that she now considered to be her guiding mantra as she shot yet another round of bullets from the Sig Sauer with perfect precision.

She pulled the trigger again and again, lost in her memories until she realized she was out of ammunition.

Selecting another gun from her collection, this time a modified Beretta with a stainless-steel barrel, she slid on her noise-canceling ear muffs and grimaced as *Under Pressure* by Queen filled her head.

She'd listened to the song every day when Dessie had been on trial for the murder of the two men who had ambushed him as he'd delivered a truckload of illegal firearms.

Of course, he hadn't been alone and he hadn't killed those men.

The memory of that fateful night played through Olga's mind as she lifted the Beretta.

Dessie's face was flushed and wet with nervous sweat as they waited for the pick-up.

He hadn't signed up for any of this.

Olga felt bad.

She'd been the one who'd gotten him involved with the cartel.

He'd been an ordinary worker at the Jacksonville Port Authority when they'd met a dozen years earlier.

She'd offered him the chance to earn a quick thousand dollars by looking the other way, and he'd agreed with some reluctance, more because of the intriguing gleam in her dark, intense gaze than the promise of easy money.

But over the years he'd found himself sinking deeper and deeper into the cartel's dirty business.

And now that their bright, inquisitive daughter was only weeks away from her thirteenth birthday, he didn't like the thought of doing anything to jeopardize her future.

He'd started talking about walking away from the cartel. About going straight for good.

Of course, Olga knew that could never happen.

Not with the blood of many of the cartel's victims on her hands. Not with all the secrets she knew about Mr. Tumba and his illegal operations.

Suddenly headlights appeared.

Two men pulled up in a mud-splattered SUV and Olga saw at a glance that they weren't the men they'd been waiting for.

Pulling out guns, one of the men raced forward and wrenched open the driver's side door, pulling Dessie down from the cab as the other came for Olga.

"Open the back," the man yelled. "We're taking the guns and-"

He never got a chance to finish the sentence.

Olga had already slipped a small Colt pistol from her waistband and put a bullet in the man's temple.

Dropping to the ground, she'd rolled under the truck, crawled commando style to the other side, and put a bullet in the second man's back.

As he slumped to the ground, she slid from under the truck and fired another bullet between his eyes for good measure.

When she stuck the Colt back into her concealed waistband holster and looked up, Dessie had been staring at her in horror.

She knew he must have heard rumors about a fixer in the cartel named the Saint, but he'd never allowed himself to believe the woman he loved and the mother of his child was capable of cold-blooded murder. Not until now. Not until he'd witnessed it with his own two eyes.

"We've got to hide the bodies and get out of here," Olga said. "I didn't have time to screw on a silencer, so someone could have heard the gunshots. The police could be on the way."

But Dessie was dazed and slow to move. He stumbled as they started to drag the first man toward the woods, falling to his knees.

He grunted in disgust as he saw the man's blood on his hands and frantically wiped it off on his jeans.

"Grab his boots," Olga ordered, her voice cold and hard. "I'll get his shoulders. Come on, one, two, three..."

Dragging the man between them, they managed to dump him behind a fallen tree trunk. But as they returned for the second man's body, headlights lit up the road behind them.

Olga turned and pulled out her Colt, but Dessie grabbed it from her hand and flung it into the bushes.

"No one else dies tonight," he said. "I didn't sign up for..."

His words died in his throat as the blue and red lights on top of the police car began to flash. Olga lunged into the bushes, dropping onto her stomach and scrambling for cover.

When she looked back, she saw Dessie standing frozen in place, a bright spotlight illuminating his solid frame and bright red blood coating his hands as he lifted them in surrender.

"Dessie!" she hissed, thinking they might still have a chance to make a run for it through the woods. "Come on, let's go!"

But the police were already racing forward, cuffing Dessie's hands behind him, barking questions that he stoically ignored.

Cursing herself for not bringing her back-up weapon, she looked around in a panic for the Colt, thinking she could probably take down both the cops before they knew what had hit them. But it was nowhere in sight.

Of course, she wasn't sure if the police had seen her before she'd taken cover, in any case. And they might come for her at any minute. If she was going to get away, she'd have to go now.

Knowing she had no other choice, she turned and ran.

A hollow click brought Olga back from the abyss of the past.

Realizing she was out of bullets, she lowered the Beretta.

Rage still bubbled up inside her as she thought of how desperate she'd been to help Dessie after he'd been arrested.

She'd arranged for him to be defended by Roderick Payne,

a lawyer who had helped more than one cartel associate get off in the past.

But Dessie had refused to answer any questions during the entire trial. Refused to defend himself even though he hadn't been the one who'd pulled the trigger.

Even after he'd been sentenced to life in prison, he'd refused to name Olga as the real shooter, insisting that Birdie needed her, insisting his appeal would be successful, and that it would only be a matter of time before they were together again.

But thanks to Cate Flynn, the appeal had been rejected, and their daughter, Birdie had become silent and despondent.

One night the distraught teen had left home, leaving a note that she would be staying with friends.

Olga had been too caught up in her own guilt and grief to question her. But when Birdie failed to return after several days, Olga had emerged from her own fog of depression long enough to realize that the teen had run away.

She'd searched Verbena Beach, then expanded her search a hundred miles in each direction while putting out feelers with all her connections. But no one had seen her daughter.

For more than two years Dessie had rotted in his prison cell, and Olga had descended into despair and madness, with no sign from Birdie.

Then one day out of the blue, Dessie had called her on a cellmate's burner phone. He'd told her that he'd been taken down to the warden's office.

"Birdie didn't run away," he'd said in a strangely expressionless voice that turned her blood to ice. "She's dead."

Before Olga could fully comprehend what he was saying, he continued.

"Our little girl was murdered. Her body was found in a crypt in Belle Harbor, Florida along with dozens of other victims," he said. "The warden told me the police suspect serial killer Carter Delaney is responsible."

"Birdie's dead?" Olga had rasped, her throat dry and tight with grief. "Our girl is gone?"

The next question spilled out before he could respond.

"They think it was a cartel job?" she asked. "They think-"

"Shut up," Dessie warned her, although his voice was listless. "They could be listening in. Maybe trying to bait me. Trying to get me to say something incriminating. Stay quiet or you'll be next."

Even over the phone, Olga could hear the change in Dessie's voice. His spirit had been broken.

While he'd been willing to suffer in silence behind bars to protect his family, now that Birdie was gone for good and Olga was working for the criminal organization responsible for her death, he'd lost the will to go on.

After that, he stopped calling. Stopped communicating with Olga altogether, taking her off his visitors list, causing her to spiral even deeper into her own outrage and despair.

Desperate to see Dessie, she had watched the news clips of his trial again and again, her rage building every time she saw Cate Flynn's smug face.

The woman was responsible for ruining her life and destroying her family. She had prosecuted and convicted an innocent man.

It had grown ever clearer that the woman had to pay.

A week later, Olga had traveled down to Belle Harbor to visit her daughter's final resting place. Beside the crumbling crypt in the old burial ground, she began to plot her revenge.

As she learned more about Cate and the city of Belle Harbor, Olga had formulated a plan, coming to the conclusion that the prosecutor wasn't the only one who had to pay.

While Cate might have prosecuted Dessie, setting the tragedy in motion, the criminal organization she'd faithfully served for years had betrayed her, taking out her own daughter when the heartsick girl had arrived in town asking questions that hit too close to home.

Birdie had paid for those questions with her life, and now it was up to Olga to find out who had killed her daughter. Once she did so, she would take her revenge.

Packing away the Beretta, she offered up a prayer to Saint Olga.

As patron saint of widows and revenge, only she could ensure that a fierce and final justice was served.

CHAPTER SEVENTEEN

The Summerset Espresso Café was humming with activity when Bailey led Ludwig inside. Ordering two mocha lattes, she snagged a table by the window and waited for the barista to make the warm drinks, wondering why Fraser had wanted to meet outside the police station.

She suspected he didn't want his new boss to know he was discussing Gayle Kershaw's homicide with her. After all, the new chief of police had already made it crystal clear that Bailey and the FBI weren't welcome to join in on the investigation.

Hearing her name called, she picked up the two coffees off the counter and turned to see Fraser push his way in the door.

"Thanks for meeting me here," he said as he took one of the cups from her hand. "I'd have asked you to meet me at the station, but I didn't want Chief Pruett to know I'm talking to you about the case. If you'd rather not get involved..."

"Don't be silly, I'm already involved," Bailey said, waiving away his concern. "And I don't mind meeting here. The coffee is definitely better than at the police station."

Sipping at the sweet, warm drink, she cleared her throat.

"Of course, I also have my own reasons for wanting to find out who was responsible for Gayle's murder," she admitted. "My sister's safety and happiness, for one thing."

Fraser raised an eyebrow.

"How so?"

"Well, if we find out Mason's guilty, I can stop my sister from dating a killer," she said. "And if he's innocent, as I suspect, I'll be able to sleep at night knowing she's safe."

As the door opened to let another stream of customers in, Bailey leaned forward and lowered her voice.

"And remember, there's also the question of the Saint Olga pendants," she said, but Fraser wasn't listening.

He was looking past her with a curious expression that turned into a frown. Bailey turned to see Dr. Jude Varney standing in line.

Once the psychiatrist had ordered her drink, she headed straight for their table. Spotting Ludwig beside Bailey's chair, Dr. Varney bent to stroke the soft fur behind the German shepherd's ears.

"I thought you would have gone home by now," Bailey said as she gestured to the chair beside her. "Are you taking a few extra days to enjoy the warmer weather?"

Dr. Varney shook her head.

"I'm staying in Belle Harbor awaiting the release of Gayle Kershaw's body," the psychiatrist explained. "I promised her mother I would accompany the body on its journey back home."

"That's very nice of you," Bailey said, surprised by the generous gesture. "You must have been very fond of Gayle."

A pink flush fell over Dr. Varney's cheeks as she shook her head.

"I wish I could say affection was the motivating factor, but in all honesty, my relationship with Gayle wasn't particularly close," she admitted. "She wasn't exactly the easiest person to get along with. But her mother is understandably devastated, and I feel as if I bear some of the responsibility for her daughter's death."

Startled by the comment, Bailey cocked her head.

"How are you responsible?" she asked. "If you were up in Virginia and she was murdered in Belle Harbor..."

"That's just it," the psychiatrist said. "She should never have been allowed to come to Belle Harbor. In fact, she should never have been allowed out of the hospital."

She ran a distracted hand through her cap of dark hair.

"I tried to talk the parole board out of granting Gayle early release but they wouldn't listen," she said. "If I'd tried harder, or maybe come up with a better explanation of the danger she presented to herself and others, maybe..."

With a sigh, she lifted her small, round shoulders.

"Of course, I hadn't seen the letter she'd written at the time. Maybe if I had known...if I'd had that letter...I could have talked the parole board out of it. Maybe things would be different. Maybe Gayle would still be alive."

"The letter *she* wrote?" Bailey asked. "The only letter I saw was the one supposedly sent to her from Mason, although I have no way of knowing if it's authentic."

Dr. Varney nodded along in agreement.

"I wouldn't be surprised to find the letter was some sort of prank. Or maybe even something Gayle arranged to send herself," she said.

"So, you don't believe Mason would have ever invited her to join him in Florida?" Fraser asked. "You don't think he might have lured her here intending to kill her?"

Shaking her head emphatically, Dr. Varney spoke with conviction.

"The evidence in the stalking case against Gayle was overwhelming. There was no doubt that she presented a clear and present danger to Mason Knox. I even spoke to him myself on the phone after the sentencing to get his take on what had happened."

She smiled at the memory.

"Not many victims are willing to take the time to help their stalker get appropriate treatment," she confided. "He'd been through a lot but didn't sound bitter, only wary. I suggested at the time that he find a therapist to help him deal with the fallout, but I never heard back."

Bailey studied the woman's plain, round face, wondering at her apparent absolute certainty that Mason Knox was only a victim and not a murderer.

She was tempted to tell the woman that Mason's prints had been lifted from the letter that had been found in Gayle's pocket and that the postmark indicated whoever mailed it had been in Belle Harbor the week before.

There was little chance Gayle could have arranged to mail the letter to herself while locked within Rock Ridge's walls, although it wouldn't be impossible with the help of an accomplice.

But how would that explain how and why she'd been killed? None of it made any sense.

After Dr. Varney left, Bailey realized Fraser had said very little during their conversation. She studied him as he sipped at his drink and stared out the window, obviously brooding over something.

"Okay, what's wrong?" Bailey asked. "Are you thinking about the case? Or are you still worried about work?"

"I'm worried I'm about to lose my job," Fraser admitted "I've got a family to consider and it's clear that Chief Pruett is looking to get rid of me."

Suspecting he may be right, Bailey fumed at the thought of the new police chief preferring a childish dolt like Rourke over a good man like Fraser.

"She'd be a fool to let you go," Bailey said.

Unfortunately, I'm not so sure Pruett isn't one.

Deciding it was best not to voice the unhelpful thought, Bailey looked up just in time to see her mother walk into the café with Mayor Sutherland.

The two were laughing and looking very chummy as they passed by without noticing that Bailey was sitting at the table.

What's Mom doing with Sutherland? Hopefully, she knows he's one of those men she claims can't be trusted.

Draining the rest of her coffee, she picked up her cup.

"You ready to go?" she asked Fraser.

He nodded and followed her toward the door, waiting as she stopped beside the table where Jackie was sitting with the mayor.

Sutherland looked past her to Fraser and raised an eyebrow.

"You're the detective who's getting us sued, aren't you?" he asked. "I had Raya Valera in my office earlier, and she's bound and determined to squeeze every last cent out of the department."

Fraser gaped at him for a long beat.

"That has nothing to do with me," he finally managed to say. "I had nothing to do with her mother's death. And I'm not to blame for any payout you might choose to give her."

"Keep your voice down," the mayor scolded. "Or we'll be looking at a libel suit as well. We'll talk about this later, I'm sure. Now, if you'll excuse us, we have matters to attend to."

"Business or pleasure?" Bailey asked pointedly, her eyes flicking to the wine glasses on the table.

Jackie's eyes widened and her cheeks turned pink, but before she could respond, Fraser put a hand on Bailey's elbow.

He guided her out of the café, obviously in no mood to linger.

"Let's get out of here," he said, looking miserable. "I want to get home so I can start updating my resume."

* * *

Once Fraser had driven away, Bailey leaned against the Expedition and checked her messages. Her pulse quickened when she saw she'd missed a call from Reverend Schroeder at All Saints Orthodox Church of Summerset County.

Tapping to return the call, she held the phone to her ear.

Reverend Schroeder answered on the second ring.

"Thank you for calling back, Agent Flynn," he said, sounding slightly out of breath. "I asked if anyone at the youth shelter had met a girl named Birdie and I believe there's someone you'll want to talk to. She's at the church now if you have time to stop by."

"That's good news," Bailey said. "I'm on my way."

It was dusk by the time she pulled up to the big building. The church was dim and cold as she walked into the narthex.

Candles lit up the cavernous room as she moved into the nave, looking up at the domed ceiling and walls which were decorated with colorful images of angels, prophets, and saints.

Moving toward the sanctuary, she stopped in front of a large wooden wall, which was decorated with religious images that flanked a closed gate, preventing her from going any further.

Footsteps sounded behind her.

She turned to see Reverend Schroeder moving toward her.

He was accompanied by a woman with long, dark hair and large brown eyes.

"Special Agent Flynn, I'd like to introduce you to Tanya Jimenez, one of our regular volunteers at the youth shelter."

Bailey smiled at the woman, noting the healed scars on her arms and the cautious expression on her face.

"It's good to meet you, Tanya. Reverend Schroeder said you might have some information for me about a teenager named Birdie who passed through here a few years back?"

Returning Bailey's smile, Tanya nodded.

"When Reverend Schroeder asked if anyone knew a girl named Birdie, I remembered her right away," she said. "She stayed at the shelter for almost two weeks. At first, I thought maybe she was a little crazy, but she turned out to be alright."

"What do you mean she was *a little crazy*?" Bailey asked.

Tanya swallowed hard and glanced over at Reverend Schroeder.

"How about I leave you two to talk in private?" he said as he backed toward the door. "Just let me know if I can be of any help."

Once he was gone, Bailey turned expectant eyes to Tanya.

"The first time I talked to Birdie, she told me she was looking for a killer," Tanya explained. "She said her father had been framed for murder. She said he was in jail but that he was innocent."

She gave a nervous little shrug.

"I thought she was making it up or that maybe she was high or delusional. But after I got to know her, I started to think she might be telling the truth. I mean, she seemed like a pretty smart girl."

"What else did she say?" Bailey asked.

Watching Tanya shift from one foot to the other, she could see that the woman was nervous.

"She said she'd heard her parents talking on the phone. Her mom said her father shouldn't be in prison because they both knew who had really pulled the trigger. Her Mom wanted to ask his boss for help. She called him Mr. Tumba."

Bailey's heart skipped a beat.

"You're sure that's what Birdie said? You're sure the name was Mr. Tumba?"

Tanya nodded grimly.

"That's the part I remember the most," she said as her fingers fidgeted with the button on her sweater. "You see, I lived at the shelter for a while myself back when I was a teen. Before that, I'd been recruited by a *bastardo* who worked for the Tumba Cartel. He had me running drugs and...other stuff."

Her big eyes appeared to darken at the memory.

"Lucky for me, I was able to break away from the cartel after he went on a job to Colombia and never came back. I heard later he'd been killed in a bar fight."

A ghost of a smile lifted the corner of her mouth.

"Did you ever meet Mr. Tumba?" Bailey asked.

Tanya quickly shook her head.

"No one around here has ever met him. At least, no one who has come back to talk about it."

Bailey swallowed back another question about the cartel. This wasn't the right time to ask about Mr. Tumba and his operation.

She couldn't afford to get distracted. She'd come here to find out what had really happened to Birdie and the woman in front of her had been one of the last people to see her alive.

With any luck, she could help them find her killer.

Sucking in a deep breath, Bailey met and held Tanya's eyes.

"What did Birdie look like?" she asked. "Can you describe

her?"

"I'll do better than that," Tanya said. "I'll show you a picture."

She turned and led Bailey out to the narthex where a notice board held a variety of announcements and photos.

A newspaper clipping had been pinned near the top.

"That's Birdie," Tanya said, tapping on the clipping. "She was here when the *Belle Harbor Chronicle* featured the shelter in an article on cuts to funding for local youth programs."

The photo accompanying the article showed a tall, lanky girl with messy blonde hair and a defiant tilt to her narrow chin.

Tanya turned to stare at Bailey with a wistful expression.

"The day they took that photo was the last time I ever saw her."

CHAPTER EIGHTEEN

Carter Delaney shuffled into the small interview room where inmates met with their lawyers when they needed to discuss private legal matters. As the guard propelled him toward a chair by the table, Delaney was surprised to see an attractive woman sitting in the chair his defense attorney usually occupied. Placing a thick folder on the table, the woman looked expectantly at the guard, obviously waiting for him to leave.

"I need some private time with my client," she said, her impatient tone implying that he was moving too slowly for her liking. "If you can give us about thirty minutes..."

Nodding at the woman's request, the guard crouched down to attach Delaney's leg iron to the sturdy metal table, which was bolted to the concrete floor.

He allowed his eyes to run appreciatively along the woman's toned, shapely calves before standing and backing toward the door.

"I'll be right outside if you need me."

As soon as the door had closed behind the guard, the woman opened the folder and began spreading out a collection of grisly crime scene photos.

"Is this your work, Dr. Delaney?"

The serial killer ignored the photos as he appraised the woman with narrowed eyes.

"Who are you?" he asked coldly. "I know you're not a lawyer. But you do look vaguely familiar."

Taking off her glasses, the woman pushed back the thick bangs covering her forehead and produced an angry smile.

Delaney's eyes widened in recognition.

"You're the Saint," he said slowly. "Saint Olga."

He couldn't keep the surprise from his voice

He'd only met the woman once during a chance meeting at Mr. Tumba's office. If he hadn't seen the pendant around her neck that day, he wouldn't have known for sure it was her.

His eyes dropped to her chest but there was no pendant now.

Suddenly, he realized that he was alone with a skilled killer and his leg was chained to the table.

Even if he was trained in hand-to-hand combat he would be at a distinct disadvantage. But he wasn't a fighter. He was a scientist.

Of course, the guards must have taken away any weapons she had before letting her through the doors, right?

"If you try anything smart, I'll call the guards," he said.

"And if you try anything stupid, I'll have you killed," she shot back. "I'll tell the big boss that you told your friend Bailey Flynn his real name. I'll tell him you've signed a nice cushy deal to go into witness protection. He'll love that."

They stared at each other over the table, sizing each other up for a long, tension-filled moment before Olga broke the silence.

"You killed my daughter," she said coldly. "You killed Birdie."

He shook his head.

"No, I didn't."

His hands were shaking slightly as he folded them on the table, knowing that if she left there believing he was her daughter's killer he was as good as a dead man.

"Tell me what happened to my daughter and I might leave you here to die in peace," she said. "But if you lie to me, I'll make sure you're lying in a carboard box next to my Dessie by morning."

Holding up his hands in mock surrender, Delaney sucked in a deep breath and sat back in his chair.

"Your daughter came to Belle Harbor a few years ago and started asking around about the Tumba Cartel," he said. "She told several people that she needed to speak to Mr. Tumba himself."

Olga's face drained of all color.

"Supposedly, she said that Mr. Tumba knew who had murdered the men her father had been convicted of killing. That he could help her father get out of jail," Delaney continued. "She said she needed the information so she could go to the police and clear his name."

He raised both eyebrows.

"It seems that she somehow had gotten hold of Dessie's phone. She actually managed to speak to Mr. Tumba himself. I guess she made some threats he wasn't very happy about."

"You can imagine what happened next."

Slowly, Olga nodded.

"Mr. Tumba himself ordered the hit. I was out of town at a convention at the time, so he called in El Monstruo."

The name brought a gleam of rage to Olga's eyes.

"He called that *monster* in to kill a *child*?"

She bared her teeth and leaned forward over the table as if she wanted to take a bite out of his throat.

"What happened next?" she gritted out between clenched teeth.

"El Monstruo did what he likes to do," Delaney admitted. "He lured her in with his good looks and charm and then he tore her apart, bit by bit until there was very little for me to clean up."

Olga's face had flushed a deep red.

"What do you mean, clean up?"

"I got a phone call when I got back from my conference," Delaney said. "Mr. Tumba didn't want the body found for obvious reasons and neither did I."

He cleared his throat.

"You see, I had a few private matters of my own that I didn't want coming to light. I wasn't interested in the feds starting a murder investigation. So, when he asked me to do him a favor, it was a win-win for us both."

His pulse quickened as he thought of the mess he'd had to take care of. The slicing and sawing and cutting of bone. The memories sent chills all through him.

Oh, how I miss those old days.

As if reading his thoughts, Olga reached over the table and grabbed the front of Delaney's orange jumpsuit, pulling him toward her with startling strength.

"I should kill you with my bare hands right now for defiling my daughter," she spit out. "If the guards weren't right outside you'd be dead, I can promise you that."

She shoved him backward, sending him sprawling into his chair.

"You should thank me for not leaving her lying on the open ground for the animals," Delaney protested. "I cleaned her up and put her in a proper crypt. She was protected from the elements. Her bones are intact. They can be buried if-"

"What's his name?" she asked, her eyes blazing with hate. "What's El Monstruo's real name?"

Delaney swallowed hard.

"I don't know," he lied. "I only know that-"

Her hand lashed out, grabbing him by the throat, squeezing so hard he couldn't make a sound. He struggled silently as she stared directly into his eyes.

"What is his name?" Olga hissed. "Who is El Monstruo?"

Releasing him, she watched as he gasped for breath.

"I won't ask you again," she said.

As he reached up to massage his throat, Delaney noticed that she wasn't even breathing hard.

"His name is Fernando Borja," he said.

He felt his throat constrict as he coughed up a drop of blood and he frowned, suddenly wishing he could kill the woman.

"You seem very angry at everyone else," he said. "But I'm pretty sure I know the truth about Dessie."

Wiping his mouth with the back of his hand, he coughed

again.

"I'd bet my life he took the fall for the murders *you* committed. So, why not blame yourself for his death? And for Birdie's. If it wasn't for you, they'd both still be alive."

Olga had been getting up to leave but she hesitated at Delaney's words, causing him to recoil. But she only shook her head.

"I don't blame myself," she said. "I blame Cate Flynn. She's the one who persecuted an innocent man. I've already managed to send her boyfriend to jail. But now that Dessie's dead, it'll need to go further than that. He'll have to die. And I'm going to kill him."

"Good luck with that," Delaney said. "Mason Knox is being kept in solitary confinement since he's helped put half the killers in here behind bars. You'll never get to him, even with Mr. Tumba's help."

She produced an angry smile.

"I already have a plan to get him out," she said.

"You'd have to break him out of here," Delaney said. "Because he'll never get bail."

"He will with my help," she gloated. "Your lawyer, Tony Brunner, is representing Knox. He's already filed a petition to Judge Inglebert asking for bail. Let's just say the good judge has no choice but to grant it. And once Mason is free, he's all mine."

Crossing the room, she knocked on the door.

"Guard? I'm ready to go."

She stared back at Delaney.

"But you? You'll never leave."

As she followed the guard out of the room, Delaney knew he would need to contact Mr. Tumba. He'd have to make it clear that none of this was his fault.

Although he had a special bond with the big boss, he knew the man wouldn't hesitate to have him killed if he thought Delaney posed any danger.

In that way, they were alike.

Rubbing his neck, he thought back to the night he'd met the man who would one day become the head of the dangerous cartel, wondering if anyone else knew why it was called La Tumba.

It had all started twenty-five years earlier at the Belle Harbor Burial Ground. The very place where Delaney had previously killed his own father.

As he waited for the guard to take him back to his cell, he closed his eyes and remembered.

Carter Delaney spun around as he heard the creak of rusty hinges.

A man stood just inside the door of the old crypt, his eyes taking in the dead body on the ground and the bones stacked against the wall.

Looking at the human remains with interest rather than horror, he held a gun in one hand but gave no indication he was in a hurry to use it.

At least, not yet.

Shocked into momentary silence, Delaney stood frozen in place.

Other than his father, he'd never encountered another living human in the abandoned graveyard.

Why had this man come, and what could he possibly want?

"Who are you?" Delaney asked, his eyes dropping to the gun. "If you're looking to loot the place, there's nothing of value in here."

"I didn't come to Belle Harbor to steal money," the man said with a laugh. "I came to earn it. Although my kind of work isn't exactly legal."

His eyes once again scanned the dim interior of the crypt.

"But perhaps that doesn't bother you. In fact, from the look of this place, I'd say you and I are in the same sort of business. Although, it appears you may have gotten a head start."

Lifting an eyebrow he nodded toward the body at Delaney's feet.

"I'm assuming that's your latest job," he said, then gestured toward the bones by the wall. "And you have been a busy boy."

"This isn't all my work," Delaney said, feeling his chest expand under the man's approving gaze. "I can't take all the credit."

The man frowned.

"You work for someone?"

Delaney shrugged.

"I guess you could say it's more of a hobby. An interest passed down to me by my father. Although he was more obsessed with buried treasure than buried bones."

A gleam entered the man's eyes.

"Your father wouldn't happen to have been looking for the stash Samuel Bellamy was rumored to have buried around here, was he?"

The question caught Delaney off guard.

"How'd you know about that?"

"Oh, there's been rumors going around Latin America for years about the lost pirate treasure," he said. "One of the missionaries, a

man of God named Reverend Cheever, went from church to church giving a sermon of one man's quest for treasure. He said it had driven the man crazy with greed and blood lust, causing his damnation."

He laughed out loud.

"But instead of scaring the local people into compliance with his teaching, the reverend only made everyone want to come to Florida to look for the treasure themselves."

Startled by the mention of Reverend Cheever, Delaney scoffed.

"Reverend Cheever is a fool. As was my father. He wasted years looking for that stupid treasure."

"And did he find it?"

The man's eyes fixed on his with intense interest.

"Nope," Delaney said, trying not to show the sudden fear that had fallen over him. "All he found for his trouble was a cold, lonely grave."

Disappointment flooded the man's face.

"Your father is dead? Is he in this tomb?"

Delaney hesitated, not sure how much he should tell this stranger.

Who knew if he would let him leave the crypt alive?

But if he was going to die, what was to stop him from revealing his darkest secrets? Why bother to hide behind his mask any longer?

"Yes, my father's dead," Delaney admitted. "But he's not in here. I buried him in the dirt. The dignity of a tomb was more than he deserved."

"Because he found no treasure?"

Delaney laughed.

"Treasure is in the eye of the beholder," he said. "And these

bones in here are mine."

The man smiled.

"Maybe I've discovered something very valuable after all," he said, sticking his gun into the waistband of his pants. "Maybe we both have found something valuable tonight."

His face appeared wolfish in the dim light.

"I'm starting up a new enterprise in South Florida," he said. "I'll need someone capable of...well, your sort of work. I'm sure we can make a lot of money together."

He gestured to the walls of the crypt.

"And we can use this tomb as our secret headquarters," he added with a grin. "We'll call our operation La Tumba, since it started in the heart of a grave. And guess what? I already have a job for you."

As the man detailed the job he had in mind, Delaney considered the man's words, then smiled, relieved he'd be leaving the crypt alive after all.

The heavy hand of the guard fell on Delaney's shoulder, wrinkling the orange jumpsuit and bringing him out of the darkness of the crypt and back into the stark, brightly lit prison.

So much had changed since his first meeting with Mr. Tumba.

He'd left the crypt that day as if nothing had happened, continuing his education and forging a career as an anthropologist.

But on the side, he'd begun working for Mr. Tumba as a contract killer, earning money doing what he did best, gathering bones for his many experiments.

And over the years, La Tumba had grown into a dangerous cartel, feared for the merciless revenge they'd take on anyone who stood in their way.

Few people knew who Mr. Tumba really was and even fewer knew the story behind the start of his operations in South Florida.

But Delaney knew that the kingpin wasn't a sentimental man.

If he thinks I've told anyone who he really is, I'm a dead man.

CHAPTER NINETEEN

Friday morning came with a cold breeze from the east that ruffled Dalton West's fair hair as he headed toward the coffee shop where Bailey would be waiting. She'd suggested they meet at the Summerset Espresso Café beside the courthouse for breakfast prior to Mason Knox's bail hearing. Dalton had readily agreed to the early morning date, knowing that it might be his only chance to see Bailey all day.

Zipping up his jacket against the chill of the February wind, he stuck his hands in his pockets and quickened his pace, joining the stream of office workers heading into downtown, most of them wearing heavy coats that hadn't seen sunlight all year.

It was rare for the temperature to fall below sixty degrees in South Florida, and when it did happen, most people used it as an excuse to bundle up as if they were heading for the arctic.

As he entered the coffee shop, Bailey waved to him from across the room. He could see right away from the gleam in her green eyes that she had news to share.

"I finally have a photo of our teenage Jane Doe," she said. "Only, she's not a faceless Jane Doe any more, she's called

Birdie."

She smiled as she slid a printout toward him.

"That photo was in the *Belle Harbor Chronicle* a few years ago," she said. "And the girl right there is Birdie."

Dalton studied the photo.

"Congratulations, that's some good investigating," he said.

As he looked up, he saw Nigella Ashworth and her son standing in the long line to order coffee.

His smile faltered momentarily, and then he looked away as if he didn't recognize them, careful not to give any sign that he was working with Neil, who was also studiously avoiding looking at their table.

"I can't wait to show this photo to the task force," Bailey said. "We've been trying to identify this girl for so long, and now it's all coming together. Once we got a match to her father in CODIS, I knew it would just be a matter of time until we figured out everything about her. And we're almost there."

As she spoke, Dalton glanced over at Neil and his mother.

An idea started to take shape in his mind.

Maybe he could figure out a way to run Neil's DNA through CODIS to find out if Chuck Ashworth's DNA was in there.

If the man's body had been found but not identified, or if he'd committed some sort of crime and run off, his DNA would likely be in the FBI's national database.

"How do you get DNA sent to CODIS to see if there's a match?" he asked when Bailey stopped to take a sip from her cup.

Blinking at him in surprise, she cocked her head.

"Well, the FBI only allows law enforcement to send in DNA profiles to be added to the database," she said. "And the law enforcement labs have to be certified. The Bureau is pretty strict."

Dalton's heart fell.

"So, if I was looking for a missing person..."

"It would have to go through an agency, such as the BHPD or the FBI lab," she said. "And it would have to be a missing person case where foul play is suspected. Why are you..."

Her words trailed off as she noticed Neil and his mother leaving the café. She grimaced as her eyes followed Nigella Ashworth toward the courthouse.

Dalton hesitated, then sighed. He didn't want to lie to her or keep secrets. He should tell her about Neil Ashworth and the case he'd taken on to find his missing father.

Although she might not like him working for the Ashworth family, he was sure she was bound to find out sooner or later.

Of course, I'll have to ask her to keep it quiet so Nigella doesn't know.

Bailey's eyes were still on Nigella and Neil when she spoke again.

"I don't know why, but I feel sorry for Neil," she said, shaking her head. "Growing up with a mother like–"

She jumped as her phone beeped and she dug it out of her purse.

"It's Cate," she said as she got to her feet. "I promised to meet with her before the bail hearing. I better go."

Picking up her coffee cup, she headed toward the door

before Dalton could say another word.

* * *

Dalton parked his pickup in front of the Belle Harbor police department and went into the lobby, where Madeline Mercer was already waiting for him.

She smiled as he approached, obviously pleased to see him, but as she led him down the hall toward the lab, he experienced a momentary flash of doubt about what he was about to do.

He and the crime scene investigator had enjoyed a brief fling not long after he'd moved to Belle Harbor.

Although their fleeting romance had quickly faded into a casual friendship and they rarely saw each other anymore except in passing, when he'd called her up asking to see her, she had quickly invited him to come to the lab to meet her.

He hoped now that she hadn't gotten the wrong idea.

"I was surprised to get your call," Madeline said. "It's been a while since I've heard from you. How have you been?"

Swallowing hard, Dalton shrugged.

"Things are okay, I guess," he said, sticking his hands in his pockets to keep from fidgeting. "Business is slow, which is why I took on a missing person case that's not my usual kind of case."

Madeline cocked her head.

"What do you mean? What kind of case is it?"

"Well, usually I take on cases where I'm looking for missing kids or young people," he said. "Maybe somebody's daughter or son. They might have run away or even been abducted."

He cleared his throat.

"But with this case, I'm looking for someone's father. A grown man...an older man...who might have run off and abandoned his family, or maybe become the victim of a crime. But there's no evidence of foul play or anything. No police involved, although his son is pretty anxious to find out what happened to him."

Madeline looked intrigued.

"That sounds like a worthwhile case," she said. "I'm sure his son appreciates you helping him."

Deciding it was now or never, Dalton sucked in a deep breath.

"It's just that we've run the son's DNA through all the publicly available ancestry and genealogy databases and haven't got a hit. And since there aren't any law enforcement agencies involved...."

A frown had started to form on Madeline's forehead.

"Well, my client was thinking...or really, I was thinking that maybe you could...you know, run his DNA through CODIS?"

He said the last part quickly, resisting the urge to wince and close his eyes so that he wouldn't have to see her reaction.

"That's not really allowed," Madeline said slowly. "We have to follow strict protocols and have limits, but..."

She hesitated.

"But, if your client filled out a missing person report, I

could submit his DNA profile to see if it matches any of the remains we've found in the Belle Harbor Burial Ground project," she said. "Once it's in CODIS, it would flag any other matches as well."

Dalton's face lit up.

"You could do that for me?"

"Sure, bring me his DNA profile and I'll see what I can do."

As Dalton turned to leave, Madeline gave his hand a warm squeeze and he found himself walking back to his truck feeling vaguely guilty.

Was his trip to see Madeline and her testing of Neil Ashworth's DNA another secret he was bound to keep?

CHAPTER TWENTY

Bailey took the elevator up to Cate's office, wondering if there was any way she could talk her sister out of attending Mason Knox's bail hearing. After all, Cate was an assistant state attorney, and even though she wasn't assigned to the case, her presence at the hearing might be considered a conflict of interest if she was seen actively supporting the defense.

Sticking her head into her sister's office, Bailey saw Cate standing by the window, staring out at the sky with brooding eyes. Running a distracted hand through her auburn hair, she tucked a wayward strand behind her ear.

"Are you still planning to go to the hearing?" Bailey asked.

When Cate spun around, she pointed to the messy stack of files and folders on her sister's desk and raised an eyebrow.

"It looks as if you have plenty of work here to keep you busy if you want to skip it," she said.

Cate surveyed Bailey with somber eyes.

"Where's Ludwig?" she asked, looking past her into the hall.

"I dropped him off at Sid Morley's house for a play date with Amadeus," Bailey said. "He's not a big fan of courtroom hearings."

Her sister nodded with satisfaction.

"That's probably for the best," she said. "Knowing how erratic Judge Inglebert has been lately, I wouldn't want to try to take a dog into his courtroom, even a good boy like Ludwig."

Gathering her bag and phone, Cate headed toward the door.

"You sure you want to do this?" Bailey asked. "Didn't Henrietta Trilby advise you to stay away?"

When her sister didn't answer, she tried again.

"And Mason said in his note that-"

"I don't need you to tell me what Mason's break-up letter said," Cate snapped. "I've got that memorized, thank you very much."

Her tone was icy but her eyes were sad.

"And whether he wants my support or not, he's got it," she added. "He doesn't have anyone else that I'm aware of in his corner. So, I'm going to the hearing. It's up to you if you want to come with me."

With that, she strode out of the room and down to the elevator, jabbing the metal button with a nervous finger.

Trying to think of something to say while they waited for the elevator doors to open, Bailey remembered what she'd been meaning to tell her sister.

"You know, I saw Mom with Mayor Sutherland yesterday," she said. "They were having wine and seemed very cozy. I just hope she's keeping her guard up around that man. I don't trust him."

But the doors had slid open and Cate didn't seem to be listening as she stepped into the elevator, which carried them down to the busy courthouse lobby.

As they stepped out into the crowd and began heading toward Judge Inglebert's courtroom, Cate called to a slim, athletic-looking woman with sleek black hair pulled back into a low ponytail.

"Dr. Chung, what are you doing here?"

The woman turned to Cate.

"I've come to support Mason during his bail hearing, of course," she said with a nervous smile. "I thought he might need someone to speak on his behalf as a character reference."

"That's really nice of you," Cate said, looking pleased. "You can sit with us if you'd like. This is my sister, Bailey Flynn."

Turning to Bailey, the therapist stuck out a small hand.

"I've heard so much about you," she said.

Her eyes flicked to Cate and she smiled.

"And I don't mean from your sister during our sessions," she clarified. "I've seen reports about your cases on the news and in the paper. Very interesting work."

Bailey returned her smile, suddenly feeling self-conscious.

Before she could reply, her eyes fell on a woman with a cap of dark hair pushing her way through the crowd.

"Dr. Varney?"

The woman turned to her, her eyes wide behind her glasses.

"What are you doing here?"

She had forgotten that the psychiatrist was still in town.

"Apparently, there was some hold-up at the medical examiner's office," the woman said. "They aren't sure when Gayle will be ready to be transported back to Crimson Falls. In the meantime, I was curious about the outcome of today's hearing."

Glancing back at Dr. Chung and Cate, who were both staring at her expectantly, Bailey made awkward introductions.

"This is Dr. Jude Varney," she said. "She's a psychiatrist up at Rock Ridge Detention Center in Virginia."

Not sure how to explain the presence of Gayle Kershaw's doctor at the hearing, Bailey stepped back to allow the two women to exchange greetings.

She thought the therapists might feel awkward meeting each other when their respective patients had shared such a violent and turbulent history, but the women seemed to hit it off right away as they all made their way into the courtroom and sat down together in a bench near the back of the room.

"All rise for the honorable Judge Brett Inglebert."

Everyone in the courtroom stood as the judge came into the courtroom and took his place on the bench.

Studying the Judge's hard, implacable face, Bailey could see no outward emotion or reaction as Tony Brunner got up to make his case for granting bail.

Cate shifted on the bench beside her as Henrietta Trilby followed, requesting that the judge deny Mason bail.

"Your honor, this man is accused of committing two serious offenses in the last week alone. He presents a very real and present danger to the Summerset County community," she said in a grave voice. "Therefore, I must request that you deny Mason Knox bail."

The judge stared at Henrietta for a long beat, then frowned.

"Mr. Knox has no previous criminal record and thus far has proven to be an upstanding citizen in our community," he said. "The State has failed to prove that he presents a danger and should thus be retained in custody pending his trial. Therefore, I will grant bail to Mr. Knox in the amount of–"

As Cate gave a happy sigh of relief beside her, an angry protest sounded from a bench near the front of the room.

Straining to see what was going on, Bailey saw Detective Killian Rourke gesturing toward Henrietta Trilby, who was trying very hard to ignore his outburst.

"Order in the court!" Judge Inglebert snapped, banging his gavel on the bench. "I will have order in the court!"

He glared down at Rourke for a long beat before wrapping up the proceedings and dismissing the court.

Bailey stood and prepared to follow Cate and the other women out of the courtroom. For once, her sister seemed to be happy with Judge Inglebert and his ruling.

They watched as Mason left the room flanked by the bailiff and Tony Brunner, then headed to the exit.

Stepping into the lobby, Bailey said goodbye to Dr. Varney, watching with a smile as Dr. Chung squeezed Cate's hand. As the therapists walked away, Bailey spotted a familiar face in the crowd.

"Look who's here," she said, grabbing her sister's arm and tugging her toward Jackie Flynn, who was standing by the elevator looking down at her phone with a self-satisfied smile.

"You look like the cat who ate the canary," Bailey said as she and Cate stopped beside their mother. "Has Duchess been giving you lessons?"

Jackie glanced up in surprise, still smiling.

"We're almost through with the negotiations on the Sun Creek Preserve purchase," she said. "I finally have Mayor Sutherland's approval to close the deal. And best of all, the entire parcel of land will be designated as a protected preserve. Isn't that fabulous?"

As her mother tapped in a message on her phone, Bailey cleared her throat and leaned closer.

"So, that's why you were getting all cozy with Sutherland yesterday," she said in a low voice. "You were trying to butter him up so he would approve the negotiation."

"Of course, dear," Jackie said. "It hasn't been easy to get that awful man to agree to the protected preserve status, you know. He wanted to turn the whole place into a strip mall."

She sighed dramatically.

"Being a lawyer can be very stressful, you know."

"Then why are you always telling me I should have been a lawyer?" Bailey asked, raising an eyebrow.

"It might be stressful but at least it's not dangerous," Jackie said. "I don't have to worry about getting killed every time I-"

Cate stepped between them and raised her hands.

"I think this discussion is over," she said. "You both just need to agree to disagree. Now, as much as I would like to wait and try to speak to Mason, I have to attend a strategy session on the upcoming case against Phillip Thayer and Kelvin Miller."

Noting Bailey's confused expression, she clarified.

"You know, Phoenix and Kato, Jordan Stone's bodyguards."

Bailey grimaced and nodded as she suddenly placed the men's real names with their sullen faces.

"I'll walk you out to the parking garage and then I've got to go."

Suddenly remembering the photo of Birdie in her bag, Bailey followed Cate and her mother out to the parking garage, eager to update the task force. With a final wave, she hurried to the Expedition and sped away.

CHAPTER TWENTY-ONE

Olga sat perfectly still in the silver sedan, watching with bitter eyes as Bailey Flynn climbed into her black SUV and drove out of the parking garage, leaving Cate and her mother to finish their conversation. Humming along to the melancholy strains of U2's *Mothers of the Disappeared*, Olga grimaced as Jackie Flynn pulled her daughter in for a hug.

Heart aching in rhythm to the poignant music, Olga closed her eyes, trying to remember the last time she'd comforted Birdie.

Had it been the day Dessie was found guilty? Or a few weeks later when he'd been sentenced to life in prison?

Everything from those days had been such a blur.

She hadn't known then that those would be the last precious moments she'd ever spend with her daughter. The last of Birdie's tears she'd ever wipe away.

The bond between a mother and a daughter was no longer hers to enjoy. What she'd once shared with Birdie was lost to her forever.

And if justice was to be served, she would have to break that bond between Cate and her mother as well. She would have to take from them what had been taken from her.

Fracture for fracture, eye for eye, tooth for tooth...

She watched Jackie leave and felt the temptation to go after her. She could enact further revenge with one well-aimed bullet. But no, first things first. She needed to concentrate on completing her first unfinished objective.

Hands gripping the steering wheel, she forced herself to remain where she was as Cate disappeared back into the courthouse.

Finally, she saw the person she was waiting for.

Mason Knox appeared looking tired and disheveled. But he wasn't alone. He was flanked by his lawyer, Tony Brunner, and Detective Fraser.

And to her dismay, a small woman followed in their wake.

Olga's eyes narrowed as she made out Dr. Jude Varney's small frame and dark hair.

What is Gayle Kershaw's therapist doing with Mason and his lawyer? Is the interfering woman trying to help him?

Had she been planning to testify that Gayle was unstable? That the woman had brought her fate upon herself?

Adjusting the listening device she carried with her to every job, Olga strained to hear what they were saying.

"It's best if you don't go back to your house," Fraser told Mason. "The media will be there. And we haven't released the crime scene yet. I don't think Detective Rourke is in any rush."

"You can get a room at the Summerset Hotel where I've been staying," Dr. Varney suggested. "You can book online and use your phone as the room key. It's all very modern and up-to-date. No one else will even know you're there."

"That sounds good," Brunner said, answering for Mason. "I'll go get my car, and then I'll drop him off there after we've had time to review the next steps."

The lawyer hurried away, then returned minutes later in a sleek BMW, stopping to allow Mason to climb into the passenger seat. The medical examiner stared straight ahead as the lawyer pulled away, leaving Dr. Varney and Fraser behind.

Olga tensed behind the steering wheel, waiting impatiently for the detective and the psychiatrist to leave, wanting to follow after Mason. She didn't want to lose sight of him but didn't quite dare to pull out of her parking spot and risk being seen eavesdropping.

"So, how long did you say you are planning to stay in Belle Harbor?" Fraser asked.

"Until Gayle's body is released," Dr. Varney replied. "I told Mrs. Kershaw I'd accompany Gayle back home. In the meantime, I plan to find out as much as I can about what happened that night. It just doesn't make sense."

Fraser nodded his agreement.

"Nothing around here makes much sense lately," he said as he headed back to his car, leaving Dr. Varney on her own.

The psychiatrist walked to a compact rental car parked halfway down the row. As she backed out of her space and drove past, Olga pulled out after her.

I'll follow Dr. Varney to the hotel and wait for Mason there.

But as she merged the silver sedan into traffic behind the psychiatrist's car, Olga began to worry. The doctor was curious and resourceful. And she asked too many questions.

If she starts poking around and talking to people who know Mason and Cate, there's no telling where her questions could lead.

Perhaps to Olga's own doorstep.

The nosy doctor could ruin everything.

Following Dr. Varney's rental car into the Summerset Hotel parking lot, Olga was pleased to see that the two-story hotel offered only rooms that opened onto outside corridors.

Good, that should make this easy.

She waited to see which room the psychiatrist was in, then pulled her silver sedan around back and parked behind the building.

Opening her bag, she pulled out a gray metal cylinder.

Her eyes rested briefly on the words engraved in the metal as she attached the silencer and opened the door. Stepping out of the car, she held the gun straight down by her side, keeping it hidden in the folds of her skirt.

Walking quickly but casually to the back stairwell, she ascended quietly and moved down the corridor to Dr. Varney's room.

She knocked twice and waited. Several seconds passed, and then the curtains flicked in the window.

A lock turned and the door opened.

As Dr. Varney stood in the doorway with a curious smile, Olga lifted the gun and pulled the trigger, putting a bullet directly into the psychiatrist's heart.

The force of the bullet sent her staggering backward as Olga stepped into the room and closed the door behind her.

A crimson stain was already spreading over Dr. Varney's blouse and Olga saw blood spatter on the door and carpet.

Looking around the hotel room, she decided it would be safe to hide there until Mason arrived.

She would make the scene look like a murder-suicide.

Make it appear as if Mason had taken out his rage on Gayle's therapist before killing himself.

But when she peeked out the front window, she froze.

Detective Jimmy Fraser was pulling up outside.

CHAPTER TWENTY-TWO

Fraser pulled up to the Summerset Hotel still trying to make sense of what he'd learned when he'd gone back to the station. As he'd passed Madeline Mercer in the hall, the crime scene investigator had pulled him to the side. She'd spoken in a low voice as if she didn't want anyone to overhear what she was saying.

"I just thought you'd want to know we found something interesting in the security video taken at the medical examiner's office the night Finola Lawson was attacked."

She'd looked around as if someone might be listening in.

"There was someone else there that night," she said. "The video was grainy, and the person was wearing dark clothes and a hat, but it appeared to be a woman. She came in just after Mason."

Madeline had gone on to say that there was no video of the mysterious figure ever leaving.

"She must have gone out the back. There's no camera at the loading dock."

She had kept her voice low, sounding almost scared.

"Rourke asked me not to tell anyone else, yet. He said it doesn't prove anything and that Tony Brunner will only try to use the tape to get Mason off the hook."

Fraser had realized then what the crime scene team leader was scared of. She was scared of Rourke.

After assuring her that she'd done the right thing and thanking her for coming to him with the information, he'd been tempted to storm down to Chief Pruett's office and demand to have Rourke answer for hiding key evidence in a murder investigation.

But he wasn't sure the new chief wouldn't bother listening to what he had to say, much less act on it.

Realizing that the person who had tried to kill Finola was still out there and that the same person may have killed Gayle Kershaw, he had decided the first thing he needed to do was warn Mason.

As he climbed out of the Interceptor, Fraser surveyed the hotel parking lot and then crossed to the lobby. Approaching the reception desk, he showed the clerk his badge.

"I need to speak to one of your guests," he said. "I'm looking for Mason Knox. What's his room number?"

The clerk studied his badge and then turned to the old desktop computer on the counter.

As the clerk began pecking out Mason's name on the keyboard, Fraser turned and looked out the window. A woman in a jacket with the hood pulled up was stepping out of a room on the second floor. The woman's face was hidden as she hurried toward the stairs.

"Looks like he's booked in Room 228," the clerk said as Fraser turned around. "But he hasn't accessed the room yet."

"Okay, thanks for checking, I'll wait for him outside."

He turned to leave, then hesitated.

"Could I also get the room number for Jude Varney?" he asked. "She should be staying here, too."

It wouldn't hurt to get some more information about the psychiatrist. After all, it seemed strange to him that she was staying in town. And why show up at Mason's hearing?

Was it just him or did the woman seem a little too curious for her own good? A little too involved?

The clerk sighed and turned back to the computer.

"Jude Varney is registered in Room 226," he said. "That's the one next door to Mr. Knox. Anything else?"

Shaking his head, Fraser left the office, stepping outside just as Brunner's BMW pulled into the lot.

Mason still sat in the passenger's seat as the lawyer rolled down his window to glare at Fraser.

"You aren't here to harass my client are you?"

"Not at all," Fraser assured him, wondering if he should tell Brunner about the woman he'd seen in the security video. "I just want to make sure he's keeping out of trouble."

"Well, he's been with me planning his defense, and now he's planning to hole up at the hotel and get some rest."

Fraser nodded as Mason climbed out. Before he could say anything else, the lawyer sped away.

"I think I'm in room 228," Mason said, looking a little less dazed than he had that morning at the hearing.

He held up his phone.

"I believe I can use my phone as a key to the room."

Looking over at Fraser, he cocked his head.

"Is there anything else, Detective?"

"I'll just make sure you get up to your room safely," Fraser said. "There's something I wanted to tell you and-"

But Mason was already heading toward the stairwell.

Following behind him, Fraser climbed the stairs to the second floor and walked along the outside corridor toward Mason's room.

As he walked past Room 226, he stopped and stared.

There was blood on the door and the pavement outside the room. Seeing that the door to the room wasn't fully closed, he stepped closer and pushed on it.

The door swung open, then banged against something lying on the floor and swung back toward him.

Squinting into the dark interior of the room, Fraser stepped inside, then jerked back with a startled yell.

"What is it?" Mason asked, coming up behind him.

"It's Dr. Varney," Fraser said, looking down at the doctor, who was lying in a pool of blood. "She's dead."

Mason looked past Fraser into the room.

His eyes widened as he saw the woman on the floor.

'This can't be happening again" he said, staring at Fraser with a stunned expression. "It wasn't me."

He stepped back and held up his hands.

"I didn't do this. And I didn't hurt Gayle or Finola, either."

Fraser looked down at a faint, bloody footprint on the carpet. It looked like a woman's high-heeled shoe.

His eyes flicked to Dr. Varney.

The psychiatrist was wearing flats and there was no blood on the bottom of her shoes.

Moving back into the corridor, he looked down to see faint

blood stains leading toward the stairwell and immediately thought of the woman he'd seen leaving the room just after he'd arrived.

"I know it wasn't you," he told Mason.

He shook his head, trying to think.

"That's what I wanted to tell you. There was a woman...she was just here. And she was seen on the camera at your office the night Finola was attacked."

Mason nodded as he processed the information.

"I knew there had to be someone else," he said. "But, who is she? Why is she doing this?"

"That's just it," Fraser said. "I don't know who she is. The video is grainy. By itself, it doesn't really prove anything."

Looking around at the scene, he imagined what Rourke and Pruett would say, then looked up at Mason.

"We need to find that woman," he said. "It's the only way they'll believe you didn't do this."

He looked again at the bloody footprints.

Sucking in a deep breath, he pulled out his phone and quickly tapped in a message to Bailey.

Come to the Summerset Hotel ASAP. Bring Ludwig. Please hurry.

CHAPTER TWENTY-THREE

Bailey's phone buzzed again and again in her pocket as she sat in the conference room at the FBI's Miami field office showing Aisha Sharma and Argus Murphy the *Belle Harbor Chronicle* article she'd brought with her. Their attention was still fixed on the photo of Birdie when Eloise Spellman arrived.

The forensic anthropologist quickly joined them at the table, studying the photo with interest, and pointing out the features of the girl that matched up with the remains.

"I knew she had to be tall," Eloise said, transfixed to finally see the girl whose remains had been sliced up and stacked against the stone walls of the crypt. "And I said she couldn't have been more than fifteen or sixteen, didn't I?"

Irritated by the incessant buzzing of her phone, Bailey dug into her pocket and pulled it out. Before she could thumb the *Do Not Disturb* icon, she saw Fraser's message.

Come to the Summerset Hotel ASAP. Bring Ludwig. Please hurry.

Bailey cleared her throat.

"Sorry, but it looks as if I'm going to have to go," she said, calling to Ludwig, who was tired after his morning playdate.

Argus caught her as she was heading for the door.

"I've done some searching for Birdie, using the last name Bolt, but so far, no luck. Although I haven't had much time."

He lowered his voice.

"I've been pulled in to assist an old friend who I understand you've been helping as well."

For a minute, Bailey wasn't sure who he was talking about.

"Our mutual friend from D.C. who's working in the area?"

"Oh, you mean..."

She stopped herself before blurting out Charlie's name.

"Yes, of course. I didn't know you were...helping."

Argus grimaced.

"I'm not sure how much help I've been, but during what little free time I've had while I've been in Miami I did attempt to find a digital trail to Birdie. Again, no luck, at least not yet."

"I keep thinking the pendant that was found with her body is the key," Bailey said as she inched toward the door. "And the fact that a matching pendant was found at the Gayle Kershaw murder scene? It's another link between the cartel and the other murders. Somehow it all seems connected."

He noticed her checking her watch.

"I won't keep you," he said. "I'm flying back to Virginia tomorrow night. If you think of anything else, call me."

"I will," Bailey promised. "And if I don't see you before then, have a good flight."

Hurrying out to the Expedition, she settled Ludwig into the back seat and then drove toward the highway.

She headed east, wondering what Fraser needed, assuming that if Ludwig was required there must be a missing or dead person involved.

Turning on the radio, she heard Sabrina West's familiar voice. The Channel 3 News reporter was interviewing Raya Valera again. The bereaved daughter of Fraser's late partner was making an appeal to the public.

"Please, if anyone out there has any information about my mother's death, call the hotline. I've been told that Detective Jimmy Fraser with the Belle Harbor Police Department was the last person who saw her alive, but he's not talking."

Bailey reached forward and turned off the radio, thinking with concern that Raya Valera's baseless accusations could end Fraser's career.

And while she felt sorry for the woman, knowing it must be devastating to lose your mother, even when there had been disagreements and an estrangement, she was sure Detective Valera's death hadn't been Fraser's fault.

Carter Delaney had caused the woman's death when he'd strangled her and pushed her car into the river with her unconscious body strapped inside.

Although the malfunction of the ventilator was strange, and it sounds as if someone was in Valera's room that night.

She pushed all thoughts of Valera out of her mind as she arrived at the hotel to find Fraser outside, along with two BHPD cruisers and an ambulance.

"I stopped by to speak to Dr. Varney and found her body," he said as she approached. "She'd been shot."

Fraser looked strained and Bailey could tell by the strange, tense look in his eyes that something was wrong."

"There are bloody foot prints leading from the room," he

said. "That's why I asked you to bring Ludwig."

Leading the tired German shepherd up the stairs to the second floor, Bailey allowed the search and rescue dog to sniff the blood-splattered door.

Ludwig nosed the doorframe and the carpet inside, then trotted over to Room 228 next door and barked.

"Not there," Fraser said, stepping in front of the dog and pointing toward the concrete corridor. "Have him sniff the shoe print."

But once again, Ludwig turned back to the room next door and once again Fraser pointed him toward the footprint.

"He's a little tired," Bailey said. "He had a play-"

Before she could finish her sentence, Ludwig caught the scent, putting his nose close to the ground and following the trail along the corridor and down the stairs.

Hurrying after him, Bailey and Fraser followed the dog to the parking lot and around to the back of the building.

He stopped beside an empty parking spot and then led them toward a nearby patch of overgrown grass and weeds.

Ludwig barked and Bailey looked closer.

The sun was glinting off something in the grass.

Looking down, she saw a metal cylinder on the ground.

Bailey bent to examine it, her heart pounding as she noted the words engraved in the metal.

Silent as the grave.

"That looks like the custom-made silencers Phoenix and Kato were carrying along with their load of automatic weapons when they were arrested. We think those two were planning to deliver the load to the cartel."

Fraser nodded grimly.

"Then it looks as if there's good cause to bring the feds into this case. It could be linked to the cartel. And that's not the only reason."

He looked around as if someone might overhear.

"I saw someone near Dr. Varney's room when I was in the lobby talking to the clerk at the reception desk. A woman came down the stairs. She was wearing a big jacket with the hood pulled up."

"I wouldn't have thought too much about it but a similar woman was also seen on the camera at the medical examiner's office the night Finola was attacked."

"Hold on, I still don't understand why you were here in the first place," Bailey said. "Were you trying to interview Dr. Varney? Was she a suspect?"

Fraser hesitated.

"Not exactly," he said, swallowing hard. "There's something else you need to know."

CHAPTER TWENTY-FOUR

Mason Knox paced back and forth beside the basketball court at Summerset Park, sweating profusely despite the mild weather. He'd left the hotel earlier on foot, just as Fraser had advised, and had kept to little-used side streets as he'd made his way to the park, which was quiet and empty as the sun began to sink toward the horizon.

He watched as a black pickup truck turned into the park and headed down the road toward him.

As it came to a stop beside the court, Dalton West waved and rolled down the window.

"Bailey Flynn sent me," he said. "I've got orders to take you to Sid Morley's house. She said she'll meet you there."

Hesitating, suddenly not sure who he could trust, Mason met Dalton's eyes. The private investigator smiled.

"Last time I was there Morley fixed an ice-cold pitcher of margaritas," he said. "I bet if we're nice to him, he might be willing to make another batch."

The thought of a frosty alcoholic drink was too much to resist. Reaching for the door handle, he climbed into the passenger seat and sat back with a sigh.

Dalton didn't ask any questions as they drove, for which Mason was grateful. Soon, the Dodge was turning onto Mariner Trail. It came to a stop in front of a modest house.

"You'll be safe here," Dalton said as Mason looked up toward the porch. "At least for now."

The front door opened and a man emerged. As he slowly navigated the porch steps and then walked with a slight limp toward the truck, Mason recognized Sid Morley.

He'd met the retired FBI agent on several occasions during recent investigations and liked the man.

And if Fraser and Bailey trust him, I guess I can, too.

Waving for the men to get out of the truck, Morley led his visitors to lawn chairs under a big tree that had twinkling lights wrapped through the branches.

Faint strains of Beethoven's *Moonlight Sonata* drifted out from the house. It was one of the few piano solos Mason could name.

He smiled as Morley called to a black German shepherd and threw a stick, which the dog immediately retrieved.

"Good boy, Amadeus," he said, throwing the stick again, further this time. "Go get it, boy!"

"I guess you're a classical music fan," Mason said, sitting back in the chair. "Will your next dog be called Wolfgang?"

Morley stopped to stare over at Mason, his expression suddenly bereft. After an uncomfortable moment of silence, the older man cleared his throat.

"Wolfgang was the first German shepherd I ever worked with," the older man finally said. "He was the best tracker I've ever had the honor to train and a faithful partner until the day he died. God bless his soul."

Morley crossed himself and lifted his eyes to the sky.

"I'd never be able to give another dog his name."

The man turned and walked back toward the house, leaving Mason staring after him with an open mouth.

As he turned back to Dalton, feeling vaguely guilty, Bailey Flynn's black Expedition pulled into the driveway.

Getting to his feet, Mason looked for Fraser, but the FBI agent's only passenger was her dog, Ludwig.

As she climbed out of the vehicle, she was holding her phone to her ear. Mason's chest squeezed as he wondered if she might be talking to Cate.

He had seen her sister at the hearing that morning and found it hard not to turn around and stare. But he'd been afraid of seeing pity in her eyes. Or, even worse, doubt.

Standing silently beside Dalton, he strained to hear.

"It looks as if the unsub may be a woman," Bailey said into the phone. "We have a grainy video and a shoe print, as well as an eye witness who caught a quick glimpse. It's not much to go on but it's something."

There was a long pause, then Bailey nodded.

"Okay, thanks, Charlie. I owe you one. See you soon."

As Bailey lowered the phone, she slowly approached, her fingers tapping rapidly on the screen.

"I've asked a colleague for help," Bailey said when she finally looked up and caught his eye. "She's sending someone we can trust."

Mason nodded, watching as she attached a photo of what appeared to be some sort of silencer to her message before she tapped *SEND*.

"Can you tell us what's going on?"

The question came from Sid Morley, who had returned, carrying two bottles of water, one of which he handed to Mason and the other to Bailey.

Unscrewing the cap, Bailey swigged down a long drink and then cleared her throat.

"Video evidence suggests an unknown woman attacked Finola Lawson at the medical examiner's office the other night. We suspect the same woman is also responsible for the murders of Gayle Kershaw and Dr. Jude Varney."

"Based on the discovery of a custom-made silencer at the latest scene, it's possible the murders are linked to a criminal cartel that traffics in illegal weapons among other things, which is why the FBI is now involved."

As she finished speaking, a dusty white Silverado pulled into the long driveway and jerked to a stop. A man Mason had never seen before climbed out. He was small but powerfully built with dark hair that curled over the collar of his leather jacket, which he wore over jeans and a lumberjack shirt.

His cowboy boots added a few inches to his height.

"I'm Special Agent Emil Lazar."

Digging into his pocket, he pulled out his FBI credentials and flashed them at Bailey.

"Thanks for coming so quickly," she said. "This is Mason Knox. He'll be the one going with you."

Mason stared at Bailey with wide eyes.

"Go with him where?" he asked.

"I'll be taking you to a safe house," Lazar said. "You can

stay there until we can figure out what's going on."

He turned to Bailey.

"What exactly is going on?"

"We think the Tumba Cartel was somehow involved with several homicides in Belle Harbor," she said. "Seems they may have been trying to set Mason up to take the fall."

Lazar turned to Mason.

"Why would they target you?"

When Mason only shrugged, the man frowned.

"Can you tell me what's happened so far?"

Sucking in a deep breath, Mason quickly recounted the nightmarish events of the last few days, beginning when he came home to find Gayle sitting at his dinner table and ending with the discovery of Dr. Varney's body in the hotel room next to his.

As he fell silent, Bailey lifted her phone.

"You left out the part about the pendant," she said.

She showed Lazar a photo of the Saint Olga pendant on the dinnerplate.

"An identical pendant was recently found in a crypt with human remains," she said. "The same crypt where Carter Delaney had dumped some of his victims."

Lazar's eyes widened.

"Looks like the work of the Saint," he said in a grim voice.

Mason frowned.

"The Saint?"

"I don't know why the cartel would send one of their top fixers to Belle Harbor," Emil continued as if Mason hadn't spoken. "But if the Saint is here, we're all in danger."

CHAPTER TWENTY-FIVE

Cate gripped the steering wheel of her Lexus with both hands as she drove toward Dr. Chung's office, fighting the urge to turn around and go home. She wasn't sure what she planned to ask the psychiatrist, or what the doctor might be able to tell her. All she knew was she needed to find out more about Mason's anger issues. And she wanted Dr. Chung to reassure her once and for all that Mason wasn't capable of killing Gayle or anyone else.

Pulling into the dark parking lot, she was relieved to see lights behind the office windows. Perhaps she'd gotten lucky and Dr. Chung was still there.

She got out of the car and walked to the door, half expecting it to be locked. But it swung open easily.

Stepping inside, she approached the reception desk to find the chair behind the counter empty.

"Cecilia's gone for the day," a voice said behind her. "I'm here on my own waiting for my final appointment."

Cate jumped and spun around to see Dr. Chung standing in the doorway to the session room.

"But what are *you* doing here?" the therapist asked as she moved into the room. "Has something happened? Is everything okay?"

Her forehead creased into a concerned frown.

"Everything is...fine," Cate said, suddenly unsure of what she was hoping to gain from the impromptu visit. "I just wanted to thank you for your help earlier. With Mason, I mean."

The therapist cocked her head.

"You came here to talk about Mason?"

Her voice had cooled on the words.

"You know I can't share any information about my other patients," she reminded Cate. "The only reason I can even acknowledge that he is a patient is because you're the one who referred him to me."

Cate nodded, her throat suddenly tight as she thought back to the comments she'd seen in his file.

"It's just that, as you know, I've been seeing Mason and..."

She swallowed hard, forcing herself to continue.

"I thought we had something special and I just wanted to know if you thought...well, you've talked to him in session so...you must have an opinion if...well if you think..."

Dr. Chung raised a hand to cut off her stammering words.

"I hope you didn't come here to ask me if I think Mason is capable of murder," she said firmly. "Because, if you did, you're wasting your time. I can't discuss his treatment or his diagnosis with you."

Her eyes softened as she took in Cate's anxious face.

"All I can tell you is that as a mental health professional, I have an obligation to report anyone who is showing signs of being an imminent threat to themselves or to others. I take that obligation seriously and would act immediately if and when needed."

Before Cate could reply, the door opened again.

Henrietta Trilby stood in the doorway.

Cate gaped at the woman, who stared back with narrow eyes.

"What are you doing here?"

Cate's surprise quickly turned to suspicion.

"I should ask you the same thing," Cate replied. "You aren't here to question Dr. Chung about Mason Knox, are you? Because if you're trying to-"

"She's not here to ask me about Mason," Dr. Chung interrupted as she stepped between the two prosecutors. "But Henrietta does actually have an appointment scheduled, unlike you, so I'll need to ask you to leave, Cate."

She gestured to the door.

"Now, please."

As Cate turned and walked to the door, she heard Dr. Chung apologizing for her.

"I'm sorry about that, Henrietta. How has your week gone?"

The door to the session room closed behind them.

Cate felt a flush of shame crawl up her neck.

Dr. Chung had obviously been angry with her.

And she'd accused Henrietta when the poor woman had only been coming to see Dr. Chung as a patient.

It looks as if I'm not the only prosecutor who's been emotionally scarred by the job.

* * *

Cate unlocked the door and pushed it open, irritated to see the lights were off. The living room lay in pitch darkness.

Reminded why she hated coming home to a dark house, she felt along the wall for the light switch.

Managing to turn on the weak lamp by the door, she dropped her bag on the floor and crossed to the kitchen.

With a heavy sigh, she pulled down a glass and poured herself the last of the wine left in a bottle she'd opened the weekend before.

She took a long drink and then opened the refrigerator, looking inside at the meager contents.

It looked as if she would be having another dinner alone.

Feeling a pang of self-pity, she reminded herself that now that she and Mason had broken up, she would need to get used to being lonely.

She grew still as she heard a sound from the living room.

Was that someone coming in the door?

Had whoever attacked Gayle and Finola now come for her?

The blood in her veins grew cold as she slowly opened a drawer and reached in to pull out a knife.

Creeping slowly to the door, she listened.

Someone was moving in the other room. She could hear footsteps. Her mouth went dry as she realized the footsteps were coming closer.

Suddenly, the door swung open and the light flashed on.

Cate held up the knife as Bailey jumped back with a terrified scream, running into Ludwig, who barked loudly.

"What in the world are you doing?"

Holding her hand to her chest, Bailey glared at Cate as she put the knife back in the drawer and sank into a chair, her eyes bright with tears.

"I don't know what I'm doing," Cate admitted. "My head is all over the place. Which is why I went to see Dr. Chung."

"That sounds like a good idea," Bailey said. "I'm sure you needed someone to talk to after every-"

Cate held up a hand to stop her.

"I didn't go to talk about my PTSD," she said. "I went to ask if she thinks Mason could be a killer. Because I looked in his file and saw she'd written notes about him."

A single tear slid down her cheek.

"Apparently he has anger issues and blackouts."

She reached for a tissue.

"I feel guilty for looking but I keep wondering if Mason actually could have done this. Is that terrible of me?"

Bailey shook her head.

"It's not terrible at all. After all the evil people you've dealt with, it's not surprising that you aren't sure if Mason could secretly be a monster masquerading as a nice guy."

"But I was coming home to tell you something that should put your mind at ease. At least, as far as Mason's guilt is concerned," Bailey said. "Unfortunately, it came to light after Dr. Varney was attacked. I'm sorry to say she's dead."

Wiping way the tear, Cate stared up at Bailey in shock.

"Fraser and I think whoever killed Jude Varney was the same person who killed Gayle and attacked Finola. We think she was trying to set Mason up. We aren't sure why."

"She? You think the killer is a woman?"

Bailey nodded.

She took out her phone.

"Fraser shared this photo with me. It's from the security camera outside the medical examiner's office. It was taken the night Finola Lawson was attacked."

Cate stared at the grainy figure in the photo.

It was impossible to make out any features, but from the view of the heeled shoes and shapely legs, it appeared to be a woman.

"Fraser also got a glimpse of a woman leaving the hotel room where Dr. Varney's body was found. She was wearing a similar jacket, so he didn't get a good look at her, but we think it could be the same woman."

Bailey scrolled to the next photo on her phone, which showed a gray metal cylinder lying in the dirt.

Zooming in, she focused on the words etched into the metal.

Silent as the grave.

Cate frowned.

"That's one of the silencers we found in Phoenix and Kato's truck," she said. "They were delivering an order to-"

"To the Tumba Cartel," Bailey finished for her. "Yes, I know. And the same kind of silencer was found behind the hotel tonight, which is why we think the cartel might be involved with these killings."

A strange combination of fear and relief flooded through Cate.

"So, Mason isn't a killer," she said, dabbing at her eyes

with the soggy tissue. “But why would the cartel target him?”

Bailey shrugged.

“We don’t know,” she admitted. “But we plan to find out.”

CHAPTER TWENTY-SIX

It was half past eight and the sun was already peeking through the gaps in the window blinds when Bailey opened Cate's bedroom door and peered inside. Her sister was still sleeping, curled up under a thick blanket, her face smooth and childlike in the darkened room. Backing away, Bailey pulled the door closed, glad that she was finally getting some solid sleep.

Finding out Mason isn't a monster or a murderer must have helped.

She called to Ludwig and grabbed his leash from the hook.

It was sunny and getting warmer fast.

Despite it technically still being winter, it was already starting to feel like spring was just around the corner.

It would be a good morning for a nice, long run.

Leading the German shepherd out the door, she ran to the end of Sanctuary Street and turned onto Grand Harbor Boulevard, following Ludwig along the wide, tree-lined street, pulling back on the leash only when they'd reached the Belle Harbor Police Station.

She was about to turn around and start back the way she'd come when she saw Dalton's black truck pull up outside the station.

She lifted her hand to wave, then dropped it again as she saw the Dodge's passenger door open and Madeline Mercer jump out.

Bailey's heart stopped in her chest as Madeline gave a playful wave at Dalton and then headed inside.

Before she could force her legs to move, Dalton spotted her.

His guilty expression visible through the dusty windshield told her everything she needed to know.

Spinning on her heel, she bumped straight into a woman striding down the sidewalk.

Raya Valera stumbled backward.

The woman appeared to recognize her right away.

"You're that FBI Agent, Bailey Flynn, right?" she said. "I've been hoping to run into you."

Bailey tried to move around her but the woman crouched down next to a panting Ludwig and began to scratch his head.

"I've seen you on the news but didn't know how to find you," she said as she straightened up to meet Bailey's eyes.

Suddenly Dalton was there behind her.

He tried to take Bailey's arm but she pulled it away.

"Please, Bailey, it isn't what you-"

"Dalton West?"

Raya was staring at him with wide, brown eyes.

"You two are the ones who tried to save my mother," she said. "I haven't had a chance to thank both of you."

Bailey tried to keep her face neutral, refusing to meet Dalton's eyes as Raya explained that it wasn't their fault her mother was dead. It was Detective Fraser's fault.

In a flash, Bailey's anger was redirected from Dalton to the woman in front of her.

"Detective Fraser had nothing to do with your mother's death," she protested. "He tried to be a good partner to your mother. He's a good man. An honest man with nothing to hide."

She glared back at Dalton.

"Unlike some men I know."

Before Dalton could reply, she turned and ran, sending Ludwig scrambling after her, leaving Raya and Dalton behind as she pictured Madeline's flirtatious smile.

Several months earlier, the CSI team leader had confided that she and Dalton had dated in the past. Bailey had been startled to feel an unexpected pang of jealousy, considering she didn't plan to stick around in Belle Harbor long enough to start a serious relationship.

She'd dealt with the revelation of Dalton's past fling with Madeline just as she dealt with all unpleasant facts.

She tried to ignore it.

But Bailey hadn't been prepared for what she'd just seen. She hadn't expected Dalton to pick up with Madeline where they'd left off.

While she and Dalton had made no commitment to each other, she'd foolishly allowed herself to believe she would have him to herself until she decided to leave town.

Caught up in her thoughts, she didn't notice the silver sedan following behind her as she ran back the way she'd come.

CHAPTER TWENTY-SEVEN

Dalton turned back to Raya Valera, still shaken by the look of hurt and betrayal he'd seen on Bailey's face, wanting to go after her but knowing it was no use. She needed time to cool down. And he needed time to decide how to explain what he'd been doing with Madeline Mercer.

"I'm sorry if I said something wrong."

Raya Valera was studying him with worried eyes.

"It's just, I get so worked up about my mother," she said. "It's so hard to move on when I don't understand what happened. And I never got a chance to say goodbye."

Dalton felt a surge of sympathy for the woman.

Perhaps he could help her find some closure.

And of course, he might have a chance to get back into Bailey's good graces if he helped clear Fraser of any responsibility for his ex-partner's death.

If he could find out what had really happened, Bailey might actually forgive him

"Listen, why don't I buy you a cup of coffee and you can tell me what it is you know about your mother?" he suggested. "I'm a private investigator. I run West Security Services. I could try to help you figure out what happened to her if you want."

Raya looked doubtful.

"I already have someone helping me," she said. "Detective Rourke from the Belle Harbor police has been helping me. He's been giving me information that everyone else has tried to hide, especially that Detective Fraser."

"What have they been trying to hide?" Dalton asked.

"Detective Rourke told me that Detective Fraser was at the hospital the night my mother died," Raya said. "But Fraser won't admit it. He must have something to hide."

Shaking his head, Dalton looked doubtful.

"I know it's true," she insisted. "I spoke to the nurse and she told me someone with the police department had stopped by just before my mother's ventilator shut down."

Raya's eyes filled with tears.

"For some reason, the alarm didn't go off as it should have. She died there all alone, gasping for breath."

"I know I should have been there...but if Detective Fraser was there...if he shut it off, I have to get justice for my mother."

"Why would Detective Fraser want to do that?"

"He didn't like my mother. He didn't want to be her partner. At least, that's what Detective Rourke told me."

"Let me check into it," Dalton said. "I often work pro bono, so it won't cost you anything. Just tell me everything you know."

* * *

After he'd spoken to Raya and had given her his contact details, Dalton tried calling Bailey. When she didn't answer, he left a message that he didn't expect her to return.

For some reason, Bailey must be thinking he was two-timing her with Madeline, but that wasn't the case.

Dalton had simply asked the crime scene technician to meet him at a nearby coffee shop so that he wouldn't be seen giving her Neil Ashworth's DNA profile to run through CODIS.

He didn't want to get Madeline in trouble.

But somehow he suspected that fact might make Bailey even more angry than she was now.

He'd have to try to explain.

Although from the look on Bailey's face, I don't think it'll make much of a difference.

Not wanting to go home, he called Summerset County Medical Center and asked to speak to Carmen Lopez, the nurse in intensive care who'd worked the night Valera had died. After a long wait, the operator came back on the phone.

"Ms. Lopez no longer works at the hospital."

The line went dead.

Figuring he'd have to go down to the hospital later and speak to the current nurse on duty, he decided that he would first attempt to face Bailey's anger head on.

He would tell her about his attempt to find Neil's father, and about asking Madeline for help.

Maybe I'll even tell her that I'm going to help Raya find out what really happened to her mother.

Debating with himself whether she would approve or not, he drove to the Sanctuary Apartments.

He didn't see either Bailey's Black Expedition or Cate's white Lexus in the parking lot.

Disappointed that Bailey wasn't home, he hesitated, then made a wide U-turn, paying little attention to the silver sedan he passed as he pulled back onto Sanctuary Street.

CHAPTER TWENTY-EIGHT

Olga parked under a shady tree and stared at Cate's apartment with angry eyes. Her fingers reached for the Saint Olga pendant, then fell away in frustration as she remembered too late that it was no longer around her neck. She would need to get a replacement soon. Without the pendant, she felt less powerful, even vulnerable as if her patron saint had deserted her.

She was furious that Fraser had shown up at the Summerset Hotel the night before. Furious that she'd had to scurry away like a rat on a sinking ship, allowing Mason to escape his fate.

And now, she couldn't find him.

She'd wanted to watch Cate Flynn suffer his loss. Wanted her to experience the pain of losing the man she loved.

But now Mason was gone.

It was as if he'd just disappeared.

Someone must be helping him, but she wasn't sure who.

She'd managed to persuade Judge Inglebert to grant Mason bail by sending him a clear message from the Tumba Cartel.

A message that the judge had likely thought came from Mr. Tumba himself.

And the judge hadn't dared disobey a direct order.

Not when Mr. Tumba practically owned him.

Mr. Tumba wasn't someone you ignored.

Oh no, not if you've seen what I've seen.

A chill rolled down Olga's spine as she recalled the last time she'd been contacted by the big boss himself regarding an associate who had blatantly defied his orders.

She could still hear the boss' cold voice in her ear as he'd given her specific instructions to follow.

"Make sure he knows who sent you," he'd said without any detectable emotion. "A single shot to the stomach should do the trick. That will give him plenty of time to contemplate the error of his ways."

Olga had willingly complied.

She'd lured the man to an isolated location where they wouldn't be disturbed.

"Mr. Tumba isn't happy with you," she'd said, once they were alone. "He asked me to give you a message."

"You can tell that bastard to-"

The rest of his words had burbled out in a rush of blood as Olga put a bullet in his gut at close range.

She'd watched him fall to the ground, clutching at his sodden shirt as he writhed in pain. She'd wondered if his act of defiance had been worth it, not sure she'd have the nerve to do the same.

The memory of the man's pathetic groans echoed in Olga's ears as Bailey Flynn's black Expedition pulled into the parking lot.

She watched as the FBI agent parked the car and ran

inside. Minutes later she was back in her SUV, speeding away.

Where's she going in such a hurry?

It suddenly hit Olga that the FBI agent was the only one who had the means and motive to help her sister's boyfriend flee the scene.

Bailey Flynn is hiding Mason.

The realization prompted Olga to start the sedan's engine.

She would have to follow Bailey.

Eventually, the agent would lead her to wherever it was she'd hidden Mason.

Of course, after Olga had taken care of Cate's boyfriend, there would be one more task to complete.

One more target to kill to ensure her revenge against the prosecutor had been served in sweet and equal measure.

CHAPTER TWENTY-NINE

Bailey had run straight home after her encounter with Dalton, fuming all the way. Now that she knew he didn't consider their relationship to be exclusive, she had the perfect excuse to end things before she returned to D.C., and before she allowed herself to get hurt again. She wasn't interested in having her heart broken by another man.

She'd suffered enough after being dumped by her former fiancé weeks before their scheduled wedding because he'd fallen in love with her best friend.

Getting involved with another two-timing Casanova wasn't in her future plans.

After a quick shower, she'd left the apartment without stopping to eat breakfast, not wanting to be there if Dalton decided to come by the apartment to plead his case.

In her hurry, she'd left her phone at home and had been forced to swing back by the apartment to pick it up.

Now, as she climbed back into the Expedition, she saw several missed call alerts on the display. One number in particular drew her attention. She returned the call using handsfree as she made a left turn onto Sanctuary Street.

Tanya Jimenez picked up the phone on the first ring.

"Thanks for calling back, Agent Flynn. I have some information for you, but I can't talk now."

She spoke loudly, her voice competing with laughter and raised voices in the background.

"But I'll be working at the All Saints Church all morning. We're having a rummage sale. It ends at noon. Meet me then and I'll tell you what I know."

Bailey quickly agreed.

As soon as she ended the call, she tapped on Jimmy Fraser's name in her contact list.

"I'm heading over to All Saints Orthodox Church to talk to someone who has information for me. I think it might be about Birdie or maybe the Tumba Cartel," she said when he answered sounding sleepy.

"Linette and the girls are out doing some Saturday shopping," he informed her. "So, I'm free if you want to stop by and pick me up for church. I haven't been in a while."

Twenty minutes later she pulled up to his house, where Fraser was waiting outside for her. Climbing into the car, he looked back and gave Ludwig a scratch behind the ears as Bailey headed toward Parish Parkway.

"I should probably tell you about my run-in with Raya Valera this morning," she said. "And I mean *run-in* literally. I crashed into her while I was out for a run with Ludwig."

"What's that woman saying about me now?" he asked.

"The same old thing about you not telling her what you know," Bailey admitted. "But I gave her a piece of my mind. She can't just go around bad-mouthing you like that."

Fraser shook his head and looked despondently out the car

window at the passing scenery.

"Chief Pruett's scheduled my performance review for Monday afternoon," he said. "I have a bad feeling she plans to put me on probation, or maybe even suspend me pending the outcome of Raya Valera's lawsuit against the city. If it wasn't for the union, she'd probably fire me straight away."

Bailey found it hard to believe that anyone would be foolish enough to let a good detective like Fraser go.

Assuring herself that proof of Fraser's innocence would eventually come to light, just as it had in Mason's case, Bailey turned the Expedition into the All Saints Orthodox Church parking lot.

It was still a few minutes before noon, and a stream of stragglers were exiting the church's event hall.

Bailey and Fraser took a detour through the church graveyard, letting Ludwig lead them between above-ground tombs and grave markers, as they killed time until Tanya was done with her shift.

As they approached the building, Reverend Schroeder was standing outside. He smiled at Bailey.

"I've been meaning to call you," he said. "I finally heard back from Reverend Zelnik at the Orthodox Church of Verbena Beach."

His cheerful expression dimmed.

"I asked him if he'd had any teenage parishioners named Birdie in his congregation. He wasn't familiar with anyone by that name, but he's only been with the church about a year, so he wasn't sure. He did say he'd check the records and get back to me."

"Thank you for checking, Reverend," Bailey said. "Would you mind if I contact Reverend Zelnick directly? It's just that we're kind of in a hurry to find anyone who knew the girl's family."

"Oh, certainly," Reverend Schroeder said. "Come to my office and I'll give you his number."

Bailey followed him inside, then carefully entered Reverend Zelnick's contact information into her phone.

By the time she went back outside, Tanya was standing in the parking lot, her dark hair pulled up into a bun as she loaded boxes of unsold items into the back of a truck.

"Thanks for coming by," Tanya said, not stopping her work as she spoke. "A friend of mine called me this morning. She's been seeing one of the guys in the cartel. I've been telling her it's dangerous, but she says she's *in love*."

She shook her head in disgust.

"Anyway, she was saying her man told her about some guy he called El Monstruo. They call him that because he's such an animal. Supposedly, this guy leaves his victims in pieces. Anyway, her man was freaking out because he saw this guy drive by on a motorcycle last night."

"This man, this El Monstruo guy...does your friend know his real name?" Bailey asked, thinking of Carter Delaney's claim that the cartel had other fixers working in the area. "Does she know what he looks like? Could she describe him?"

Tanya shrugged.

"I don't know," she said. "I don't even know if it's true. There's always rumors going around. I can try to find out."

"That would be great," Bailey said. "Thanks for passing on

the information."

As she headed back to the parking lot, her mind churned over the information Tanya had shared.

She never saw the motorcycle parked behind the building or the handsome man standing under the shady tree. When she pulled back onto Parish Parkway, she didn't see the silver sedan merge into traffic several cars behind them.

CHAPTER THIRTY

Fernando Borja kept watch from his position outside All Saints Orthodox Church. Mr. Tumba's brief on his mission had included an address where the Saint could be found, and he had followed his fellow fixer around Belle Harbor most of the morning before he'd finally figured out that she was tailing an FBI agent named Bailey Flynn.

The agent was young and attractive, with dark blonde hair and earnest green eyes. She was just the type of diversion Borja would have enjoyed if he hadn't had a job to do.

Having hidden his motorcycle behind the big church building, he was standing under the cover of a shady tree, where he'd used a long-range listening device to hear the conversation between the two women who'd been talking in the parking lot.

He had been startled to hear himself mentioned as the FBI agent questioned the woman named Tanya, who apparently had friends within the cartel. Friends who liked to talk.

And while Bailey Flynn had been busy sticking her nose into his business, Borja had also managed to attach a tracker to the bottom of the FBI agent's black SUV, deciding it was the best alternative to putting a tracker on the silver sedan.

The Saint was sticking close to Bailey Flynn, so it would be like tracking two targets for the price of one.

And it wouldn't do for the Saint to find a tracker on the crappy car she was currently driving. That could give her forewarning of his presence in Belle Harbor.

He assumed she had a habit of checking under her car each time she got in since it was prudent to look for tracking and incendiary devices. If you were a contract killer, a little healthy paranoia came with the job.

He hadn't figured out yet why the Saint was following the FBI agent or why Mr. Tumba had sent him to Belle Harbor to kill her. All he'd been told was that she'd gone rogue.

Whatever she'd done had obviously put the cartel into jeopardy and she needed to be stopped.

It would be his pleasure to do just that.

His amber eyes turned toward the church.

But first, I think it's time to introduce myself to Tanya.

The door to the event hall swung open silently, and he stood for a moment watching as Tanya picked up discarded items from the floor on her way toward the church office.

Something in the air must have shifted, or perhaps she could smell his cologne. As if Tanya sensed him, she turned around with a half-smile.

Borja figured she'd been expecting to see old Reverend Schroeder. He watched as her eyes lit up with pleasure when she saw him standing by the door instead.

"Am I too late for the rummage sale?" he called out in a deep voice that had set many hearts to trembling with both pleasure and pain in the past.

"I'm sorry, but it's over," she said, looking around the empty room as if she may be able to conjure something up to entice him into staying.

Walking slowly forward, his mouth spread into a teasing smile that revealed straight white teeth.

"So, everybody left you all alone?"

His lips formed a playful pout.

"That wasn't very nice of them."

She laughed but as he continued to draw closer she took an instinctive step back as if suddenly sensing danger.

"Have you called your friend yet?" he asked.

Tanya frowned.

"You know, the one who told you about El Monstruo?"

The gleam of interest in her eyes had turned to fear.

Funny how quickly that always happens.

Stopping directly in front of her, he studied her large dark eyes. She looked tired. It had been a long day. And it was going to be a very long night.

"Your friend's man didn't tell her that I don't look like a monster, did he?" he said.

Slowly, as if in a trance, Tanya shook her head.

"Well, unfortunately, you won't be able to tell her either."

He reached out and ran a long finger down the side of her soft cheek and then across her full lips, anticipating the screams that would come.

But there was no rush.

He had all night.

Tanya would be a gift he gave to himself for all the hard work he'd done lately.

Yes, he would take his time killing this one.

And when he was through, he would leave her on the altar for the big-mouthed reverend to find when he came in to give his Sunday sermon the next day.

Hopefully, Tanya's death would send a message to her friend in the cartel that she should keep her mouth shut in the future. And then tomorrow, it would be time to find Olga and finish his business in Belle Harbor.

CHAPTER THIRTY-ONE

Fraser stared out of the Expedition's window at the passing scenery, impatient to get home. He was sure that Linette and the girls must have already gotten back from their shopping trip and would be wondering where he was. They'd made plans to order a pizza and watch a movie. As the SUV approached Goswell Road, his thoughts were interrupted by the buzzing of his phone.

Looking down at the display, he saw that someone from the Summerset County Medical Center was calling. He answered the call on speaker, holding it up so that Bailey could hear, too.

"Detective Jimmy Fraser?"

The woman's voice was warm and friendly.

"Finola Lawson is awake. She's asking to speak to you."

By the time he'd ended the call, Bailey had already made a frantic U-turn and was racing back toward the hospital.

Twenty minutes later, they stepped off the elevator into the ICU, quickly walking to Finola's room, where they found her still attached to a variety of machines.

Her mother, who had driven down from Orlando days before after getting the news that her daughter wasn't expected to survive, looked tired but relieved as she stood up to greet them.

"Finola's been asking for Detective Fraser ever since she woke up," she said. "I'll leave you alone to talk. Don't stay too long."

Fraser turned to the bed and looked down at Finola.

"Hello, Finola," he said softly. "I'm glad you're feeling better. We've all been very worried about you."

"Mason?"

The name came out in a raspy whisper.

"I think she needs some water," Bailey said.

Picking up a cup of water from the bedside table, she held it for Finola so she could take a small sip from the straw.

"Is Mason okay?" Finola said, sounding clearer.

"Yes, Mason's okay," Fraser said. "Did he do this to you?"

Finola gave a slight shake of her head.

"It wasn't Mason," she said. "It was a woman. She attacked both of us. She hit Mason over the head."

A surge of satisfaction rolled through him at the news.

"Do you mind if I take a statement?" he asked. "And I'd like to record it as well."

She nodded and he took out his phone. By the time they were done, her eyes were drooping closed and Fraser was feeling much better.

Surely there was no way Rourke or Pruett could try to railroad Mason Knox now. Was there?

Of course, they could always try to suppress the interview.

After a moment's thought, Fraser took a deep breath and stepped out of the room.

He scrolled to a name in his contact list that he had rarely used. With a sigh, he tapped on *Sabrina West*.

"This call is off the record," he said. "I'm at the Summerset County Medical Center and if you want a major scoop, I suggest you get down here now. Finola Lawson is talking and she says she saw her attacker."

Twenty minutes later, Sabrina stepped out of the elevator and hurried down the hall wearing jeans, an oversized sweater, and tennis shoes.

It was the first time Fraser had seen her without heels on.

"I didn't take time to change," she said as she skidded to a stop beside him. "I didn't want anyone else to get to her first."

Fraser hoped he hadn't made a terrible mistake. But it was too late to back out now.

As he ushered the reporter into Finola's room, Bailey looked over in surprise and stood up as if ready to protest.

He stopped her by holding up a hand.

"How did she know..."

Her voice trailed off as she saw the guilt in Fraser's eyes.

"This is the only way to make sure Pruett and Rourke don't try to suppress the truth."

Bailey raised both eyebrows and exhaled.

"I hope you know what you're doing," she said once she'd followed Fraser back into the hall, leaving Finola and her mother alone with the eager-faced reporter.

As they walked toward the elevator, Fraser saw a nurse hovering in the hall.

"Are you Detective Jimmy Fraser?"

"Yes, I am."

"A man was in here earlier," she said. "A private investigator. He said I should tell you what I know. He said I should only speak to you or Agent Bailey Flynn."

"Well, you've got us both here. How can we help you?"

The nurse exhaled nervously.

"My friend used to work here. Her name's Carmen Lopez and she was working the night Rita Valera died."

Fraser's heart stopped.

"Carmen told me she saw an officer with the Belle Harbor police coming out of Ms. Valera's room the night she died. When she asked him what he was doing, he said to leave her alone, that she was sleeping peacefully. But when Carmen went to check on her later, the ventilator was off. The alarm hadn't sounded."

Staring at the young woman's wide eyes, Fraser could see that she was terrified.

"How could Carmen be sure he was Belle Harbor police?"

"It said so on his uniform," she said. "Besides, Carmen went to the Belle Harbor police station to report what she'd seen the next day. Only the same officer was there."

"He said he would take her statement, but he acted really weird. Carmen was scared and left without making a statement. Then the guy came into the hospital the next morning and asked for her."

"I saw him myself. She asked me to tell him she had called in sick and she hid in the break room. She quit that afternoon without notice. She was terrified he'd come back."

Fraser pulled up the Belle Harbor PD website on his phone.

"Can you remember what the officer looked like?"

"He was wearing a hat, but from what I could see, his hair was sort of reddish. And he was pale, with lots of freckles."

The description sounded a lot like Rourke.

Fraser showed the nurse a page full of headshots. Each officer had their own photo.

"Do you see the man on this page?"

Her eyes scrolled down the page, then stopped to rest on a photo of Detective Killian Rourke.

"That's him," the nurse confirmed. "That's the officer who came in asking for Carmen. The one she said was in Rita Valera's room the night she died."

Fraser saw Bailey's eyes flick to the open door behind him.

He turned to see Sabrina West exiting the hospital room, aiming her camera in their direction.

The red light beside the viewfinder confirmed she was still recording.

"Looks like I got two scoops for the price of one trip to the hospital," she said. "Detective Fraser, is there anything you want to say on the record about the recent attack on assistant medical examiner Finola Lawson, or the death of Detective Rita Valera?"

Fraser turned to Bailey, not sure if he should call Chief Pruett right away or if he should wait for Sabrina West to break the news for him on the nightly broadcast.

He turned back to face the reporter.

"No comment."

CHAPTER THIRTY-TWO

Bailey rode down in the elevator with Fraser in stunned silence, ignoring the renewed buzzing in her pocket until she was standing outside the Summerset County Medical Center. Pulling out her phone, she looked down at the display, surprised to see a name and phone number she'd added to her contacts earlier that day. Reverend Zelnick from the Verbena Beach Orthodox Church was calling.

"Is this Agent Flynn?" a tentative voice asked when she answered the phone. "With the FBI?"

"Yes, this is Bailey Flynn. I'm glad you called, Reverend Zelnick. I was hoping to talk to you. I wanted to ask you about-"

The reverend cut in.

"About Birdie," he said. "Yes, I know. Reverend Schroeder was kind enough to pass on your message."

He cleared his throat.

"I'm fairly new to the congregation here in Verbena Beach, but I've asked around and believe I have the information you've been looking for."

Pressing the phone to her ear, Bailey listened closely, not wanting to miss a word of what he was saying.

"Our choir director confirmed there was a girl named Birdie Sadler in the children's choir but apparently she stopped attending several years ago," he said. "The director isn't sure where she is now, but I did check our baptismal records."

Bailey's pulse quickened.

"The girl's name is Bernadette Sadler. According to our records, she will be turning eighteen in April."

A pang of sadness filled Bailey at the thought that Bernadette "Birdie" Sadler wouldn't be alive to celebrate her eighteenth birthday. That she would never become an adult.

"The record shows that she was born to a woman named Olga Sadler," Zelnick said. "No father is listed."

A chill rolled down Bailey's back.

"Olga Sadler?"

"That's right," the reverend said.

"Apparently, Olga Sadler was a parishioner here as well, but she stopped attending around the same time as her daughter."

After thanking Reverend Zelnick for calling, Bailey told him she would like to drive up to interview his choir director and other members of the congregation who might have known Birdie.

"You don't think something's happened to her, do you?" he asked. "She's almost an adult now. Perhaps she and her mother just moved away. Perhaps they wanted a fresh start."

"I wish it was that simple," Bailey said. "But unfortunately, we suspect foul play."

She didn't tell him that the Birdie they were looking for

was dead.

Better to break the news in person to anyone at the church who knew her. Perhaps she even had extended family or friends in the congregation. If so, they may be able to provide much-needed information about her mother's current whereabouts.

After telling the reverend she would drive up to Verbena Beach the following day, Bailey ended the call.

She thought a minute, then sent the information she'd learned to Argus and asked him to call her when he got a chance.

Within minutes her phone was buzzing in her hand.

"I know you're flying back to D.C. today but I'm hoping you can add the name Bernadette Sadler to your data and use it to rerun your algorithm. I believe she may be our Birdie. And a woman named Olga Sadler may be her mother."

Argus was quiet for a long beat.

"*Olga* Sadler? As in, *Saint* Olga? As in *the* Olga on the pendants found in Birdie's grave and at the scene of Gayle Kershaw's murder?"

"That's the one," Bailey confirmed. "If we can track Olga down, we just may find our killer. Or at least find out who may be killing people in the name of her patron saint."

* * *

When Bailey dropped Fraser off at home, his wife and their two little girls, Sasha and Tiana, were bringing in groceries from the car.

Based on the tight expression on Linette's face, Bailey figured the detective would be having a cold dinner.

She gave him a consoling smile as he climbed out and shut the door. Before she could drive away, he turned to look back in the window.

"If you want me to go with you to Verbena Beach tomorrow..."

Bailey shook her head.

"No, it's Sunday. You stay with your family," she said. "I'll get Agent Sharma to ride up there with me."

She didn't add that he would probably have plenty of questions from Chief Pruett to answer once Sabrina West's report hit the late-night news.

Another scandal was about to hit the Belle Harbor Police Department, and Jimmy Fraser would once again be in the middle of it.

Once she left Fraser's house, Bailey drove to Claremont Street. She had promised to have dinner with her parents, and Jackie and Christopher Flynn were already sitting at the dinner table when she and Ludwig arrived.

Duchess, her mother's Siamese cat, pretended to ignore them both as usual while Ludwig immediately crossed over to her father, staking out a position where Christopher could sneak him bites of table food.

After dinner, Bailey asked her father to turn the television to Channel 3 News. She'd been correct in suspecting that Sabrina West wouldn't be able to keep her big scoops under wraps until morning.

The reporter was on air live, holding out a microphone as

she followed Chief Pruett and Mayor Sutherland into a restaurant downtown.

"Chief Pruett, is there anything you'd like to say to our viewers about the recent attack on assistant medical examiner Finola Lawson?" Sabrina asked. "And will the charges against Summerset County medical examiner Mason Knox be dropped?"

Chief Pruett had obviously been caught off guard.

"I have no comment on ongoing investigations," she said, trying to wave the reporter away.

Holding a microphone by Pruett's face, Sabrina prodded.

"So, you have nothing to say about the investigation into Detective Rita Valera's death? Are you aware that a witness has come forward?"

"A witness?"

Chief Pruett sounded indignant.

"Yes, a witness contacted our station," Sabrina confirmed. "Were you aware that, according to this witness, an officer from the Belle Harbor PD was the last person to have been in the room with Detective Valera the night she died?"

As the mayor hurried into the restaurant, leaving Pruett on her own, the police chief held up an irritable hand.

"As I said, I can't comment on active investigations."

Turning off the television, Bailey turned to see her parents staring at her in consternation.

"So, Mason has been cleared of all charges?" Jackie asked. "And that woman who works with him is going to be okay?"

"Well, Mason's not officially been cleared yet," Bailey admitted. "But, I'm confident he will be. And yes, Finola

Lawson should make a full recovery."

Christopher frowned.

"But do they still think Mason killed the other women?" he asked. "What about the one who was found at his house?"

"He means the crazy woman who was stalking him," Jackie added helpfully. "And, if it wasn't Mason, who was it?"

Not sure how much more she should say, Bailey hesitated.

"New evidence suggests a woman is responsible for the attacks," she said, choosing her words carefully. "Although that information hasn't been made public yet, so keep it to yourselves for now."

After they finished eating, her father stood and stretched.

"I'm off to bed," he said. "I've got an early round of golf."

Bailey gave him a hug, then turned to her mother.

"You really think a woman has been attacking all these people?' Jackie asked, looking troubled. "What could possibly be her motive?"

"I'm not sure, that's what we're still trying to figure out," Bailey said. "But we identified a teenage girl's body in the Belle Harbor Burial Ground crypt and based on information I just learned today, I'm starting to think her mother might have been involved in the murders."

Picturing the pendant on the dinner plate, she nodded to herself. Yes, Olga Sadler must be involved.

Saint Olga is the patron saint of revenge after all. So maybe this is all about revenge.

"I'll be driving up to Verbena Beach tomorrow," Bailey said. "I may find out more then."

Jackie's frown deepened.

"That sounds dangerous."

"Don't worry, I'm not going on my own. I'll ask Agent Sharma to go with me."

Surreptitiously checking her watch, she hoped Aisha Sharma would be amenable to making last-minute plans.

Either way, tomorrow she would go to Verbena Beach and she would find out what Olga Sadler was up to.

CHAPTER THIRTY-THREE

The morning sun was obscured by a thick cloud as Olga drove toward the Sanctuary Apartments in her silver sedan. Looking in the rearview mirror, she smiled when she saw the man on the motorcycle behind her. He had been waiting for her outside Cate and Bailey's apartment, knowing she would show up eventually, biding his time.

She finally had Fernando Borja exactly where she wanted him. Mr. Tumba had played right into her hands.

After Carter Delaney had told her who had killed Birdie, she knew the incarcerated serial killer would snitch on her and tell Mr. Tumba she'd gone rogue.

And once the big boss decided she posed a risk to him and his operations, she'd known he would send for El Monstruo.

It may have been the only thing that would guarantee he'd summon the monstrous man back to Belle Harbor.

Who else would be capable of taking out his best fixer? Who else could be trusted to take out the elusive Saint Olga?

So, she hadn't been surprised when, less than forty-eight hours after she'd spoken to Delaney, Borja had arrived in the little town, just as she'd anticipated.

And she'd made sure he had no trouble finding her.

Most likely the sadistic killer had been instructed to make her disappear without drawing any attention to himself or the cartel.

He'd want to follow her for a while to better understand her current situation before he made his move.

What he doesn't know is that I'm one step ahead of him.

Starting the engine, she pulled onto Sanctuary Street, confident that El Monstruo would be right behind her.

The man who was feared throughout the cartel for his sadism was about to find out what pain really was.

Leading him to Summerset Park, she drove down the narrow, twisting service road that led to the lake.

As Olga rounded a bend just before the head of the nature trail, she made a sharp turn onto a dirt path. It was practically impossible to see it if you weren't looking for it.

But she had explored the park from end to end over the last few months as she'd formulated her plan, and she knew exactly where she was going.

Pulling forward until the car was concealed by a cluster of overgrown bushes, she waited until she heard Borja's motorcycle rumble past before quickly putting the sedan in reverse.

Once she was back on the service road, positioned behind El Monstruo just as she'd planned, she quickly continued toward the lake.

Coming up behind the big motorcycle, she jammed her foot on the gas pedal and accelerated forward at full speed, sending the heavy silver sedan crashing into the back of Borja's motorcycle with a deafening crunch.

The impact sent Borja flying over the motorcycle's handlebars. He landed hard on the grassy bank of the river.

To Olga's surprise, the big man got to his feet.

Stomping on the brake, she brought the sedan to a screeching halt, then jumped out, her Beretta already in her hand.

As Borja turned and lunged toward the river, she pulled the trigger, putting two bullets into his back.

He plunged under the water as she ran forward.

Before she could shoot again, someone shouted.

Looking up, she saw a boat on the other side of the lake.

She turned back to the car and jumped in. As she raced back the way she'd come, she wondered if she should have chosen another method of destruction for the monster.

She could have spent more time with him. She could have tortured him the way he'd tortured her daughter.

But no, she couldn't risk being seen.

Not when she still had one more target to take care of.

She would have to be satisfied with the thought of his body being torn apart by the alligators that lived in the dark water of every Florida lake.

Sticking her gun back into the glove compartment, Olga headed toward Claremont Street.

* * *

Olga pulled up outside a large, comfortable-looking home and climbed out of the sedan, stopping to inspect the dented bumper before she walked up to the front door.

She knocked and waited as footsteps sounded in the hall.

The door swung open to reveal an attractive woman with short, silvery hair and an inquisitive smile.

"Hello?"

Clearing her throat, Olga returned the smile.

"Jackie Flynn? I'm sorry to bother you on a Sunday, but I was hoping to talk to you about your daughter. May I come in?"

Jackie hesitated, then nodded and stepped back to allow her visitor inside the foyer. Olga's smile faltered as she caught sight of a white Siamese cat perched on a table by the door.

She was allergic to cats. Had always hated them. She glared at the animal, who glared back with wide blue eyes.

"I saw you at the courthouse the other day," Olga said, turning to Jackie, unable to keep the bitterness from her voice. "You're very lucky to have two such accomplished daughters. I envy you."

Scooping up the cat to hold it against her chest, Jackie smiled. She seemed oblivious to the hostility underlying Olga's words.

"Yes, I'm quite proud of them both," Jackie said, glancing down at her watch. "But I'm afraid I was just heading out, so what exactly is it you wanted to discuss?"

Turning curious eyes on Olga, she waited.

"How about we start with Cate?" Olga suggested. "How about we start with how your daughter ruined my life?"

Drawing a gun from her pocket, she thrust it toward Jackie, earning an angry scratch from the cat in her arms.

"You nasty little beast," Olga hissed, using her free hand to swat at Duchess, who yowled in anger as Jackie dropped her to the floor.

Blood from the scratch dripped onto the marble floor as Olga kicked out at the cat, who scurried away.

"Don't try anything stupid," Olga ordered, keeping the gun trained on the pale skin between Jackie's startled green eyes. "If you do as you're told, you may still get out of this alive."

CHAPTER THIRTY-FOUR

Dalton West frowned at his reflection in the coffee shop window as he approached the Summerset Espresso Café. He already looked tired and out of sorts despite the early hour. Running a hand through his windblown hair, he arranged his face into a smile and pushed through the door to find Neil Ashworth sitting at a table in the corner.

Since the man was currently his only paying client, Dalton had decided to indulge his request to meet at the café at eight a.m. on Sunday morning.

"Sorry about this," Neil said as Dalton sank into the chair across from him. "It's just that my mother goes to the early service at church, so she won't be asking any questions about where I've been."

Biting back a question about why a forty-year-old man would need to explain his constant whereabouts to his mother, Dalton nodded and gratefully accepted the steaming cup of black coffee Neil slid toward him.

"My mother says all the rich, successful people in Summerset County attend the early service," Neil explained as he sipped at his own small cup of green tea. "According to her, only the lazy people sleep in. She says church is where she makes the most lucrative business contacts."

Dalton decided he'd heard enough of what Nigella Ashworth had to say, but he managed to keep his expression neutral as he took a long sip from his cup, hoping the caffeine would give him enough energy to get through the meeting.

"Listen, Neil, I've got some good news," he said. "I've arranged to run your DNA profile through another database."

He'd already decided he wouldn't tell Neil that the database was CODIS or that the DNA within it was associated with crime scenes, criminals, and victims.

"If we're lucky, we'll have some information on your father in the next few weeks."

Suddenly, Neil's face flushed a deep red.

He stared past Dalton with wide eyes.

"What have you done, Neil?"

The shrill voice made Dalton jump.

He turned to see Nigella Ashworth standing behind him.

From the horrified look on her face, it was obvious she'd heard his last comment about Neil's father.

"How dare you go behind my back?" she screeched. "Haven't I told you that your father is dead to me? Haven't I been hurt enough for one lifetime?"

Resentment flashed across Neil's face so quickly Dalton wasn't sure he'd even seen it. Then it was gone, leaving behind his usual placid, stoic expression.

"I'm sorry, Mother. I wasn't thinking..."

Neil's words trailed away as Nigella turned blazing eyes on Dalton.

"How dare you take advantage of my son," she hissed in a low, hard voice, suddenly aware that she was drawing attention from the other customers in the café. "Trying to exploit his grief for your gain, are you? Trying to make a buck out of other people's pain?"

Refusing to dignify the woman's accusations with a response, Dalton shrugged his wide shoulders, pushed back his chair, and got to his feet.

"Let's pick up our conversation another time."

He addressed the words to Neil, keeping his voice calm.

"When you're ready to talk, you know how to reach me."

Ignoring Nigella's huff of outrage, Dalton dropped his empty coffee cup into the trash marked *Recycling* and headed out the door.

* * *

After leaving the Café, Dalton decided to try his luck again at Bailey's apartment, although he didn't have much hope.

She hadn't answered any of his calls or responded to his text messages for the last twenty-four hours.

Seeing her Expedition sitting in its usual space outside, he parked and went up to knock on the door, wondering if he should have stopped first and bought flowers.

No, that would just make me look guilty, and I'm not.

He managed a smile as the door swung open but it faded when he saw Cate standing just inside with her arms crossed over her chest.

"Bailey's not here," she said.

"Then why is her car out there?" Dalton asked.

"Agent Sharma from the Miami field office picked her up."

Checking her watch, she started to close the door.

"Hold on. Where did she go?" he asked. "Do you know when she'll be back?"

"I think she's going to interview a potential witness in Verbena Beach," Cate said. "I don't know when she'll be home but I'll let her know you stopped by."

Dalton frowned, wondering why Cate was being so curt with him. Had Bailey told her sister what had happened? Had she told her they were through?

He turned to leave, then stopped and turned back.

"I don't know what Bailey might have told you," he said, feeling instantly foolish. "But when she saw me with Madeline the other day she got the wrong idea."

Raising an eyebrow, Cate remained silent.

"All I did was ask Madeline to help me with a missing person case I'm working on. I think Bailey misunderstood and I just wanted a chance to set her straight."

"Whether she believes it or not, I'm not interested in seeing anyone else, and I hate wasting the time we could have together before she moves back to D.C. for good."

He turned again to leave.

This time, Cate reached out a hand to stop him.

"Listen, I appreciate you helping out with Mason," she said, her voice no longer cold and formal. "Bailey told me you were there for him the other day."

"And I appreciate you saying that," he replied, feeling his shoulders relax. "I was just doing what Bailey asked me to do.

I may sound like a complete fool, but I'd do just about anything your sister asked of me."

"I think she just wants you to be honest," Cate said, trying to soften the words with a smile. "She's got to deal with enough secrets and lies at work. Next time you talk to her, just tell her the truth."

Figuring she was right and that there wasn't much more to be said, he nodded and left. This time for real.

He had just reached his truck when his phone buzzed in his pocket. Sabrina's number appeared on the display.

"The stupid van won't start again," she wailed into the phone as soon as he answered. "A woman's body has been found on the altar of All Saints Orthodox Church and I don't have a way to get there."

"I'm on my way."

CHAPTER THIRTY-FIVE

Bailey listened closely for the sound of Dalton's deep voice. Hearing only silence, she opened the door to the study and stepped out into the hall, then winced as she saw Cate standing in the middle of the living room waiting for her.

Her sister's arms were crossed over her chest and there was a familiar put-upon expression on her face that didn't bode well.

"Okay, I did what you wanted. I told him you weren't here," Cate said with a heavy sigh. "Although, you and I both know that hiding from your problems won't fix anything."

Bailey opened her mouth to explain, but Cate wasn't finished.

"Dr. Chung says that the only way to overcome your fear is to face it head on. You should take her advice."

"Fear?" Bailey asked indignantly. "I'm not afraid of Dalton."

Cate snorted.

"Well, you're certainly afraid of getting close to him. Anyone with two eyes and half a brain can see that."

Deciding it was pointless to argue with a person who made

a living out of arguing complicated criminal cases in court, Bailey crossed to the front window and looked outside, wondering what Dalton was really up to.

She'd overheard everything he had said earlier but she couldn't imagine what missing person case he'd been working on with Madeline Mercer.

And why wouldn't he have told me about it?

She wasn't sure it even mattered.

If I can't trust him to be honest then...

Her brooding was interrupted by Cate calling her name.

"Bailey? Did you hear me? I said why don't you go after Dalton? Give him a chance to explain. Why not talk it out?"

"I can't," Bailey said. "I don't have time. I'm driving up to Verbena Beach today, remember?"

Cate followed after her as Bailey went back to the study.

Her sister watched suspiciously as Bailey slid her Glock into her holster and strapped her smaller Ruger to her ankle.

"Is Agent Sharma picking you up?" Cate asked. "Or are you taking the Expedition?"

Ignoring the question, Bailey picked up Ludwig's leash and called to the German shepherd

She hadn't mentioned to Cate that Aisha Sharma had driven down to Key West with her boyfriend for the weekend.

Bailey would be going up to Verbena Beach on her own.

The idea wasn't exactly comforting, but what could she do?

Besides, how much trouble can I get into interviewing a reverend and a few elderly parishioners at a church?

Wanting to get away before Cate could ask further questions, she hurried out to the Expedition, made sure

Ludwig was settled into the back seat and climbed behind the wheel.

But before she could pull away, Cate appeared beside the driver's side window. She held up Bailey's phone.

"You forgot this," she said, arching an accusatory eyebrow. "Just like you forgot to tell me that Agent Sharma isn't going with you."

Bailey stared at her phone, seeing that a text message from Sharma had popped up on the display.

Sorry I can't join you today. Be careful!

Avoiding her sister's disapproving eyes, Bailey sighed.

"It's no big deal. I'll be fine on my own."

"I'm coming with you," Cate stated flatly.

Her stubborn tone made it clear Bailey had no hope of changing her sister's mind.

Still holding the phone, Cate circled the vehicle and climbed into the passenger seat. Once she was all buckled in, she peered over at Bailey with an *aren't-we-having-fun-now* smile.

"If we've got to drive four hours on a Sunday morning, we might as well make the best of it," she said with forced cheerfulness. "We haven't been on a road trip in a while so let's make an adventure out of it, just like Thelma and Louise."

"We've *never* been on a road trip together," Bailey reminded her. "And didn't Thelma and Louise drive off a cliff at the end? That's not my idea of an exciting adventure."

"Lucky for you, there are no cliffs in Florida," Cate said.

As Bailey headed for the highway, Cate's phone buzzed.

"Mom's asking us to go over to her house," she said as her thumbs tapped in a response. "But today's *our* day. I'm not going to let her ruin our trip by guilting us for not going over there."

"What did you tell her?" Bailey asked once Cate's thumbs had stopped moving.

"I told her we were together, heading up to Verbena Beach for the day. I said I was putting our phones in *do-not-disturb* mode and that we'll call her when we get back."

With a self-satisfied smile, Cate turned off the ringers on both her phone and Bailey's and shoved them into the glove compartment.

Turning the radio to a classic rock station, she rolled down the window, leaned back, and let the cool wind and Tom Petty's *Runnin' Down a Dream* flood over them as they sped north up the coast.

* * *

It was well past noon by the time they pulled into the sprawling parking lot of the Verbena Beach Orthodox Church.

Bailey saw that most of the parishioners who'd attended the morning service had already left. Only a handful of cars remained parked along the chain-link fence that cut between the big lot and the church graveyard.

Parking next to a silver sedan, Bailey let Ludwig out of the back seat as Cate climbed down and stretched her legs.

She gave the German shepherd time to take care of business after the long drive before heading toward the big building.

As they approached the entrance, Bailey looked up at the church's stone walls, domed roof, and arched windows, which gave the building a medieval vibe.

Resisting the sudden urge to run back to the car and drive away, Bailey opened the door and followed Ludwig inside.

The interior of the church was dimly lit by banks of candles blazing from small altars along both sides of the cavernous room, and sunlight that filtered through the narrow, arched windows.

Bailey could see a man in an elaborate white robe standing before the main altar at the front of the church.

He was talking to several members of the congregation who had apparently stayed after services for choir practice.

Not wanting to interrupt, Bailey and Cate stood quietly, listening to the choir's peaceful, melodic chanting.

Once the practice was over and the choir members began to disperse, the reverend came over to greet them.

"Special Agent Flynn? I'm Reverend Zelnick."

He was tall and lanky, with a scraggly beard and longish blonde hair that had started to thin. His narrow face was solemn, although his eyes were friendly and welcoming.

"Thank you for seeing us, Reverend," Bailey said. "I hope you don't mind that I brought along my sister, Cate Flynn, and my search and rescue dog, Ludwig."

Reverend Zelnick greeted Cate, then smiled at the German shepherd, who politely wagged his tail.

Turning to the departing choir members, he waved to a woman heading toward the exit.

"There's someone I think you'll want to meet," he said as the woman approached. "This is Mrs. Sadler. She's Bernadette Sadler's grandmother."

Bailey's eyes fell to the silver pendant hanging on a chain around the woman's neck.

"It's good to meet you, Mrs. Sadler. I'm Special Agent Bailey Flynn with the FBI, and this is my sister, Cate Flynn. She's an assistant state attorney down in Summerset County."

Bailey gestured toward the necklace.

"That's not a Saint Olga pendant, is it?"

Glancing down at the pendant, the older woman shook her head.

"No, this is Saint Cecilia, the patron saint of musicians. She's my namesake, and my inspiration for joining the choir."

She looked at Bailey with a curious smile.

"But I do have a daughter named after Saint Olga."

Her smile faded.

"It's a tradition in my family for each child to take the name of their patron saint."

Cate had gone still beside Bailey and was staring at the woman with a confused frown.

"You're *Cecilia*?" Cate asked. "Cecilia Sadler?"

"Yes, I am," the woman confirmed.

Before Cate could reply, Bailey cut in.

"And your granddaughter is Bernadette Sadler? The daughter of Desmond Bolt and Olga Sadler?"

A wary look entered Cecilia's eyes.

"We call my granddaughter Birdie," she said slowly. "And yes, Dessie is her father. But he's in jail. He was convicted of murder a few years ago. Not long before..."

She sighed.

"Well, not long before Birdie ran away. Is that why you're here? Have you found Birdie? Has she gotten into some sort of trouble?"

Bailey hesitated.

She would have to tell the woman that her granddaughter was dead. And she would have to ask the woman if she knew who might have killed her.

But first things first.

"Where's Birdie's mother?" Bailey asked. "Where's Olga now?"

Cecilia opened her mouth, then quickly closed it again as if unsure what to say.

"My daughter hasn't been well for some time," she finally managed. "Not since Dessie was sentenced to life and Birdie ran off. Naturally, Olga was devastated. She sank into a terrible depression. I mean, she's always been moody but I've never seen her that bad."

Tears welled in the woman's eyes.

"And then a few months back, after I hadn't heard from her for several days, I stopped by her house. It was empty. She had packed up and was gone."

She raised her hands in a helpless shrug.

"I keep trying to reach her on her phone, but she won't pick up," she said. "I haven't heard from her since."

"Did Olga ever file a missing person report for Birdie?"

Cecilia shook her head.

"Oh no, she said the police wouldn't help. She blamed them for locking up Dessie. Called them all scum, although, in my opinion, *he* is the scum."

Bailey cleared her throat, realizing that the older woman hadn't heard yet that Dessie was dead. Perhaps she didn't listen to the news, and the prison obviously hadn't contacted her.

"Do you have a photo of Birdie and her mother?" Bailey asked.

Cecilia nodded.

She dug into her purse and pulled out an oversized keychain with a faded photo of a smiling woman and child.

She handed the keychain to Bailey, who stared down at the image with a sinking heart.

The girl in the photo was a younger version of the girl she'd seen in the *Belle Harbor Chronicle* article that had been pinned on the message board of the All Saints Orthodox Church youth shelter.

Cate leaned over to study the photo as Bailey turned somber green eyes to Cecilia.

Clearing her throat, she steeled herself to deliver the bad news.

"What is it?" Cecilia asked.

Her lips had started to tremble.

"Do you know something about my Olga or my granddaughter?"

Bailey gave a reluctant nod.

"I'm sorry, but a teenage girl's body was found down in

Belle Harbor, Florida several months ago. A DNA test has since confirmed that the girl was the biological daughter of Desmond Bolt. We believe she was your granddaughter, Bernadette Sadler."

"Birdie's dead?" Cecilia gasped, putting a hand to her mouth. "Are you...are you sure it's..."

Suddenly her knees gave way, and both Bailey and Cate sprang forward to grab her arms before she could crumple to the floor.

"Come, sit down over here," Bailey said.

Leading the distraught woman to a chair by the wall, she called to Reverend Zelnick, who was saying goodbye to the last of the choir members.

"Can she get some water?"

The reverend hurried through a door behind the altar before returning minutes later with a full glass. He murmured words of comfort as Cecilia sipped the cool liquid.

"I'll drive her home," he said. "She shouldn't be on her own."

As he helped Cecilia to her feet, Cate pulled Bailey to the side.

She pointed to the photo keychain in Bailey's hand.

"I've seen Cecilia's daughter before," she said in a hushed voice. "I've met Olga Sadler. Only, that's not the name she's been using."

* * *

Cate and Bailey helped Cecilia Sadler out to the parking lot and into Reverend Zelnick's roomy Buick, then watched the big car drive away. As they turned toward the Expedition, Bailey realized she still held the distraught woman's car keys in her hand.

Looking after the departing Buick, she noticed the silver sedan parked by the fence. As it was the only other vehicle left in the lot, she decided it must belong to Mrs. Sadler.

Before she could ask Cate what they should do about the keys, her sister grabbed her arm and swung her around to face her.

"Did you hear what I said inside?" Cate demanded.

She grabbed the keychain from Bailey and held it up.

"I've seen Olga Sadler in Belle Harbor," she said. "She started working at Dr. Chung's office a few months ago after the regular receptionist got into an accident."

Bailey's eyes widened as she realized what Cate was saying.

"The Olga in this photo looks a lot younger than the Cecilia Sadler who works at Dr. Chung's office," Cate continued. "The woman in Belle Harbor has gray hair and glasses now, but I'd bet my life she's the same woman that's in this picture."

Her face was flushed with emotion, and the photo in her hand shook as she held it out to Bailey.

"Olga Sadler must have used her mother's identity to get a job at Dr. Chung's office. She's been working there for months."

Horror filled her voice.

"That would explain how she knew about Gayle's

obsession with Mason. If she'd been reviewing the notes from the charts, she'd know pretty much everything about Mason...and about me."

Grabbing Bailey's arm, she pushed her toward the Expedition.

"Let's get going," she urged. "We need to get to Belle Harbor."

"Okay, just slow down," Bailey said, trying to make sense of what Cate was saying as she opened the SUV's door and reached into the glove compartment to retrieve her phone. "I need to get Ludwig. He's still inside the church."

She plucked Cecilia's keychain from Cate's hand.

"And we can't take this with us. I'll leave it inside for now."

Starting back toward the big building, she turned on her ringer and checked her phone, noting that she had over a dozen missed calls and messages.

The latest text message was from Argus Murphy.

Olga Sadler served time in prison for manslaughter. Call me.

There was also a message from her father.

Do you know where your mother is? I got home and she and Duchess were gone. And there's blood on the foyer floor.

She turned back to see Cate hurrying toward her, holding up her phone with a look of panic on her face.

"You need to see this, it's from Mom."

Dropping anxious eyes to the phone in Cate's hands, Bailey saw a photo of her mother and sister standing outside the courthouse.

"It looks as if someone took that from a distance," Bailey

said. "Someone who was at the courthouse Friday morning."

A message accompanied the photo.

A mother's last embrace.

Bailey frowned as she looked down at her father's message, her heart starting to pound hard in her chest.

"How'd she get that photo?" Cate asked. "And what does she–"

Holding up a hand to stop her sister's words, Bailey gestured for her to listen. Slow, solemn music was drifting from the church.

Bailey frowned as she remembered the church was supposed to be empty. Sliding her Glock from its holster, she motioned for Cate to follow her back inside.

As they pushed through the big door, she recognized Chopin's Piano Sonata No. 2 in B-flat minor. She saw movement up ahead as the dramatic music spilled from the speakers to fill the sanctuary.

A woman with thick gray hair and glasses stood in a patch of the fading light coming in from the tall, narrow windows.

She was aiming a gun in their direction.

"Did you know this sonata was played at Chopin's graveside during his burial almost two hundred years ago?" the woman asked in a conversational tone. "It's a funeral march. Which is why I played it during Gayle Kershaw's last meal."

Cate gasped beside Bailey.

"You're not Cecilia Sadler," she called out, pointing an accusing finger toward the altar. "You're Olga, her daughter."

"That's right," the woman admitted, pulling off her

glasses. "But I had you fooled, didn't I? A little hair dye, my mother's glasses, and some old clothes was all it took."

Bailey's pulse quickened but her eyes remained fixed on the gun.

"Why did you do it?" she asked.

She needed to stall for time. Needed to find out what the woman had done with her mother before anyone started shooting.

"Why kill Gayle Kershaw and the others?" she added. "What did they ever do to you?"

"They didn't do anything."

Olga raised a hand to point at Cate.

"*You* caused all this suffering."

Her eyes gleamed with hate.

"*You* chose to prosecute Dessie when he was an innocent man. Birdie's dead because she tried to exonerate her father."

Olga's face twisted into a grimace as she took a step forward.

"*You* made me a widow and *you* broke the most precious bond on earth, the bond between a mother and her child."

A terrible smile lit up her face.

"You might have succeeded in sending Dessie and Birdie to their graves, but with the help of my patron saint, I have come here to take my revenge in accordance with the holy text of Leviticus."

She began to recite the verse in a low, menacing voice that sent a chill down Bailey's spine.

"Anyone who inflicts a permanent injury on his or her neighbor shall receive the same in return: fracture for fracture, eye for eye,

tooth for tooth. The same injury that one gives another shall be inflicted in return."

Olga reached into the pocket of her jacket and pulled out Jackie's bright green phone case.

She brandished it with satisfaction.

"I'm afraid there'll be no more mother, daughter time for either of you, ever again," she said. "Your mother is now lost to the grave, just like my daughter, Bernadette."

CHAPTER THIRTY-SIX

Jimmy Fraser stood at the door of All Saints Orthodox Church of Summerset County. Needing a break from the bloody crime scene behind him, he watched two uniformed Belle Harbor PD officers cordoning off a special area for the press. Looking back over his shoulder, he saw Killian Rourke standing beside the altar, staring down at what remained of Tanya Jimenez.

The detective had been the first on scene after Reverend Schroeder arrived early that morning to find the battered body of the church volunteer laid out on the altar.

The older man had managed to call 911 and report the crime before going into a state of shock that had since prompted responding paramedics to take him to the hospital for observation.

As agitated voices erupted in the parking lot, Fraser turned back to the crowd, figuring they must be getting restless.

Then he saw Sabrina West pushing her way through the throng.

The Channel 3 News reporter had been at the scene for hours, jockeying for position behind the yellow crime scene tape as she broadcast live. She was now pushing bystanders out of her way as she made a beeline toward a white SUV that had pulled into the lot.

Reaching the vehicle just as Millicent Pruett stepped out, Sabrina shoved a microphone toward her, only to be blocked by two uniformed officers who had jumped out after the chief of police.

The officers cleared a path toward the church entrance where Fraser stood, and Chief Pruett began making her way toward him.

Fraser grimaced inwardly as she approached, wondering if Rourke had once again summoned their new boss to do his bidding.

But what does the man have to complain about now?

Forcing the thought from his mind, Fraser steeled his resolve, determined to focus on the task at hand.

He had to investigate a gruesome murder and interview dozens of potential witnesses in the congregation. He couldn't afford to worry about Pruett and what she might say or do.

Worrying wouldn't help him find the monster who'd killed Tanya Jimenez. He'd need all the experience, skill, and luck he could muster to solve the case. And even that might not be enough.

And if this is my last day on the job, I intend to make damn sure I've done everything I can. I won't be leaving anything on the field.

He watched Chief Pruett dodge Sabrina once again.

Giving a dismissive shake of her head, she ignored the camera and microphone the reporter held out and ducked under the tape.

Fraser stepped back into the building, remaining silent as the police chief followed him inside and looked around the scene with obvious distaste.

"I've been trying to reach you all morning, Fraser," she said in a low voice. "Is there somewhere we can talk in private?"

Fraser raised an eyebrow, then nodded and led the chief down the aisle to a small alcove. Luckily, the cozy nook showed no signs of the bloody attack that had taken place the night before.

"I conducted an interview with Carmen Lopez this morning," Chief Pruett said. "She's the nurse who was working at the Summerset County Medical Center the night Rita Valera died."

"I know who she is," Fraser said with a frown. "What I don't know is why you felt the need to come down here to tell me you interviewed her. Couldn't you have updated me later?"

"I realize this isn't ideal timing," the police chief said. "But Ms. Lopez has identified Killian Rourke as the man she saw leaving Rita Valera's room the night she died."

As she met Fraser's eyes full on, he saw tension in her face.

"I'm going to have to suspend Rourke from his position pending an investigation and take him in for questioning," Pruett said.

"Now?" Fraser asked, unable to hide his shock.

"Right now," Pruett confirmed. "Which is why I brought a couple of uniformed officers with me. We'll try to do this as quickly as possible so as not to impede your investigation here."

Her voice held a respectful tone he hadn't heard from her before.

Not waiting for his reaction, Pruett turned and headed back up the aisle. She stopped in the doorway and nodded at the two male officers waiting outside.

The men hurried forward as Pruett made her way over to Rourke.

"Detective Rourke, I am suspending you from your duties with immediate effect," she said without preamble as he turned to stare at her in surprise. "I need you to come with me for an interview. Several serious allegations have been made related to the death of Detective Rita Valera."

At her words, Rourke stiffened indignantly.

Glaring at the two brawny officers standing behind the chief, Rourke balled his fists as if contemplating a fight, then stomped past them toward the cruiser.

As he passed by Fraser, Rourke's face flushed an angry red and his mouth set into a hard line.

"As you were, Detective," Chief Pruett said before turning on her heel and following the procession out of the church.

Fraser sucked in a deep breath, trying to calm his nerves, which were on edge after the unexpected turn of events.

Recalling Pruett's comment that she'd been trying to reach him all morning, Fraser pulled out his phone, deciding he should probably check his voicemail and missed calls.

He was surprised to find several messages from Argus Murphy. The FBI behavioral analyst and profiler had flown back to D.C. the night before. As he tapped to open the first message, Fraser suspected something must have gone wrong.

His concern grew as he read Argus' text.

I need to get in touch with Bailey Flynn regarding the recent murders in Belle Harbor. I have urgent information for her.

That message had been quickly followed by another.

Olga Sadler is a convicted killer with a possible connection to the Tumba Cartel. She should be considered armed and dangerous.

The final message made Fraser's heart drop.

Agent Sharma said Bailey planned to go to Verbena Beach to talk to Olga Sadler. She may have gone alone.

Fraser's anxiety grew as he checked the time stamp on the message. The text had come in hours before.

Tapping on Argus' name in his contact list, he held the phone to his ear, exhaling in relief when the profiler answered the call on the first ring.

"I just read your message," Fraser said. "I'm at a crime scene. A homicide. I'm handling it on my own and Bailey isn't answering her phone and I don't know what to-"

"I've already requested back-up," Argus cut in. "When I didn't hear back from you, I called SAC Ramsey. He assured me agents will arrive in Verbena Beach soon. Hopefully, they'll get there in time."

CHAPTER THIRTY-SEVEN

Olga Sadler clasped the silver chain that hung around her neck. Gently lifting the pendant from its resting place under her shirt, she gazed at it with burning eyes. She'd stopped by her house before coming to the church, wanting the added protection of her patron saint as she ended the journey of revenge that had kept her from her home and what was left of her family for the last two months.

Descending the altar steps one at a time, she walked slowly forward, holding the Sig Sauer pistol out in front of her.

"Where's my mother?" Bailey asked.

The FBI agent stepped in front of Cate as she spoke, keeping the big Glock aimed squarely between Olga's eyes.

But the gun didn't bother her. There was no need to be afraid.

"You won't shoot me," Olga sneered. "Because if I die, you'll never know what happened to your mother. You'll never be able to find her body and bring her home."

Reaching the bottom step, she stopped.

"I have to admit, I was surprised to hear you were headed to Verbena Beach this morning. It took some effort to get here in time and I had to once again adjust my plan."

She studied Bailey's face, looking for any signs of weakness but saw only a steely resolve in the agent's eyes.

"I'm surprised you figured out what's going on," she admitted. "Most people don't catch on to me until it's much, much too late."

"That's probably because your actions don't make sense to sane people," Bailey said. "If you believed Cate made a mistake prosecuting Dessie, why kill Gayle Kershaw or Dr. Varney? Why attack Finola? Or my mother, for that matter?"

As Bailey spoke, keeping her gun steady and pointed straight ahead, she took a small step forward.

"You still don't get it, do you?" Olga asked, feeling the familiar resentment and anger stirring in her chest. "You think I'm doing this because I'm crazy. But in that, you're wrong."

"Ok, then explain it to me," Bailey said. "Help me understand."

Lifting her gun, Olga tightened her grip, making sure Bailey knew she was ready to fire at a moment's notice.

"Someone like you could never understand. You think only in terms of courtroom justice while I think only of retribution."

"Is that why you wear that pendant?" Bailey asked. "Because you want Saint Olga to take vengeance on anyone who wronged you or made you mad? I didn't know saints were spiteful."

Olga's jaw clenched.

"You know nothing about it. Nothing about Saint Olga."

"I know more than you think," Bailey assured her. "I know your saint was once a young woman named Princess Olga of Kiev, and that she lived over a thousand years ago."

The FBI agent's voice had taken on a soothing quality that Olga knew was intended to set her at ease. To take her off guard.

"I know that after Princess Olga's husband was betrayed and slaughtered, she held a funeral feast for those responsible," Bailey continued. "She tricked them into coming, then killed them all."

"And that was just the beginning. Many more people had to die to quench her thirst for revenge," she continued. "But what I don't understand is why they made her a saint. After all that death and destruction? It's hard to comprehend."

"She did what was necessary to purge her land of traitors. She slaughtered those who'd made her a widow. And she showed no mercy for her enemies," Olga said indignantly. "And once she'd gotten her revenge, she converted her people to the true religion."

She lifted her chin defiantly.

"That's why she's a saint, and why I follow in her footsteps."

It felt good to finally speak the truth that had been burning in her heart. Despite the ten centuries that lay between them, Olga and her patron saint were the same.

"We've both been wronged and have suffered in our own ways. And we've both been left with nothing but revenge to comfort us."

Gripping the gun so hard it hurt, Olga thought back to

everything she'd been through. Every injury she'd suffered.

"You know, after your sister sent Dessie to jail, my poor Birdie tried to exonerate him," she said, wanting Bailey Flynn to understand why all this had to happen. "She went down to Belle Harbor trying to find evidence to clear his name."

"She believed her father was telling the truth when he swore to her he hadn't pulled the trigger. But she must have overheard us talking about asking Mr. Tumba for help."

The thought of Birdie's innocence and her naïve attempt to save her father brought angry tears to Olga's eyes.

"Her questions reached the wrong ears," she continued. "Mr. Tumba isn't a man who'd let a teenage girl put his freedom in jeopardy. I know now that he ordered Birdie to be eliminated. He sent in the nearest fixer at the time. A man known throughout the cartel as El Monstruo, *the Monster*, for his cruelty."

Rage dried the tears from her eyes.

"The man tortured our sweet girl and left her body to be found. But another monster lived in Belle Harbor and he had other plans."

Picturing Carter Delaney, Olga's face twisted with contempt.

"That monster had been using the Belle Harbor Burial Ground as his own personal graveyard and he didn't want to draw attention to the town. He didn't want the FBI to start a murder investigation."

"He cleaned up after El Monstruo, leaving Dessie and me waiting for our daughter to return. Even though I was also a fixer for the cartel, I was kept in the dark. I didn't know that my girl had died a terrible death. I didn't know she was rotting in the crypt."

Olga shook her head, trying to dislodge the images that had haunted her ever since she'd learned her daughter's fate.

"Only after Dessie had gotten the call in prison, informing him of Birdie's death, did I find out she was truly gone for good."

Grabbing her pendant, she held it up.

"Poor Dessie spiraled into despair, but I was taken over by the spirit of my patron saint. Taken by the need for retribution and revenge. And as I watched the replay of my Dessie on trial again and again, I realized that Cate Flynn was the one who was responsible. She'd sent an innocent man to jail, causing the series of tragic events to take their course."

Her eyes again flicked to Cate, who hovered behind her sister, as if thinking she could still escape the consequence of her actions.

"That's when I knew she had to pay. Not just with a quick and easy death. Not the kind of death I had delivered on behalf of the cartel plenty of times in the past."

Olga shook her head.

"No, I knew the retribution must be paid according to the rules laid out in Leviticus. Nothing less than an eye for an eye would do."

"That's when I drove down to Belle Harbor and scoped out the town, following Cate around, waiting for a chance to get close enough to learn everything about her."

A nasty smile spread across her face.

"But I'm not a patient person, so I decided to orchestrate a little accident for Dr. Chung's receptionist. It put her in the hospital and gave me the chance to take her place."

"Of course, I couldn't hope to be hired in with my background, so I presented myself as Cecilia Sadler, knowing there'd be no problem with hiring a respectable older woman with no manslaughter conviction on her record."

Lifting her free hand, she ran it through her hair.

"Gray hair dye and granny glasses sealed the deal. After that, I had a front-row seat to Cate's life story and her new relationship with Mason Knox, who was also a patient at the practice."

"With his crazy stalker in the picture, he made it easy to come up with a plan to put Cate's boyfriend in prison for a murder he hadn't committed, just as Cate had done to my Dessie."

"Why are you so sure Dessie was innocent?" Cate called out from her hiding spot behind Bailey.

She ignored her sister's whispered warning to stay quiet.

"How do you know he didn't kill them?"

Olga laughed.

"Because I killed those men myself," she said. "*I* was the fixer for the cartel, not Dessie. He was just a delivery man. A good-hearted man trying to make a living for his family."

"I was the one who knew how to kill. I was the one who had worked for the cartel since I was seventeen. And when they tried to ambush us, I was the one who knew what had to be done."

The answer was followed by a shocked silence from the prosecutor. Then Cate spoke again.

"And you were the one who sent Gayle Kershaw the letter?"

"Of course," Olga said. "Mason may be a fool but he's not crazy. He would never have told her where he lived and asked her to come down and join him. That was all me."

"I even blackmailed the head of the parole board to release her early. And I had access to Mason's records and personal history. From there it was easy to figure out the passcode to the security system at his house."

"And just like Princess Olga, I knew no limits in what I was willing to do to get my revenge. Once Gayle was on her way to Florida, I entered Mason's house and I set up a feast."

Thinking back to that night, she could still smell the fresh rose petals and see the flickering of the candlelight.

"I made sure Gayle had the letter I'd written to her in her pocket and dropped the phone I'd used to arrange the meeting into the pocket of one of Mason's coats on my way out. I had it all perfectly arranged."

"But then you had to get involved," she said, lifting her chin at Bailey. "You and your detective buddy had to ride in and try to save the day. You tried to exonerate your sister's boyfriend. Tried to save her heart from breaking as mine had broken."

"You even went to the prison and talked to my Dessie, ensuring that the cartel would get jumpy. Making them suspicious he was talking. Within twenty-four hours of your visit, he was dead."

Her voice became brittle as she thought of the last call she'd had with Dessie. He'd been broken beyond repair. And the women standing in front of her were responsible for his suffering.

"Once Dessie was dead, it was clear Mason would have to die, as well. I followed him into the medical examiner's office with the intent to kill him. I ended up finding his assistant there instead."

She glared at Bailey.

"Once again, *you* showed up to put a wrench in my plans. Then on my way to the Summerset Hotel to finish the job, I decided Dr. Varney was too big a risk to leave alive."

"The stupid woman had made a vow to find out what had happened to Gayle. She was already starting to ask too many questions. I figured she'd end up going into Dr. Chung's office sooner or later. I couldn't risk her asking questions about my background. I had to take her out, too."

Her voice took on a plaintive tone.

"That's when Detective Fraser showed up at the hotel, forcing me to scurry away like a rat on a sinking ship, letting Mason slip away. It wasn't one of my prouder moments. But it only made me more determined than ever to get my revenge."

Meeting Bailey's eyes, Olga produced a triumphant smile.

"But now story time is over," she said. "Your friends in law enforcement will be riding to the rescue any minute I'm sure, so we'll have to hurry. But I think we'll have time for one final act of retribution."

She cocked her head.

"You were asking about your mother, weren't you? You want to know what I've done with her? You want to have her body to bury?"

The tortured expression of hope and fear on Bailey's face was sublime. It was everything Olga had been working toward all these months. The only thing that had kept her going.

"Of course, it would have been better if Cate had a daughter for me to take," Olga said. "I mean, Jackie Flynn is no match to my Birdie. But your mother will have to do. The payment of her life for Birdie's, and your suffering for mine, will have to be enough."

"Where's my mother?" Cate demanded, stepping out from behind her sister. "How do we know you really have her?"

Olga shrugged.

"Oh, I have her all right. It was actually very easy," she said, trying to decide if she should shoot Cate between the eyes or in the heart. "When I called on your mother this morning and told her you needed help, she went along without hesitation. As I know too well, a mother's love knows no bounds."

Deciding to go for the heart, Olga adjusted her stance.

"And now your mother shares the same fate as my Birdie. She's dead and tucked away where you won't find her for years. That was the only way to make things right. Now my revenge is complete."

A shadow moved behind Olga.

The barrel of a gun pressed against the side of her head before she had the chance to spin around.

"Not quite," a deep voice said. "Your grief made you sloppy, *Saint Olga*. When you ambushed me at the lake, you should have gone for the head, not the back."

The gunman produced an ugly laugh.

"Didn't anyone tell you that El Monstruo always wears a bulletproof vest?"

CHAPTER THIRTY-EIGHT

Bailey pulled Cate down behind the nearest pew as the man stepped up behind Olga and held the gun to her temple. He wore no mask, and she could see straight, white teeth in a tanned, laughing face. Could the handsome man beside the altar really be El Monstruo, the sadistic killer Tanya Jimenez had told her about? The man known for the torment of his victims?

He called out to Bailey in a jovial voice.

"I saw where the Saint put your mother, Agent Flynn."

There was a singsong taunting rhythm to his words that set Bailey's teeth on edge. Whoever he was, the man was clearly enjoying himself.

"Your mother's out in the parking lot," he continued. "She's trapped inside the trunk of that shitty silver sedan Saint Olga has been driving. If it had been me, I'd have chosen something with a little more style and a lot more horsepower."

His mocking tone deepened into a threatening growl.

"Mommy Dearest may still be alive, you know. If you listen to me, you can still save her."

Smiling at Bailey, he pressed the gun hard against Olga's

head.

"I'll give you a knife and you can slit the Saint's throat," he said.

The gleam in his eyes suggested the offer was meant to be tempting. Some sort of sick reward.

"Once the Saint is dead, you can get into her car and drive away. You can take your mother straight to the hospital."

He pursed his lips in an exaggerated pout.

"She could be hurt you know. She may be bleeding out as we speak," he added. "But you could save her. No one else will have to know that any of us were ever here. Other than Olga, of course."

The wide grin was back.

"But she won't be alive long enough to tell anyone, will she?"

Shifting the gun in his hand, he shoved Olga forward.

As he did, the door to his right banged open.

Instinctively, El Monstruo spun toward the door, swinging his big gun out in front of him. In an instant, Olga lifted her Sig Sauer and shoved it up and under the man's chiseled chin.

Without hesitation, she pulled the trigger.

Blood spurted into the air as Olga dropped to the floor alongside El Monstruo. Using the dead man's body to shield herself, she took cover behind the altar, then disappeared through the heavy curtain behind it just as a second man burst into the room.

Cate started to stand up but Bailey jerked her back down.

"Stay here until I give you the all-clear," she hissed.

Scooting along the pew, she crawled out into the aisle,

holding her Glock out in front of her, using the thick wooden pew for cover.

"Bailey?"

Startled by the deep voice, Bailey peeked up and over the back of the bench. Dalton West stood on the stairs leading to the altar.

He held a gun in the ready position with both hands.

"I'll go after her," he said. "Stay here with Cate."

As he pushed through the curtain after Olga, Bailey jumped to her feet and then turned to look back at her sister.

"I've got to find Mom," she said, already moving toward the altar. "Keep Ludwig here. I'll come back for you."

Cate nodded and grasped the German shepherd's leash.

Slipping through the opening in the curtain, Bailey caught up to Dalton at the back exit, grabbing his arm as he reached for the door.

"The woman out there is a contract killer for the Tumba Cartel," she warned him. "She killed Gayle Kershaw and Dr. Varney. She attacked Finola and she's taken my mother."

"I know," Dalton said. "I heard most of what she said. I even managed to record some of it. I'll be careful. I promise."

He found her free hand and squeezed it.

"Now, come on. Let's go find her."

Pushing open the door, he lifted his gun and stepped outside.

Bailey followed after him, her eyes scanning the back lot. Sticking close to the building, they made their way around the side to the fence along the cemetery.

When they reached the parking lot, Bailey saw Olga up

ahead. She was already climbing into the driver's seat of her silver sedan.

"Stop or I'll shoot!" Bailey yelled as she aimed her Glock.

But Olga ignored Bailey's cry and slammed the car door shut.

Remembering El Monstruo's words, Bailey hesitated.

Could her mother really be trapped in the trunk of the sedan? She wasn't sure, but she had to stop Olga from driving away.

Maybe I can shoot out the back tire.

Bailey tightened her finger on the trigger, then released it. She couldn't shoot at the car if there was any chance Jackie was inside. She couldn't risk a bullet piercing the trunk and hitting her mother.

Lowering the Glock, she started running forward again just as Olga started the engine.

Instantly, the car ignited.

Bailey jerked to a stop and screamed in horror as the sedan exploded into a ball of flames.

"Mom!"

Her scream was followed by hurried footsteps, and then Cate and Ludwig were there beside her, staring at the burning vehicle.

"What happened?" Cate yelled. "Where's Mom?"

Bailey turned to her sister, trying to form an answer, but her throat was too tight and her mouth wouldn't cooperate.

Flames danced in Cate's wide green eyes as she stared at the fire.

"Where's Mom?" she repeated with growing panic.

Suddenly, Ludwig barked and jerked on the leash. Pulling the end of the leash out of Cate's hand, the German shepherd ran toward the burning vehicle.

"Stop, Ludwig!" Bailey yelled, but her words were drowned out by the roar of the flames.

She took a dazed step after the dog before she realized he wasn't running toward the flames. He was heading toward the two figures emerging from the shadow of the trees lining the cemetery.

"All clear!" Dalton called, waving his arms. "You can come out!"

Suddenly, a black German shepherd darted from the trees, racing to meet Ludwig, who barked excitedly in return.

"Is that...*Mom*?" Cate asked from behind her.

Bailey stared, unable to believe her eyes as Jackie stepped onto the pavement, followed by Sid Morley.

Rushing forward, she took her mother's hand, leading her away from the heat of the flames as Cate fumbled for her phone and dialed 911.

"You saved her," Bailey said, turning to look at Morley in stunned gratitude. "How did you know where she was?"

"When we first got here, I went into the church with Dalton," Morley said. "We saw a man sneaking around and followed him inside. We wanted to find out what he was up to."

"As soon as I saw Borja and heard him say Olga had your mother trapped in the trunk, I brought Amadeus back out here to look for her, while Dalton stayed to watch over you."

"Borja?" Bailey asked. "Is that his name?"

Morley nodded.

"Fernando Borja works for the Tumba Cartel. I've only seen him once before, and that was quite a few years ago, but I could never forget that face. He's a weirdly good-looking guy."

"He isn't good-looking anymore. He's dead," Dalton said, his voice hard. "And he won't be working for the cartel or anyone else ever again. He won't be able to kill anyone else, either."

Relief surged through Bailey as she squeezed Jackie's hand.

"I'm just glad he told us Mom was in the trunk. He saved her life, although I'm sure that wasn't his intention."

The realization of how close she'd come to losing her mother made Bailey's knees suddenly go weak. She swayed on her feet just as Dalton's warm hand settled on her back to steady her.

"I have a feeling Amadeus would have found her if Borja hadn't spilled the beans," Morley said, bending over to pat the dog. "He was pulling me toward the car almost as soon as we got outside. That's when I heard someone yelling and kicking in the trunk."

"The doors weren't locked so I just opened the trunk and your mother popped out like a jack-in-the-box. She told me a crazy lady kidnapped her. I figured we should hide until the coast was clear."

Looking back at the flames, he shivered.

"I never suspected Borja had rigged a bomb under the car. Maybe I should have. The cartel has done it before."

"And I should have been suspicious when he offered to let

me kill Olga and use her car to take Mom to the hospital," Bailey said. "He must have planned for us all to be blown to bits."

Catching movement out of the corner of her eye, Bailey turned to see a black Lincoln Navigator with tinted windows turn into the church's parking lot.

Dusk had started to fall and the vehicle's headlights were already on. As the SUV stopped beside Bailey, a woman with short, dark hair rolled down the driver's side window.

"What happened here? Is everyone okay?"

The woman studied the still-blazing fire and scanned the parking lot, closely assessing the situation as Bailey stared at her, trying not to show any sign of recognition.

Meeting Charlie Day's guarded gray eyes, Bailey spoke in a brisk, official voice, giving no indication that they had ever met.

"I'm Special Agent Bailey Flynn with the FBI," she said, loud enough for the others to hear. "We've got a man down inside and a woman trapped in the vehicle. We're just calling for back-up now so it's best if you two leave the scene."

Bailey glanced over at the man in the passenger's seat. She recognized Special Agent Tristan Hale even though his dark curls had been shorn and tamed into a crewcut and his chiseled jawline was concealed by a thick beard.

Realizing Argus Murphy must have notified the two undercover agents that she was in serious trouble, Bailey felt a combined surge of guilt and gratitude.

Charlie and Hale had risked blowing their cover to come to her rescue. SAC Roger Calloway up in D.C. and SAC Ford

Ramsey in Miami would undoubtedly be furious if the undercover operation had been compromised.

It would be best for everyone involved if they left the crime scene before the local police showed up.

"We've got it from here," Bailey said, mouthing a silent *thank you* to Charlie as the SUV drove away.

Once the fire department, paramedics, and local police were on the way, Bailey turned to see Cate comforting her mother.

Jackie looked dazed but uninjured.

As Bailey started forward, Dalton stepped into her path.

Before he could speak, Bailey lifted a hand to stop him.

"Just because you came to my rescue again doesn't mean I forgive you," she said. "Besides, I had everything under control."

"I'm sure you did," Dalton agreed solemnly. "But when Cate told me you'd gone to Verbena Beach, I got worried. I mentioned it to Morley and he suggested you might need back-up."

A gruff voice sounded behind them.

"What am I getting blamed for now?"

Bailey turned to Morley and shook her head.

"Nothing at all," she said. "You saved my mother's life. If it wasn't for you-"

"Let's give the credit to Amadeus," Morley cut in. "That boy wouldn't give up. If anyone saved the day, it's him."

Bailey smiled over at the German shepherd, who was standing companionably beside Ludwig. Both dogs were happily wagging their tails as sirens sounded past the dome of the church.

A firetruck sped into view, its lights flashing in the darkening sky. As the firefighters parked the vehicle and jumped out, Morley limped over to tell them he thought the blaze had been started by an incendiary device.

"Must have been attached to the engine," he said as Bailey started to move away, once again heading toward her mother.

A big hand took her arm, stopping her.

She spun around to face Dalton, who was staring down at her.

"I'm sorry that I didn't tell you-"

"Not here," she said. "Not now."

She softened the words with a weary smile.

"How about we just get through this first?"

Turning on her heel, she crossed to where her mother stood with Cate and pulled them both in for a hug.

CHAPTER THIRTY-NINE

Cate Flynn studied the stack of documents she still needed to review in the lead-up to the trial against Phil Thayer and Kelvin Miller, which was scheduled to start the following week. She hoped she wouldn't find any surprises in the arrest reports, crime scene photos, affidavits, evidence logs, and an assortment of other materials that would be needed to support the trafficking case against the two men, who were better known in criminal circles as Phoenix and Kato.

Roderick Payne had filed a motion to dismiss the case just that morning and she needed to file her traverse to counter the lawyer's motion as soon as possible.

But as she picked up a folder and opened it, footsteps and voices sounded in the hall.

Checking her watch, Cate got up from her desk and crossed to the open door. Millicent Pruett and Jimmy Fraser were coming down the hall. They were early for their scheduled meeting.

I guess my response to the motion to dismiss will have to wait.

As the police chief and the detective filed into her office, she waved them toward a round-top table in the corner.

"Thanks for coming in on such short notice."

She waited until they were seated in comfortable chairs before explaining why she'd wanted to meet.

"I've decided to present the case against Killian Rourke to the grand jury," she said. "I wanted to review the evidence collected and make sure we're all on board before moving forward."

"I'm happy to assist in any way I can," Chief Pruett replied.

Settling back into her chair, she crossed her legs.

"Detective Rourke is on suspension with pay at this point and will remain so until the case is resolved in court. Our budget won't allow us to hire another detective until he's officially terminated, so I'm hoping we can expedite the process."

Cate raised an eyebrow.

"You do realize we'll be charging Rourke with murder? And based on his initial statement, I expect him to strenuously fight the charges. He's hired Roderick Payne, who knows every delay tactic in the book. There's little hope of the case going to trial this year."

Clearing his throat, Fraser leaned forward and propped his elbows on the table.

"Couldn't you negotiate some sort of plea deal?" he asked. "We do have some pretty convincing evidence to work with."

"A plea bargain is always possible," Cate admitted. "In fact, it's the most common outcome in these types of cases. But at this stage, Rourke refutes all wrongdoing. He claims he's completely innocent and appears ready to go to court."

She opened the file in front of her.

"As for the evidence we've collected, I agree it's convincing but of course, a jury may feel otherwise."

Flipping through the pages in the folder, she stopped and looked down at a hand-written statement.

"I'd say the sworn statement from Carmen Lopez is highly credible. Ms. Lopez stated that she saw Killian Rourke coming out of Rita Valera's hospital room at the Summerset County Medical Center the night she died."

"And there's a witness ready to testify that Detective Rourke came to the hospital to intimidate Ms. Lopez on several occasions after that, resulting in Ms. Lopez quitting her job out of fear of retaliation."

She turned to the printout of the forensic report Madeline Mercer had sent her the day before.

"And the CSI team collected the ventilator in question for testing in the lab. The unit was suspected of being faulty, so it was pulled from service directly after Detective Valera's death and kept in a secure room pending analysis."

"The team was able to lift several fingerprints from the ventilator that perfectly matched Detective Rourke's prints."

Chief Pruett nodded eagerly.

"Yes, and when we interviewed Rourke, he insisted he'd never been in Detective Valera's room and had never touched the ventilator, which clearly contradicts the evidence."

"That's right," Cate said. "He has no plausible explanation as to why his prints would be found on the device."

She hesitated, then frowned over at Fraser.

"There's still the question of motive," she said. "It's not

something we have to prove but juries want to hear it. Especially if they're going to send a defendant to prison for the rest of his life."

"In this case, they're going to want to know why Rourke would turn off the ventilator. They'll want to understand why he would kill an unconscious, helpless woman. What was his motive?"

Searching Fraser's eyes, she waited.

"I think it's pretty obvious if you listen to Rourke during his initial interview with Chief Pruett," he said. "The bitterness in his voice speaks louder than the words he's saying."

Cate thought for a minute, then turned to her computer. She clicked on the screen several times, navigating to the audio recording Fraser had referenced.

Once she'd found the file, she clicked *Play*.

As the exchange between Chief Pruett and Rourke began, Cate followed along using the typed transcript, quickly picking up on the resentment in Rourke's responses that Fraser had detected.

"I've never been treated fairly by this department. It took ten years for your predecessor to get his head out of his ass and promote me. And now you're trying to use a bullshit charge of shutting off a medical device to get rid of me for good? Is this some sort of joke?"

Rourke ended the statement with an angry laugh and Cate decided she'd heard enough for the time being.

She clicked *Stop* and looked up a Fraser.

"So, your theory is Rourke was a frustrated uniformed officer looking for a promotion to detective?"

Fraser nodded slowly.

"As the chief said, budgets are tight. Rourke knew he wasn't going to get a promotion until one of us was gone."

He sat back in his chair and exhaled.

"I think when he heard about Valera going into that river, he got excited. Then when he found out she was expected to make it, he decided he couldn't wait any more. He decided to take matters into his own hands. A few weeks later...he's a detective."

Replaying Rourke's whining voice in her head, Cate nodded.

"It's a reasonable theory," she said. "Let's just hope the grand jury buys it. If they go for it, a trial jury might do the same."

"What would the official charge be?" Fraser asked.

"Well, if Rourke intentionally went to the hospital in the middle of the night, slipped into Valera's room undetected, and disabled the ventilator, I would have to say that the appropriate charge would be first-degree, premeditated murder."

Both Fraser and Pruett looked startled.

"Has anyone spoken to Detective Valera's daughter yet?" Fraser asked. "Has she been updated on the investigation?"

"Mayor Sutherland has been in contact with Raya Valera," Cate confirmed. "And I believe a settlement has been reached."

The news seemed to satisfy Fraser. He stood and followed Chief Pruett out of the room with a lighter step as if he'd finally set down a heavy burden.

After they had both disappeared into the elevator, Cate hurried to the breakroom in desperate need of a refill on her coffee.

She hadn't been sleeping well due to recurrent nightmares that often featured Olga Sadler and Fernando Borja.

Stifling a wide yawn, she stopped short when she saw Henrietta Trilby standing at the sink rinsing out a coffee mug.

The prosecutor turned to look at her.

"I must have died without realizing it," she said dryly. "Because you look as if you've seen a ghost."

Cate summoned a weak smile for her fellow prosecutor, sensing that Henrietta was trying to make peace.

"I hadn't expected to see you back so soon," she said. "I know you were in court this morning and-"

"And my petition to dismiss all charges against Mason Knox was granted," Henrietta finished for her with a smile.

Relief flooded through Cate at the news.

She couldn't wait to go see Mason. Maybe now they'd have a chance to pick things up where they'd left them.

"I was surprised how quickly Judge Inglebert granted the petition," Henrietta continued. "He didn't even give me a hard time like he usually does. Something must have gotten into him."

Holding back the snide comment that came to mind at the mention of the judge, Cate crossed to the coffee maker.

She didn't like or trust Inglebert, especially since he'd dismissed the bribery charges against Nigella Ashworth so quickly, but she decided it was best to keep her opinion to herself.

After all, you never know who you can trust or who's out to get you.

The dark thought was unsettling.

And it wasn't like her to be so paranoid and pessimistic.

But ever since she'd discovered Olga Sadler had been killing people in a crazed attempt to take revenge on her, Cate had become suspicious of everyone's motives, and she was starting to wonder if the nightmares and paranoia were Saint Olga's real revenge.

* * *

The lobby of the medical examiner's office was empty when Cate pushed through the door and crossed to the reception desk.

Seeing no one behind the counter, she slipped into the back unannounced and walked down the hall to Mason's office, trying to ignore the smell of death and formaldehyde that greeted her.

"Hello?" she called out, sticking her head into the room.

Mason started and spun around as she stepped inside.

"You scared me," he said, putting a hand to his chest. "I guess I've been a little jumpy since coming back to work. I keep expecting someone to spring out at me every time I walk into a room."

"I'm sorry," Cate said, realizing she might not be the only one Olga had damaged during her campaign of revenge. "I just saw Henrietta Trilby and wanted to help you celebrate the good news."

Crossing his arms over his broad chest, Mason frowned.

"What good news?"

"Haven't you heard? All remaining charges against you have been officially dismissed. Judge Inglebert granted Henrietta's petition this morning."

She waited for some sort of reaction but he only shrugged.

"Yeah, I know. Henrietta already called me up and told me."

"Aren't you happy it's all over?"

Mason considered the question.

"I'd be happier if it'd never happened at all," he finally said. "And if no one had to die. It all seems like such a stupid waste."

Stepping closer, he managed a faint smile.

"But I am glad to see you."

His words were soft as he took her hand.

"It was hard staying away."

"Then why did you?"

The question slipped out before Cate could stop it.

"I wanted to be there for you," she added. "I wanted to help."

"And *I* didn't want to ruin your career," Mason countered. "Dating an accused serial killer isn't exactly something you'd want on your resume, is it?"

Cate smiled despite herself.

"Okay, I get it. But what are you planning to do now that you're a free man?" she asked. "You aren't thinking of moving back to Crimson Falls, are you?"

Her heart dropped when he gave an uncertain shrug.

"I never thought I'd go back there," he admitted. "But now...well, I know it sounds terrible...but now that Gayle is no longer part of the equation, it does seem like an option."

Staring down at their entwined hands, he didn't seem to notice her dismayed expression.

"On the other hand, Finola is making a remarkable recovery."

He suddenly sounded more cheerful.

"I saw her yesterday and she's excited to get back to work. I'd like to be here when she returns to the office."

He lifted his eyes to hers.

"I guess I've gotten kind of fond of this town. It'd be hard to leave it behind. And even harder to leave *you* behind."

"I thought you were afraid to start a new relationship," Cate reminded him. "I mean, after Gayle and everything that happened."

"I guess I'll have to listen to Dr. Chung's advice," he said, pulling her closer. "The only way to overcome my fear is to face it."

CHAPTER FORTY

Bailey waved to Officer Boswell as she pushed through the visitor's entrance of the Summerset Detention Center. The big man returned her greeting with a cheerful smile and bent down to ruffle Ludwig's fur, ignoring the eye-roll of his fellow guard, who maintained a grim expression as he led Bailey through the door and down the wide hall toward the interview room where Carter Delaney was waiting.

The serial killer's dark hair had started to grow out again after his initial crewcut, and his narrow jaw was covered in a patchy beard that emphasized the strange pallor of his face.

"Thanks for coming," Delaney said, waving her toward the chair across from him as if she was joining him for a business meeting.

"I have to say I was surprised to get your invitation," Bailey said as she sat down. "Tony Brunner indicated that you had information about Olga Sadler that might be helpful in wrapping up the case?"

She looked at him expectantly.

"Yes, well Brunner is a master at spinning a situation, isn't he?" Delaney said. "I actually wanted to get information from you about the Saint. And about El Monstruo. I hear they're both dead."

Raising her eyebrows in surprise, Bailey wondered where he'd gotten his information about the two contract killers.

Although the explosion of Cecilia Sadler's sedan and the deaths of two people at the Verbena Beach Orthodox Church had been in the news, the identities of the deceased hadn't officially been released to the press or public yet, pending further investigation.

"What else were you hoping to find out?" Bailey asked, deciding to play along with his game for the time being.

"First of all, how can you be sure the woman who was blown up in that car was actually Olga Sadler?" he asked, getting straight to the point. "She was a master of disguise from what I've heard. Hadn't she already fooled everyone in Belle Harbor into believing she was a sixty-year-old temp worker with a spotless record?"

Inhaling a calming breath, Bailey refused to be baited.

"Someone has been filling you in, I see."

As she exhaled, she wondered how much she should share.

If she gave him a little information about Olga and Borja, he might give her more details about the Tumba Cartel.

"Apparently, your source is unaware that we were able to positively identify Olga using DNA," she said.

"I thought she was killed by an explosion," he said, raising an eyebrow. "So, how'd you get DNA if she was blown up and then burned to a crisp?"

He looked genuinely curious.

"You're right, she was blown up," Bailey admitted. "In

fact, I saw her get in the car myself and watched as the car exploded."

Blinking hard, she tried to ignore the image of flames and flying debris that suddenly flashed behind her eyes at the memory.

"And yes, it was impossible for the CSI team to collect a DNA sample from the remains at the scene," she continued. "But we were able to collect DNA from blood found at a secondary scene where she had abducted a hostage that morning. The woman she abducted had a cat and...well, let's just say the cat won."

Bailey suppressed a shudder as she thought of the blood on the floor of her parents' foyer and poor Duchess hiding in the bushes with blood on her claws.

Luckily, Duchess had made it possible to get a DNA profile from the spilled blood, which proved to be a familial match to Cecilia and Birdie Sadler.

"The DNA we collected was matched to DNA obtained from the remains of Olga's daughter, as well as from her mother," Bailey confided. "There's absolutely no doubt that the woman who died in the explosion was Olga Sadler of Verbena Beach."

Delaney nodded as if satisfied.

"Okay, and what about Borja?" he asked. "Is El Monstruo really dead? Or has he only managed to disappear again? Will he be coming back from the dead as he's done so many times before?"

"The man known as El Monstruo is in a drawer in the Verbena Beach medical examiner's office," Bailey said. "I was there for his autopsy and watched as they collected a DNA sample."

She could still picture the big killer's body on the metal table.

"They ran the profile through CODIS and it was a match for Fernando Borja, a wanted killer who has eluded police for years."

Keeping her voice neutral, she met Delaney's dark eyes.

"I can safely say, unless he's a ghost, Borja won't be back."

At this, Delaney produced a pleased smile.

"And I can say I won't mourn the man," he admitted. "Fernando Borja was no friend of mine. In fact, I'd consider him a rival. Same goes for Saint Olga. I always thought she was highly overrated."

Bailey sat forward in her chair.

"Okay, now, I have a question for you."

She saw Delaney's thin shoulders tense.

"Certain information found in Borja's phone leads us to believe he may have been responsible for the death of Lando Gutierrez. What do you know about that?"

Delaney gave an indifferent shrug.

"I know nothing about Gutierrez," he insisted, not for the first time. "If the cartel had him killed, it had nothing to do with me."

Deciding she believed him, Bailey moved on.

"Okay, then what about Jordan Stone? We're still trying to figure out his role in all this. What can you tell me about him?"

"Who says I know anything about the man?"

"He wired money into your bank account."

Delaney shook his head, suddenly irritable.

"Jordan Stone is a charitable man," he snapped. "Everyone knows that. He must have made an anonymous donation to support my research. I study bones and human remains, remember?"

"Can you at least tell me if Jordan Stone is involved with the Tumba Cartel?" Bailey asked. "Is he working with Mr. Tumba?"

Delaney crossed his arms over his chest.

"The only thing I can tell you about Mr. Tumba is that all his best fixers are now out of commission," he said. "I'm locked up in here, Saint Olga's been turned to ash, and El Monstruo is heading for a cardboard box. But the big boss? Well, he's still in the wind."

The realization seemed to unsettle him.

"Just be warned," he said, lowering his voice. "Mr. Tumba will already be looking for our replacements. He'll soon find other fixers to do his dirty work and I don't want any of them coming for me."

Pushing back from the table he called for the guard.

"We're done here," he said. "I have nothing else to say."

As she watched the guard lead Delaney away, Bailey realized he was scared. If the cartel thought he was talking, they would try to take him out, despite the locked doors and guards all around him.

Boswell was surprised she was back so soon to pick up Ludwig.

"I've started volunteering at the local shelter," he said,

lowering his voice as if afraid he might be overheard. "I bet some of those dogs would make good search and rescue dogs. They just need a chance, you know?"

He looked down at Ludwig with obvious affection.

"You're probably right," Bailey said, digging a card out of her pocket. "And I bet you'd make a good handler. I know the best trainer in South Florida. Give me a call and I'll put you in touch."

With a final wave to Boswell, Bailey led Ludwig out to the parking lot. She wasn't surprised to find Charlie Day's Navigator wedged in beside her Expedition.

She'd told the undercover agent about Delaney's request to talk to her and had agreed to find out what she could about the cartel.

"Delaney obviously knows who Mr. Tumba is," Bailey said through the open window. "But he's still too scared to tell me and I don't have much to offer. I tried to use the information I had about Olga and Borja, but he already knew they were dead."

Charlie nodded slowly and looked away.

"We're getting close," she said, making an effort to hide her disappointment. "Hale and I have informants within the cartel. It's just a matter of time until we infiltrate the inner circle. That's when we'll meet Mr. Tumba. That's when we'll have a real chance to finally take him down."

She turned back to Bailey.

"But we need to have a few people we can trust nearby," she said. "We can't do it on our own."

"I'm guessing that means Calloway will be asking me to

stay in the Miami field office for the foreseeable?" Bailey said with a sigh.

Charlie laughed.

"*Asking* is a nice way to put it," she said. "But it shouldn't be long. Maybe just a few more weeks...perhaps a couple of months."

Bailey nodded.

"I'll stay as long as you need me," she said "Just, be careful."

She watched as Charlie pulled away, keeping her eyes on the big vehicle until it had disappeared into the distance.

* * *

As Bailey walked into the Belle Harbor Police Department, she saw Fraser waiting for her in the lobby.

"Madeline told me you were coming," he said. "She asked me to bring you to the lab when you got here. Asked me to come, too."

Following the detective down the hall, Bailey wondered why the CSI team leader had summoned them.

Normally, when Madeline had news, she waited for a task force meeting so she could update the entire team.

It must be important if it couldn't wait.

As they stepped into the lab, Madeline turned to them with a strained smile. Lifting a hand to smooth back her dark hair, she gestured for them to join her at the computer.

"We've found a partial DNA match for one of the unidentified victims in the crypt."

Bailey blinked in surprise.

"That's great," she said. "Which victim?"

Turning to the computer screen, which displayed a visual diagram of the layout within the crypt, Madeline pointed to the skeletal remains of a man who had been found lying within several feet of Birdie Sadler's skull.

"Eloise and her team have confirmed that the remains belong to an adult male. He had a broken hyoid bone indicating he could have been strangled or maybe hanged. They believe his remains have been in the crypt for approximately twenty-five years."

She cleared her throat.

"The shoes he was wearing were expensive and the rubber soles looked new, but the brand hasn't been sold since the nineties."

Bailey studied the screen with growing excitement.

"And you said you've found a DNA match for the remains?"

"Yes, the DNA profile is a partial match to a profile in CODIS."

Sucking in a deep breath, Madeline turned to look at Bailey.

"It's a partial match to Neil Ashworth," she said. "You know, the son of councilwoman Nigella Ashworth?"

"I know who Neil is," Bailey said slowly. "But, how is he related to the victim in the crypt?"

"According to the DNA, the victim in the crypt is Neil's father."

Bailey stared at Madeline in shock, trying to absorb the

unexpected information, then looked back at Fraser, who appeared to be as surprised as she was.

Suddenly, Bailey frowned.

"But I thought you'd already run all the DNA for the remains in the crypt through CODIS and didn't get any hits."

"That was months ago," Madeline said, not quite meeting her eyes. "Based on new information that came to light, I decided to try again. We got lucky."

"New information?" Fraser asked. "What new information?"

Looking toward the door, Madeline lowered her voice as if someone might be listening in.

"Off the record, I can tell you guys that Dalton West's been working with Neil Ashworth, trying to help the guy find out what happened to his father. He asked me to run a DNA sample from Neil through CODIS."

Her face flushed pink as she met Bailey's startled eyes.

"I know it's against the policy but Dalton's such a sweetheart, always trying to help people. I just couldn't say no."

Momentarily lost for words, Bailey tried to make sense of the information. She turned to Fraser.

"Don't look at me," he said. "CODIS is the FBI's database. And Dalton is your special friend. I'd say this is in your court."

Rolling her eyes, she turned back to Madeline.

"So, you were helping Dalton with a missing person search for Neil Ashworth's father?"

Madeline nodded.

"And based on the results, it appears his father was one of the victims killed and dumped in the crypt."

"Did you check to see if a missing person's report was ever filed?" Bailey asked.

Madeline shook her head.

"There's nothing in our system," she said. "It's a mystery."

* * *

Bailey was still brooding over the news Madeline had shared as she and Fraser walked back down the hall to the lobby.

The police station was busy, and she didn't recognize Raya Valera until the woman was standing directly in front of them.

"Detective Fraser?"

Raya's voice was subdued and her expression contrite.

"I was hoping to get a chance to talk to you before I left town," she said. "I just wanted to say that I'm sorry for the way I acted."

A soft flush of color filled her cheeks.

"I accused you without having all the facts," she said, biting her lip. "I was wrong for thinking you had something to do with my mother's death."

After a surprised pause, Fraser nodded.

"I appreciate that. And I'm sorry about your mother. I know it must have been hard to lose her without getting a chance to clear the air or say goodbye."

Tears sprang to Raya's eyes.

"Thanks for understanding. Not many people do."

She blinked hard.

"And thanks for investigating my mother's death. Chief Pruett told me the man who's responsible has been arrested and will face charges of murder. I owe it to you for finding out who was really responsible. You and Dalton West."

Bailey frowned.

"What did Dalton West have to do with it?"

The words slipped out before she could stop them but Raya didn't seem to mind.

"Mr. West went and spoke to the nurse at the hospital and convinced her to give an official statement," she explained. "That's what started the real investigation."

"So, you hired him to look into your mother's death?"

Raya shook her head.

"I didn't hire him. He volunteered. And he didn't charge me anything to get involved. He's a really nice guy. Without him, I may never have gotten a settlement from the city."

A sad smile lifted the corner of her mouth.

"I know my mother could be a hard woman to like at times. But her life was just as valuable as yours or mine. And I'm sure she and I would have eventually mended our differences if we'd had the chance. She would have been glad to know I'll be taken care of."

"I'm sure she would be," Bailey agreed, thinking of how close she'd come to losing her own mother.

After bidding Raya goodbye, Bailey walked with Fraser to the parking lot, sensing his relief that he no longer had to worry about being fired or falsely accused.

"I didn't know Dalton had been involved with the Rita Valera investigation," she said as they stood beside the Expedition.

Fraser nodded.

"If he hadn't taken it upon himself to track down Carmen Lopez and talk her into giving a statement...well, we might never have realized what Rourke had been up to. And I might have been looking for another job."

With a sigh, he checked his watch.

"I've got to go pick up the girls," he said. "Linette will kill me if I'm late again. But be sure to thank Dalton for me if you see him."

"I'm not sure I'll see him anytime soon," she replied with a heavy sigh. "I haven't heard from him lately, and I guess-"

But Fraser had already turned and was jogging toward his car.

She watched him drive away, still thinking of Dalton.

It looked as if her jealousy and insecurity had managed to push him away for good this time.

It didn't take training as an FBI special agent to figure out she'd been sabotaging their relationship ever since they'd met.

Climbing into the Expedition, she thought of Zach's betrayal and wondered if she'd ever be able to trust anyone with her heart again.

Maybe I'm destined to be alone forever. Maybe that's for the best.

She jumped at a sharp knock on the window.

Looking over, she saw Dalton smiling in at her.

"Fancy seeing you here," he said as she rolled down the window. "I was just dropping my sister off."

Bailey looked through the windshield to see Sabrina West chasing after Raya Valera's retreating figure.

"She's nothing if not persistent," Bailey said, shaking her head.

"I bet she'd say the same about you," Dalton countered. "It's one of the things I admire about the both of you."

When Bailey didn't answer, he straightened and stepped back from the window.

"Well, don't let me keep you," he said. "I'm sure you have places to be and people to see. I'll catch you later."

Lifting his hand in a half-hearted wave, he turned to go.

"I don't have anywhere to be," Bailey called out a little too loudly, earning curious looks from several people in the parking lot.

She cleared her throat as Dalton stopped and turned around.

"And there's no one else I want to see," she said as he moved back toward the window. "Although, Morley invited me and Ludwig over for dinner. I'm sure he wouldn't mind if you tagged along."

Her face felt warm as he hesitated and cocked his head. Then his face lit up with a grin.

"No need to ask me twice."

Circling the car, he climbed into the passenger seat.

"I'm all yours."

Bailey started the engine and turned on the radio. It was

still tuned to the classic rock station Cate had put on the day they'd driven up to Verbena Beach.

The harmonica riff from Neil Young's *Heart of Gold* blasted from the speakers as they pulled onto Grand Harbor Boulevard.

Glancing over at Dalton, she smiled as she saw him singing along with his eyes closed and his fair hair blowing in the wind from the open window.

Like everyone else, they were both searching.

And maybe, if they were lucky, their search was over.

Turning up the volume, she sang along with him as they headed into the setting sun.

The End

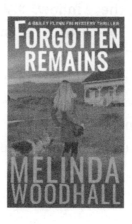

In the mood for your next thriller?
Try Melinda Woodhall's
Lessons in Evil: A Bridget Bishop FBI Mystery Thriller.
In the first book of the series, criminal psychologist and FBI Profiler Bridget Bishop tackles a chilling string of homicides that bear a startling resemblance to a series of murders committed by a man since convicted and executed for the crimes.

Read on for an excerpt of Lessons in Evil!

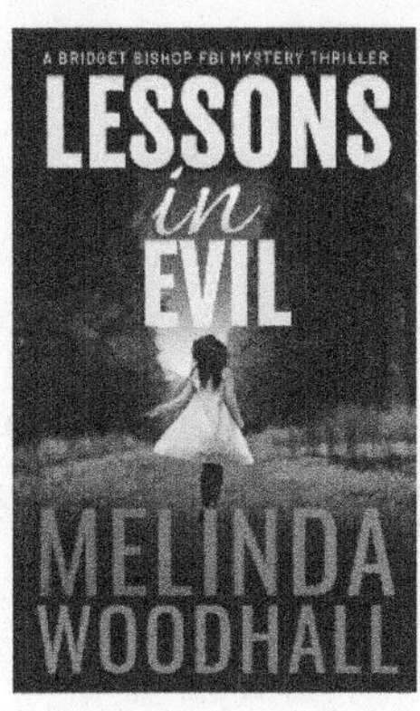

LESSONS IN EVIL

A Bridget Bishop Thriller: Book One

CHAPTER ONE

The needle on the gas gauge hovered on empty as Libby Palmer steered her mother's old Buick down the Wisteria Falls exit ramp. The heavy traffic on the interstate had added an extra hour to her drive back from D.C., and Libby had just decided she was going to run out of gas when the Gas & Go sign came into view.

Eyeing the gas station with relief, Libby turned into the parking lot, brought the car to a jerking halt beside an available pump, and shut off the engine with a resigned sigh.

Her trip into D.C. certainly hadn't turned out the way she'd hoped when she'd left home that morning. Despite her new clothes and valiant efforts to impress the hiring manager at the Smithsonian, she was still woefully unemployed.

So much for showing Mom once and for all that majoring in art history wasn't a colossal mistake.

A fat drop of rain plunked onto the windshield and slid down the glass as Libby opened the door and stepped out into the dusky twilight, credit card in hand.

A hand-written note had been taped over the card reader.

Machine broken. Pay inside.

Looking up at the darkening sky in irritation, Libby pulled the hood of her jacket over her dark curls and hurried toward the store. She hesitated as she saw the missing person flyer taped to the glass door.

It was the third time that day she'd seen one of the flyers with a picture of the pretty blonde girl who'd gone missing from her apartment near Dupont Circle the week before.

Brooke Nelson hadn't been seen since; foul play was suspected. The FBI had been asking anyone with information to call a dedicated tip line, and a slew of the flyers had been posted around Washington D.C. and the surrounding area.

"You going in or not?"

A man in a black jacket and faded jeans held the door open, waiting for Libby to pass through.

"Uh...yeah, sorry about that," she said, ducking her head as she stepped into the brightly lit building.

Wrinkling her nose against the pungent scent of stale coffee which hung in the air, Libby made her way to the counter and presented her credit card to the clerk.

"Twenty dollars on pump one," she said, hoping her card wasn't maxed out. "And can I get the key to the restroom?"

The clerk looked her up and down, taking in her disheveled curls and rain-spattered jacket as he handed her a receipt and a silver key on a red plastic keyring.

His eyes held a suspicious gleam.

"Restrooms are outside to the left." He held up her credit card. "You'll get this back when you return the key."

Libby nodded and stepped back, bumping into the solid figure of a man in line behind her.

"Sorry," she murmured, avoiding eye contact as she turned and headed outside.

Keeping her head down against the spitting rain, she hurried around the little building to the restroom, stuck the metal key in the lock, and found the tiny, tiled room surprisingly clean.

She stopped in front of the chipped mirror over the sink, wiping at the mascara smudged under her disappointed brown eyes.

"You didn't want to work at that stupid museum anyway, did you?" she asked her reflection. "I mean, who'd want to live in boring old Washington D.C. when they could live in exciting Wisteria Falls?"

Rain was falling in a steady downpour by the time Libby had returned the key to the clerk, retrieved her credit card, and pumped twenty dollars' worth of gas into the Buick's big tank.

Dropping back into the driver's seat, she started the engine and pulled back onto the highway, lowering the volume on the radio as she picked up speed, uninterested in the local weather and traffic report.

As she drove over Landsend Bridge, she glanced down toward the Shenandoah River but could see nothing of the dark water churning below the metal and concrete structure.

Always fearful the ancient truss bridge might suddenly give way beneath her, Libby drove cautiously, holding her breath until the Buick's wheels were back on solid ground before pressing her foot toward the floor, eager to get home.

She didn't see the girl standing on the side of the road until she rounded the sharp curve just past Beaufort Hollow.

Stomping on the brakes as the Buick's headlights lit up a pale face framed by sodden blonde hair, Libby brought the car to a sudden stop in the middle of the empty road.

Worried another car may round the curve behind her and plow into her rear bumper, she steered the Buick onto the shoulder and shut off the engine.

With a quick glance in the rearview mirror, she climbed out into the rain and ran toward the girl, who stood beside a black sedan. The car's trunk was wide open, and the emergency lights were blinking.

"Are you okay?" Libby called as she approached the car.

The girl's face was hidden in shadow, no longer illuminated by the Buick's headlights, but the jarring blink, blink, blink of the sedan's emergency lights revealed the outline of her bowed head and thin shoulders.

"Did your car break down?"

Libby's question was met with silence. She wondered if the girl had been in an accident. Perhaps a tire had blown.

Maybe she hit her head on the dashboard. Or maybe she...

The thought was interrupted by the girl's raspy whisper, but Libby couldn't make out what she was saying.

Stepping close enough to put her hand on the girl's thin

shoulder, she inhaled sharply.

"You're trembling," Libby said, impulsively pulling off her jacket and draping it over the girl's shoulders. "You must be hurt. Come with me to my car and..."

"Help...me."

As the girl lifted her head, the emergency blinkers lit up a heart-shaped face, which looked strangely familiar.

Libby stared into the girl's tormented blue eyes, her pulse quickening as she pictured the missing person flyer on the door at Gas & Go.

"You're that girl, aren't you? You're Brooke Nelson."

"I'm...sorry," the girl croaked and swayed on her feet as if she no longer had the strength to stand. "I'm so sorry."

The crack of a branch behind Libby sent her spinning around just as a dark figure loomed up in front of her.

A scream froze in her throat as she stared up, gaping in terror. The man's face was half-hidden by the hood of his jacket, but she recognized his cold stare.

Adrenaline shot through her as she saw the knife in his hand. Lunging toward the road in a desperate bid to get back to the safety of the old Buick, she slipped and fell to her knees.

An iron fist reached out and grabbed a handful of her hair.

Snapping her head back, the man pulled her to her feet and wrapped his free arm around her neck.

He tightened his hold until Libby could no longer breathe.

"Brooke and I were...waiting for you," he hissed, his breath coming in excited gasps. "The time...of reckoning is...here."

Waves of dizziness washed over Libby as she scratched and pried at the unyielding arm around her throat, and hot tears blurred the flashing lights around her.

"Stay still...or I'll break your neck."

His breath was hot in her ear as he dragged her toward the open trunk of the sedan, then forced her inside.

She opened her mouth to scream as she looked back and met Brook Nelson's anguished eyes but could only manage a raspy cry before the trunk slammed shut, throwing her into darkness.

* * *

Water trickled somewhere nearby as Libby struggled to open her eyes. Her throat burned, and it was hard to swallow as she blinked around the dimly lit room.

Where am I? What is this place?

Rough walls and a cracked wooden floor held a small metal-framed bed and a straight-backed chair. Rickety stairs led up to a small landing and a narrow door.

"You awake?"

She jumped at the man's voice.

"I thought maybe I'd squeezed too hard."

A dark figure stepped into view. The man who'd forced her into the trunk of his car stared down at her.

"It'd be a shame to go through all that trouble to snatch you only to kill you off so soon."

Studying her face, he reached out a hand to tuck a still soggy curl behind her ear.

Libby cringed in terror but found she couldn't pull away. Her hands were bound to the chair with bright blue duct tape, as were her ankles.

"Where am I?" she croaked, wincing at the pain in her throat. "Why are you doing this?"

He appeared not to have heard her questions as he moved toward the stairs. Propping a booted foot on the bottom step, he stopped and cocked his head as if listening.

"I know what to do," he finally said, giving a resolute nod. "I've read the handbook. I won't take any chances."

Libby looked around the room, confused.

Who's he talking to?

She suddenly remembered Brook Nelson's terrified eyes. The poor girl must have been abducted, too. Was she being held in the same place?

"Where's Brooke?" Libby wheezed out, ignoring the stabbing pain in her throat. "What have you done to her?"

Turning to face her, the man frowned.

"You're not gonna try anything stupid, are you?" he asked, shifting his weight on the creaking wooden floor. "My mentor warned me you'd cause trouble. He told me not to be fooled."

"Who warned you?" she asked, looking up the stairs toward the door. "Is someone else here?"

The man cocked his head.

"I guess you could say that. Now stop asking so many questions. I've got important work to do."

"Please," Libby called out as he turned away. "Tell me what you did to Brooke. Tell me where she is."

Looking over his shoulder, the man shrugged.

"She's served her purpose," he said softly. "As will you."

ACKNOWLEDGEMENTS

SUMMER IS A PERFECT TIME FOR READING and I was excited to be able to release this book in the heart of a long, hot Florida summer. I couldn't have done it without the tireless support and love of my incredible husband, Giles, and my five adored children, Michael, Joey, Linda, Owen, and Juliet.

I am also grateful for the ongoing encouragement and support of my extended family, including Melissa Romero, Leopoldo Romero, David Woodhall, and Tessa Woodhall.

The positive feedback from readers continues to inspire my writing, as do the treasured memories of my mother and sister, who both live on in my heart.

ABOUT THE AUTHOR

Melinda Woodhall is the author of heart-pounding, emotional thrillers with a twist, including the *Mercy Harbor Thriller Series*, the *Veronica Lee Thriller Series*, the *Detective Nessa Ainsley Novella Series*, and the *Bridget Bishop FBI Mystery Thriller Series.*

When she's not writing, Melinda can be found reading, gardening, and playing in the back garden with her tortoise. Melinda is a native Floridian and the proud mother of five children. She lives with her family in Orlando.

Visit Melinda's website at www.melindawoodhall.com.

Other Books by Melinda Woodhall

Her Last Summer
Her Final Fall
Her Winter of Darkness
Her Silent Spring
Her Day to Die
Her Darkest Night
Her Fatal Hour
Her Bitter End
The River Girls
Girl Eight
Catch the Girl
Girls Who Lie
Steal Her Breath
Take Her Life
Make Her Pay
Break Her Heart
Lessons in Evil
Taken By Evil
Where Evil Hides
Road to Evil
Valley of Evil
Save Her from Evil
Betrayed by Evil
His Soul to Keep
His Heart of Darkness
Vanishing Angels
Gathering Bones

Made in United States
North Haven, CT
22 July 2024

55311105R00182